SINS OF SEVIN

Penelope Ward

SINS OF SEVIN
First Edition, September 2015
Copyright © 2015 by Penelope Ward

Cover Photographer: Scott Hoover
Cover Model: Chase Mattson
Cover Design: Letitia Hasser, RBA Designs
Formatting by Polgarus Studio

PROLOGUE

He was more painfully handsome than I'd remembered. Sevin hadn't noticed me yet as I stood in the doorway taking in the sight of him while he sat there amongst the crowd.

I shouldn't be here.

There was no place for me in Dodge City anymore. But the one thing that I knew would force me back happened. Now, there was no choice but to face him. His gaze moved to the floor as he twiddled his large thumbs, and that bought me more time to look at him.

Someone called my name, and just like that, his head full of shiny black hair lifted to meet my frightened expression.

No smile.

No warmth shone through his gorgeous face.

His eyes instead met mine with an almost vicious-looking stare.

The adrenaline running through me only solidified what I always knew; that even after all this time, my feelings for him hadn't wavered. Despite the fact that he hated me, I was still staring into the eyes of the only man I'd ever loved.

My sister's husband.

CHAPTER 1

SEVIN

Her warm breath tickled my ear. "Sevin, I'm gonna need a strong set of hands to set up the hall for the after-service breakfast."

That was code for something else. My strong set of hands would be doing a lot more than just setting up tables and chairs, and we both knew it. But it amazed me that no one *else* seemed to know. She'd come around to the end of my pew at the same time every Sunday, about forty minutes before church ended. We'd leave together and yet, no one seemed to figure out what was really going on.

Sunlight streaming through the stained glass windows shined around her blonde updo. Candace curled her index finger for me to follow her into the building adjacent to the church.

As I walked behind her down the long hallway, the sound of the sermon faded away. My dick hardened at the sight of her ass wiggling through her long conservative pencil skirt. I was most definitely going straight to hell.

If these people only knew.

Upon entering the hall, the smell of coffee percolating hit me. We passed the table of baked goods that were already set up. The utility closet door creaked as she opened it, and my cock twitched in anticipation.

I pressed my body against her chest in the dark, enclosed space as the door clicked shut.

Candace pulled a string above us, turning on a small overhead light. She

2

smiled and wasted no time unbuttoning my shirt.

"Hey, what do you think you're doing? I'm all dressed in my Sunday best, and you're messing it up," I teased as I removed the pin holding up her hair and watched the tresses unravel down into a sexy mess.

"*Naked* is your Sunday best, baby. The light is gonna stay on this time. I need to see your body, Sevin. I've been waiting all week for this. God, I missed you. Seven days is too long." She pulled my shirt off of my arms and threw it on the ground. "You're so beautiful, baby," she whispered. "So beautiful."

I closed my eyes as she kissed down my chest. "Feels good," I muttered.

She spoke over my skin, "I hate the way they look at you. All those teenage girls in church. They all want you, Sevin. And I'm the only one that gets to have you like this, the only one who gets to see what lies beneath those clothes, the only one who gets to see this body that looks cut from stone...made for sin. I *am* the only one, right?"

"Yeah. Of course you are," I lied. Some of those girls *had* seen me.

As she undid my pants and took my engorged cock out, a familiar feeling of guilt started to creep in, but it passed in a fleeting moment.

She lifted off her shirt and took a condom out of her black lace bra before ripping the package open with her teeth. Candace looked up into my eyes as she slid the ribbed rubber onto me carefully. She looked at me like she owned me. It made me uncomfortable but not enough to stop.

"Turn around," I said so that I didn't have to see her face.

She placed her hands against the closet wall as her skirt fell to the ground.

Faint organ music in the distance was the only sound until the loud gasp she released as I buried myself inside of her.

"Shhh," I warned.

What was she fucking crazy, letting out a noise like that? I couldn't imagine the repercussions if someone found us in here.

With each thrust, though, I was reminded of why I kept coming back for more with Candace. In the small time we were in here, I could close my eyes and pretend that she was someone else, someone that meant something. I liked pretending that I was wanted, that I was loved by someone important. In reality, she was using me just as much as I was using her. But for someone who grew up without any kind of affection, sex was the closest thing I had to love, the closest thing to a connection with another human being. Unlike real love, which usually ended in pain, no one had to get hurt in this situation. When we walked out of here, it was like it never happened.

The other reason I kept doing this: it was simply exhilarating. Doing something I knew was wrong was addicting. That was the problem with me. Acting badly always gave me a high even from a very young age. At twenty, you'd think I would have had the highest morals given my sheltered upbringing. But with me, it all backfired.

Growing up, I was the kid who collected the money in church only to take a handful for myself out of the donation basket to go buy cigarettes. I was the boy who would go back to my room after a Bible lesson about lust only to jerk off to the Playboy magazine hidden under my bed. I guess I've always been a sinner by nature. But these encounters with Candace were definitely a new low.

"Shit. Sevin. Harder!" she moaned.

The sound of police sirens on the street outside the hall vaguely registered. I pumped into her with all my might until she let out a familiar muffled scream, her mouth against the wall. That was when I let myself come.

Soon after, the coldness of reality would slowly seep in as we rushed to put on our clothes in order to get back to the church service before it ended. Soon enough, people would be filling this room faster than I'd filled Candace.

She fastened her last button, licked her lips and said, "My beautiful boy. Thank you so much. That was amazing."

What had felt so good just seconds ago now made me feel sick.

The next fifteen minutes were spent doing what we were supposedly here for, setting up the tables and chairs.

The commotion in the church upon our return was a shock to my system. People were rushing around flustered. Bright red lights from emergency vehicles flashed through the stained glass windows.

My stepmother was wailing in a corner while my half-brothers attempted to hold her limp body up.

What was happening?

I spotted paramedics hovered over someone. It took me a few seconds to realize it was my father.

Preacher Thomas rushed toward me, stopping me from moving any further. "Sevin…son. I'm so sorry. Your father…he collapsed in the middle of service. The paramedics just confirmed that they couldn't save him. He's no longer breathing. He's gone to be with the Heavenly Father."

No.

No.

No.

My father was gone?

It felt surreal. Amidst my shock, all I could think about was the fact that eventually your sins catch up with you. Bad things happen to bad people. Dad was a good person. He didn't deserve this. But *I* did. This was my punishment, and it was a long time coming.

Candace stood frozen with her hands over her mouth.

"I'm so sorry," the preacher repeated.

I looked him in the eyes and stood there speechless. I wanted to tell him that he shouldn't be sorry for me. I was the sorry one. This was my fault. Because while my father lay dying, I was next door fucking the preacher's wife.

CHAPTER 2

SEVIN

The month that followed my father's death was torturous. Being left alone in the house with my stepmother and half-brothers became a situation I needed to get myself out of. I just didn't have an exit strategy yet. I'd been saving the wages I'd earned from working a maintenance job at the town stables, hoping to put myself through college and had planned to move away as soon as I had a little money in the bank. Now, with Dad gone, the need to get away from here seemed urgent.

My father, Brent, had been the only voice of reason, the only person I could somewhat relate to, even though he was pretty much brainwashed by my stepmother. At least he cared about me. My stepmother was cold, close-minded and never a true replacement for my own mother. Dad's main fault was that he was weak and didn't know how to stand up to Lillian.

My father married her five years after my mother died. Religion hadn't even been a small part of our lives until Lillian came into the picture. She convinced my father to pull me out of public school so that she could homeschool me. She felt that being around public school children would have a negative impact on me because they came from families that hadn't yet accepted Christ. Sheltering me was her way of making sure I was taught everything the way she wanted without outside influences. She'd teach us that life was about living in fear of God and that the Bible was meant to be taken literally. We had very little interaction with other children unless they came from strict Christian families. I had to get very creative, often sneaking away to hang out with the "regular" kids in the middle of the night or during detours taken on the way to run an errand for Stepmommy Dearest. My father went along with everything Lillian wanted. He was lost after losing my mother—his one true love—and fell easily into my stepmother's web.

Dad and Lillian had three sons together, my younger brothers, Luke, Isaiah and John. They were the spitting images of their mother, blond clones of each other that resembled the Children of the Corn. On the other hand, with my black hair, dark blue eyes and high cheekbones, I looked exactly like a male version of my dead hippie mother, Rose. I stuck out like a sore thumb and never felt a bond with my brothers.

Feeling like I owed it to my father, I pretended to go along with all of Lillian's rules. By all appearances, that made me the perfect Christian boy. In reality, behind closed doors, I was the antithesis of that. Lillian always taught me I could go to hell just for having inappropriate thoughts. She didn't realize that very warning was what convinced me to act out in secret. If merely having impure thoughts would guarantee me a ticket to hell, I might as well have been gaining the satisfaction that came from acting on them.

A light knock on the door prompted me to shove the sketch I'd been working on under the bed.

Lillian pushed her way into my room. "Sevin, we have guests, and I'd like you to meet them. Do something with that hair please, put a clean shirt on and come downstairs." She slammed the door shut.

I was in no mood to put on an act right now for her guests. Grabbing the sketch from under the bed, I took my sweet time finishing what I was working on before heading down.

With small circular strokes, I carefully shaded in the nipples of the breasts I'd drawn. This would be one of dozens of nudes I had stashed away in a box hidden inside a hole in the wall I'd drilled into the back of my closet. It seemed like I'd been drawing naked women since the beginning of time, but I knew the exact moment it started. In fact, a shrink would have a field day with it.

One day when I was thirteen, I'd been left alone in the house, which was a rarity. I'd decided to start rummaging through my father's things to try to find something of my mother's. I was desperately looking for pictures or any memento. I was fairly certain Lillian had either hidden all traces of Rose or had her things destroyed. To Lillian, my mother—a non-religious free spirit—was a sinner who deserved no respect.

Searching my father's office, I'd come up empty-handed with the exception of one small box that was hidden inside a larger one. The outside box was the packaging of a Craftsman drill and was clearly meant to deter people from snooping.

Inside the smaller box was some jewelry and a nude sketch of a woman with a small waist, large hips and perfectly round breasts. Lillian would have blown a gasket if she knew my father had it. It took me a few seconds to confirm that the woman was my mother. The thing is, it should have grossed me out, but knowing that my father was keeping it in secret made me happy. I assumed he'd been the artist.

That night in my room, I started to draw my first female body. I wasn't in any way trying to recreate the naked image of my mother. But I think I fell in love with the idea of creating something that was so forbidden, so intimate. I loved the idea of imagining what my father was feeling when he drew it, an intense love and appreciation. Sketching nudes became a pastime, an escape. Each one I'd create was different and more beautiful to me than the last. While some might have seen it as fucked up, over the years, I came to the conclusion that the process of drawing a naked woman was more fulfilling to me than being inside of an actual woman who was just using me.

"Sevin, what's taking you so long?" I heard Lillian yell from the bottom of the stairs.

I slipped the drawing under my bed. "Coming," I yelled.

Running a comb through my hair, a deep sigh escaped me. There was nothing I hated more than putting on a show for houseguests. My brothers were innately sweet and respectful. For me, it was always a fucking performance.

I threw on some khakis and a blue button-down shirt, rolling up the sleeves. I ran down the stairs and stopped short at the sight of a girl around my age. She had long medium brown hair and was wearing a flowy skirt down to her ankles. She was cute. Not exactly the houseguest I was expecting.

I coughed. "Hi."

"Hi. I was just looking for a bathroom," she said shyly.

"I'm Sevin. Who are you?"

Blushing, she said, "I'm Elle."

I reached out my hand and just as she extended hers, a man appeared and pushed her arm down to stop us from touching.

"I see you've met my daughter, Elle."

Turning to him, I replied, "Yes, sir. And you are?"

"I'm one of your father's oldest friends, son. We've never met." He offered me his hand. "Lance Sutton."

I shook it. "Sevin." Glancing over at the girl then back at him, I said, "Yeah…my father mentioned your name once or twice. Where are you living now?"

"We've come a long way, actually…from Kansas. Your father and I grew up together there. He and I were practically like brothers at one time. He moved away when he met your mother. Rose was a drifter and took your father with her. He lost his way for a bit back then. But we reconnected a couple of years ago, started keeping in touch again."

"What brings you all this way?"

"Actually, I was hoping you and I could sit down and talk."

Lillian was standing in the corner and gave me a slight nod of approval, which meant I probably should have been worried. Whatever this was, she was in on it.

"Okay…yeah. Sure."

Lillian placed her hands on the girl's shoulders. "Elle, honey, why don't you come help me prepare lunch for everyone?"

"Sure, Mrs. Montgomery."

When Lillian and Elle were out of sight, Mr. Sutton nudged his head toward the sliding glass door leading out to our backyard. "Why don't we go outside."

"Alright," I said, squinting my eyes suspiciously.

After a few seconds of silence, we stood facing each other on the deck as a breeze blew moss around in the air.

I was the first to speak. "What's this all about, Mr. Sutton?"

"Please...call me Lance."

"Alright. Lance. What's going on?"

"Brent and I had been discussing some things before he passed away."

"Things?"

"Yes. Your father was concerned about you, that you might be getting into some situations...certain temptations...that would not befit a good Christian life."

"Okay..."

"He told me you were saving up for college on your own, and I respect that. But I have a proposition for you."

I crossed my arms. "A proposition..."

"Yes. See, your father really did want the best for you. He knew that I had been looking for someone who I could groom, mentor and train to take over my business."

"What kind of business?"

"Meat packing. I own a beef plant back in Dodge City. Sutton Provisions."

"You want me to take over your business when all I've been doing for the past year is shoveling horse shit?"

He chuckled. "It wouldn't be overnight. I'd take you under my wing for several years until you were ready. The company would also pay for business school."

"What's the catch?"

"Well, obviously, you'd have to move."

"That's not a catch. Getting out of here is a major incentive. What's the *catch*?"

"There is something else. It's not really a catch. At least, I'm hoping you won't see it that way."

"I don't understand."

"I wouldn't ask just anyone to take over my business—something I've worked for my entire life. You would have to be a part of my family. I don't have a son of my own, Sevin. I have three daughters. Your father...he wanted the best for you. He knew you weren't happy here, that you might be getting into some trouble. But I know you're a good kid because you're Brent's son. This plan...it wasn't supposed to come about so soon, but after Brent died, I didn't think it should wait."

"What are you getting at?"

"You met my daughter, Elle."

"Yeah...nice girl. What about her?"

"Sevin, in our community, we don't just let our daughters date men. The women are courted."

"Courted?"

"Yes. As a father, it's my responsibility to find a good Christian man to court my daughter with the best of intentions."

"What does that involve?"

"Well, one thing it does *not* involve is physical contact of any kind. Under this scenario, a young man spends several months getting to know the girl. Then, eventually, if he's far away, he would move closer and outings would be chaperoned."

"What if I don't want to court Elle?"

"Then, this situation wouldn't work."

"That's part of the deal with this job?"

He hesitated. "Yes."

"You talked about this with my father?"

"Yes. He wanted this life for you."

"So, what happens if the courting doesn't work out?"

"Sevin, I can't give up my empire to someone who isn't even a part of my family."

"So, we're not just talking about spending time with Elle. When you say court, you really mean—"

"Marry," he interrupted. "You would marry my daughter."

CHAPTER 3

SEVIN

The phone rang every night at the exact same time. It was cute how consistent she was. It wasn't even necessary to look at the caller I.D.

"Hey, Ellebell."

"Hi. What are you up to?"

"Just starting to pack up some things, actually."

"You don't move out here for another month, though. I thought you said you don't have that much stuff."

"I guess I'm just a little eager to get outta here."

Elle and I had been talking on the phone every day for three months. After Lance and she left the house that first day, I spent a couple of weeks mulling over his offer before accepting. Agreeing to marry someone I didn't even know seemed like an insane thing to do at first. But in the end, the opportunity handed to me on a silver platter was really hard to turn down. My outlook was also different now since Dad dropped dead of a heart attack. I wanted to change my life, be a better person to honor his memory…basically, stop fucking around.

The timing of this opportunity seemed to be heaven sent. It felt like a now or never situation. I kept telling myself that I could always back out if it didn't feel right. With each day, though, it seemed to make more sense.

For one, the fact that I didn't know Elle enough to love her was irrelevant. I had no desire to fall so crazy in love with someone that losing

12

them caused me the same kind of irreparable damage my father experienced after my mother died. I was too young then to remember much about the years before Lillian but not too young to know that my mother's death wrecked my father.

Even though a part of me wanted to experience the intensity of love just once in my life, it wasn't worth the risk. Having a healthy mutual respect was more important to me. Love was fucking crazy. Marriage, on the other hand, was basically just a business arrangement. Elle made it easy to want to follow through with it. She was sweet as hell and easy enough to talk to. If I did end up falling in love with her, then I'd deal with that when it came. If I didn't, then at least no one would get hurt, and there was some good in that, too. Things were moving a little faster than they probably should have, but then again, nothing about this situation was typical.

"Well, I know Daddy is really eager about you coming out here. He says he's gonna put you to work before you even take your coat off."

"Seriously, anything will be better than working at the stables. You might not want to marry me right now if you knew what I smelled like."

"There is nothing that would make me not want to marry you, Sevin Montgomery."

"Really? Nothing? What if I were secretly a serial killer?"

"Of animals or humans?"

"Humans."

"Then, there could be a problem. But Daddy is a hunter, and I love him. So, animals would be okay."

"He hunts? Really?"

"Yes. He'll probably want to take you out sometime with him."

Shit. That better not have been another job requirement. It was then that it really hit me that I'd be working for a fucking beef plant, and that meant that I was essentially going into the business of dead animals. I'd have to suck that up, but there was no way I was going to kill one myself. *Wow. I guess I did have some morals.* I could look into another man's eyes after fucking his wife, but shooting a bunny for enjoyment was out of the question.

I changed the subject. "So, tell me what else there is to do in Dodge City besides killing animals."

"We have a movie theater."

"Man, that sounds exciting. You're killing me here. I can't get there fast enough."

She laughed. "Honestly, it's really not the most exciting place to live."

If Elle weren't so conservative, I might have flirted with her and told her that I could think of a number of things we could do to pass the time there together. But after three months of feeling her out, I knew better. Maybe once we were formally engaged, I would test the waters a little more. I planned to give her my mother's engagement ring soon after I got out there. The marquise diamond had two small sapphires on each side. It was one of the pieces of jewelry my father had stashed away in that box. He hadn't officially given it to me, but I was taking it. Anyway, the ring was just a formality. It was pretty much understood that my moving meant Elle and I were definitely getting married.

Swallowing the urge to say something suggestive, I said, "Well, you're lucky I like you. It won't matter what we're doing."

"I really can't wait to start a life with you, Sevin."

I knew that she meant it, even though I couldn't quite figure out what exactly it was she saw in me. Our conversations never ran deep enough for her to know the real me. She probably wouldn't want to marry that guy. So, was it physical attraction? Whatever it was, I knew she was the type of girl who would be loyal. She would worship me. She'd be a good wife. Yet, there was a part of me that wanted to shake her, wishing she'd just tell me a dirty secret, cuss, tell me that she couldn't wait to fuck me or just tell me to fuck off once in a while.

"We'll be good together, Ellebell. You have a very calming way about you. You don't let anything get to you. I need someone like that to balance me out. It's been a tough year. I've had a lot of anger inside of me. But meeting you has been the best thing to happen to me in a really long time."

She was silent for a while before she said, "I love you, Sevin."

Elle hadn't ever used those words before. My heart started to pound because I honestly didn't know how to respond.

When I didn't say anything, she continued, "I know it's maybe too early to say that, and it's a little strange because we haven't even spent physical time together. But it's how I feel. I truly believe becoming your wife is God's will for me."

Wow. That was profound, but I just couldn't tell her I loved her. I wasn't there yet. But I didn't want to insult her or lie to her.

"That's one of the nicest things anyone has ever said to me. I hope I can live up to that."

I was gonna damn well try.

***

My last month at home in Oklahoma flew by. The time was spent saying final goodbyes to friends and co-workers at the stables and spending some quality time with my little brothers, which was not typical of me. I also researched the hell out of the meatpacking industry so that I didn't seem like a total idiot walking into Lance's company on the first day.

The final day before I had to leave, I made sure to seize the small box my father kept hidden away which contained my mother's jewelry and the naked sketch I'd found long ago. I was packing up the last of my things when Luke, the oldest of my half-brothers, walked in.

"Hey, buddy."

"Don't forget us, Sevin."

"I promise. I won't. You guys have each other, though. Stick together like you always do. Just remember that someday if you figure out that things aren't exactly the way Lillian taught you, you can always come to me wherever I am. There will always be a safe place for you."

There was a reason why I chose to say that to him. I had more than a strong inkling that Luke didn't exactly share my vast appreciation of the female form. His mannerisms and some of the questions he would ask led me to believe that he was gay. And knowing how Lillian was, that scared the living shit out of me. I'd heard the way she spewed hate toward gay people, and I'd study the look of fear and shame on his face whenever he'd hear her talk negatively about them. If there was only one reason to stay behind in this hell hole, it was to protect Luke from her wrath. He'd once asked me why gay people were going to hell if God made them that way. That was when I knew. But Luke was only thirteen now and didn't seem ready to admit his sexuality to anyone.

I placed my hands firmly on his shoulders and looked him straight in the eyes. "You can come to me with anything, alright? *Anything.*"

"Thank you. I'll remember that." He hugged me tightly. "I'll miss you."

"I'll miss you too, Luke. I'm sorry I've always been a shitty brother. Just know my attitude here had nothing to do with you. I love you."

Those three words had come out very easily, and that shocked me. It was the first time I'd ever used that term toward one of my brothers. It felt right in that moment. When I spotted the tears in Luke's eyes, it only confirmed I'd made the right decision. Poor kid had probably been starving for my affection all these years, and I'd chosen to give it to him only because I was walking out of his life.

"I love you too, Sevin."

***

The next morning, I'd quickly gone to put gas in my father's old Ford 100 pickup, which I inherited after he died. I prayed hard that it would make it all the way to Kansas without breaking down. As soon as I started earning some real money, the first purchase would be a new car.

I'd packed most of the large boxes into the truck already and was just doing a final inspection of my room when Lillian entered.

"I'm checking in to see if you're all set."

"Yup. I'm all ready to go. Just taking a last look around."

"I really am proud of you for making the right decision. Your father is surely smiling down from heaven that you've found a nice Christian girl and that you'll be living the kind of life that the Lord intended for you."

"I guess," I said, packing the last of my smaller items and keepsakes.

"Let me help you carry these last two containers downstairs." She lifted one of the boxes.

"No! Don't touch that."

As soon as the words came out of my mouth, I knew I'd made a big mistake. Playing it cool would have been the smart move. Instead, Lillian was now clearly aware that there was something in there I didn't want her to see.

Her eyes slowly moved toward mine in a suspicious side glance. "What exactly are you hiding in here that would cause such a knee jerk reaction?"

"Nothing."

"Then surely you won't mind my taking a look?"

"Actually, I do—"

Before I could plead with her, she opened the box.

Fuck.

She placed the box down on the bed and covered her mouth with one hand, lifting one of the sheets of paper with the other. "What is this, Sevin?"

"It's exactly what it looks like."

She sifted through the pile. "This is sick. Who…who are these women?"

"They're not real."

"They look real to me."

"Thank you."

"That wasn't a compliment," she shouted.

A slight nervous laughter escaped me. "What do you want me to say?"

"I want you to explain why you have all of these drawings of naked women in this box when you're about to be entering into a marriage with someone who is pure and innocent. This is disgraceful!"

I looked into her eyes—something I rarely did—and said honestly, "I think they're beautiful."

"How do you think your father would feel if he saw this?"

Digging inside the other remaining box, I located the sketch my father had drawn of my mother all those years ago. Then, I walked over to Lillian and handed it to her.

"Here's your answer, a parting gift from Dad." My voice was shaky. "You thought you destroyed all traces of her, didn't you? But as you can see…I learned from the best."

I grabbed the last two boxes, leaving her with nothing but the picture of a naked Rose as I walked out the door and never looked back.

CHAPTER 4

SEVIN

"Good girl." I patted the dash of the old truck. Entering the final stretch of the long drive down US-281, I thanked my lucky stars that she hadn't broken down.

Off the highway, I continued down a long seemingly endless dirt road that was supposed to lead to the Suttons' ranch. The area reminded me of a wild frontier straight out of an old Western movie. I had actually read that the show *Gunsmoke* was filmed right in Dodge City.

On top of all this, my truck decided to start backfiring every once in a while. So, it was easy to imagine that I was in the middle of a gunfight. Maybe, I was just delirious after six hours in the car. After tearing through all of the snacks I'd brought, I was getting hungry. And horny.

I was so fucking horny.

I hadn't been with anyone since Candace—the day my father died. And I knew that it was going to be several months before Elle and I were married. So, my hand and I would have to get even more acquainted than we already were. Thank God I'd have my own private space to take care of things. The small guesthouse next door to the Sutton residence was going to be my temporary home until Elle and I moved out after the wedding.

It was about five in the afternoon, and the sun was still shining brightly. A set of white wind turbines were the first sign of movement after miles of driving down the vast open space.

Eventually, there were more signs of life: cattle on the sides of the road, an occasional car passing by, and some houses began to sparsely appear. Grateful for the daylight, I couldn't imagine breaking down out here in the middle of the night because there seemed to be no such thing as a cell phone tower in these parts. I hadn't had service since exiting the highway. It was a good thing I had written directions instead of relying solely on the GPS app on my phone. I estimated that I only had a few miles left.

Something began to move toward me in the distance. At first, it looked like it could have been a stallion galloping with strands of wild black hair blowing in the wind. As it got closer, I realized it was a girl on a bicycle. She slowed down as she approached my truck, and I followed suit. Our eyes locked for a few brief seconds as she passed me in what seemed like slow motion. My eyes stayed glued to the rearview mirror as she rode into the distance. When my truck suddenly backfired, I hit the brakes after I noticed that she'd crashed the bike and had fallen onto the dirt road.

Shit!

I put the truck in reverse, backed up and rushed out to help her.

"Are you okay? Let me help you up."

"No, no, no. I'm fine," she said as she got up without looking at me.

"You had me scared there for a minute. What happened to you?"

She seemed to stop to catch her breath for a second after she finally looked me in the eyes. I wasn't sure what it meant. Framed by the heavy raven strands of hair was a stunning face now covered in dirt. She looked around my age.

She finally spoke, "It was your truck. When it backfired, it scared the bejeezus out of me. It sounded like a gunfight at the O.K. Corral."

"Yeah. I know. It's funny you say that. I thought the same thing earlier. But I've just gotten used to it."

"That clunker is a hazard."

"It's not a clunker. It's a classic, actually."

"Oh, I know. That's a '56 Ford 100."

"Very good. How could you tell what year it was?"

"You were wearing a seatbelt when I drove by you. The '56 was the first

20

model where a seatbelt was an option."

"Wow. Impressive."

"Why is that?"

"Most girls wouldn't know that."

"Well, I'm not most girls. And I happen to know a lot more about cars than just that."

"No, you're definitely not most girls."

"Are you being facetious?"

"No. It's not every day you meet a girl with dirt on her face that knows a thing or two about cars."

"Dirt?"

"You should see yourself. Go look in my mirror."

She put the kickstand down and walked over to the truck. Leaning into the driver-side mirror to examine her face, she laughed. "You weren't kidding."

I stood behind her, staring at her reflection. "You're a mess."

Truth was, even with filth on her face, this girl was so amazingly beautiful that my heart was palpitating.

She brushed her fingers along her cheeks then straightened her back suddenly and accidentally knocked right into me. I hadn't been paying attention to anything but her face in the mirror and had gotten too close.

"Sorry," she said.

"That was my fault. Let me…get you something to clean your face."

Reaching into the open window of my front seat, I grabbed a piece of paper towel and wet it with some water from my bottle. "Here."

"Thanks." As she wiped her cheeks, she looked down and said, "Oh no."

"What?"

"There's blood seeping through my skirt. I think I cut my knee."

"Let me see."

She backed away. "No. I can't let you."

"Oh. I'm sorry. I was just trying to help. I didn't mean anything by it."

"I know you didn't. It's just…I'm not allowed to—"

Holding up my palms, I said, "I get it."

A car started to approach. I nudged my head toward the grass on the side of the road. "Let's get out of the way. Go over there and check your leg. Make sure it's okay."

She walked to a grassy area several feet away and lifted her long skirt with her back toward me. She yelled over to me, "Can I have a clean paper towel with some water?"

"Yeah…yeah, of course." I fumbled through my truck for the items, unable to figure out why I was suddenly on edge and nervous. Wetting the paper towel, I walked over to where she was now sitting down on the grass.

"Thanks." She took the paper towel and stuck it under her skirt to clean the wound.

"Are you alright?"

"Yeah. It's just a scrape. I'll put some antibiotic on it when I get home later."

When she stood up, there was an awkward silence as we just looked at each other. I could sense that I was making her nervous, yet there was something unspoken between us that kept her from running back to that bike.

Suddenly, it was like a light switch went off inside of her. "I have to go."

"Alright." I stood frozen in the same spot just watching her leave.

As she hopped on her bike and started to pedal away, I got in my truck and attempted to start it. I kept turning the ignition over and over, and nothing was happening. It was embarrassing because the girl was still within earshot. She'd called it a clunker, and I'd defended it. Now, this was proving what a piece of shit the truck really was—classic or not.

I heard her voice behind me. "Has this ever happened before?"

She came back.

"No. It's always started for me."

She walked around to the front of the truck. "Lift the hood."

"I was going to do that myself. You don—"

"Open it up."

I couldn't help laughing at her persistence. "Yes, ma'am."

I was pretty good with cars but intentionally let her have at it, watching it all unfold like a show.

I could see she was checking the fuel pump.

"It's not the fuel pump," she said.

I stuck my hands in my pockets, amazed at her knowledge. "Alright."

After a few minutes, she said, "I just checked the butterfly valves on the carburetor. That's not the issue, either."

Where the hell did this girl come from?

If she were smart, she'd check the electrical. I decided to test her. "What will you be looking at next?"

"The plug wires."

Good girl. Wow.

A couple of minutes later, she turned around with grease on her face. "Two of them came loose. It must have happened from the vibration on the highway. That's why the truck won't start now. Stopping it was a big mistake."

Actually...I was thinking that stopping the truck was the best decision I made all day.

I couldn't contain my smile. "What are you gonna do next?"

"Reconnect them."

I watched every movement of her hands until the wires were connected.

"All set. You should be good to go. Wanna test it?"

"I trust you." Truth was, I didn't want to get in the car and leave just yet. Instead, I stalled. "Where did you learn to do all this?"

"It's kind of a secret."

We both leaned against the truck.

She flinched when I lifted my hand to her face and swiped my finger along her cheek. "You had a ton of grease right there," I said.

"Oh...thank you."

"So, what do you mean...a secret?"

"I have this friend, Adelaide. She owns a car repair shop. I was actually going to visit her when I passed you on the road."

"She taught you how to fix cars?"

23

"Yeah. My parents…they don't like me going over there at all. They think I'm going to visit another friend when really, I go see Adelaide and hang out with her and the other mechanics. They all taught me everything I know."

"Why don't your folks like you hanging out there?"

"It's kind of a long story."

"I have time. Let's go sit on the grass."

What was I doing? I was so late in getting to Elle's. But I wasn't ready to leave this girl. She fascinated me. We both sat down, and she started to open up.

"My parents just don't think that Adelaide shares the same values as they do. And they don't think that fixing cars is a suitable career for a woman."

"I think it's badass."

"Me, too."

"How old are you, anyway?"

"Twenty," she said. "How old are you?"

"We're the same age. I'll be twenty-one in a week, though."

"Happy birthday."

"Thanks." I picked at the grass. "Thank you for fixing my truck and for trusting me with your secret."

"Well, we've known each other for like…a whole forty-five minutes, after all." We both laughed. Her smile lit up her entire face and when it faded, it was like the sun going down. She continued, "So, anyway, I feel really badly about lying to my parents, but I just feel like they're wrong, you know?"

"What they don't know won't hurt them. You're not hurting anyone by doing what you love and being around people that make you happy."

"Adelaide and her friends…they're good people."

"I have no doubt. Your parents sound unreasonable, kind of like my stepmother. You're not doing anything wrong. Don't ever believe that."

"That's what I try to tell myself. I just hate keeping secrets."

"Everyone has secrets."

"Tell me one of yours." Her words were abrupt and caught me off guard. Her eyes were searing into mine with a patient curiosity.

I'm heading to the house of the girl I'm going to marry. I'm supposed to be starting a new life right now, but all I want to do is stay here on the dirt and talk to you until darkness falls. How's that for a secret?

I definitely couldn't tell her that. And let's face it; we could have had a field day with the possible answers to her question. My life was a smorgasbord of inappropriate and bad things kept secret.

"Hmm...gosh, I don't even know where to begin." I chuckled and looked up at the sky, thinking long and hard about what to tell her. "Okay. So...since I was about thirteen, I've been drawing these pictures."

"Pictures?"

"Yeah...um..." I hesitated. "Pictures of women. Not distasteful. They're just drawings of the female form."

Her face turned red. "They're...naked?"

"Yeah. You think I'm a big pervert now?"

She burst out laughing. "No, I didn't say that. I guess it would just depend on the context."

Over the next several minutes, I told her the story of finding the sketch of my mother and how the drawing all started.

"That's more like art," she said.

"Exactly. But I still had to hide it because my stepmother would have kicked me out of the house or gotten me exorcised or something," I joked. "So, anyway...see? We all have secrets."

Her reaction made me feel relieved, like I wasn't crazy. Still, I'd never told anyone about my hobby or how it started.

"Thank you for sharing that with me."

"Well, you make me want to share things with you for some reason. I don't know. You seem...familiar to me or something. I'm not used to this."

"Yeah. Me, neither. Actually, I'm not even allowed to be talking to guys unless they come preapproved."

"Well, I won't tell anyone if you won't."

"Okay." The smile on her face was so beautiful it hurt. When the sunlight caught the gold speckles in the brown of her eyes, I had to look away to grab my bearings.

I never even asked her name. But what's the point? I needed to leave.

I just want to know her name.

Then, I'll leave.

"We know each other's secrets, but we haven't even exchanged names. What's yours?"

She hesitated then said, "Sienna."

"Sienna? That's nice."

"Thank you. What's yours?"

"Sevin."

The color seemed to drain from her face. "What did you say?"

"Sevin. I know. It's like the number, but it's spelled like Kevin with an S. My mother was unconventional, and she had the name picked out before I was even born. I—"

Sienna suddenly got up and straightened her skirt. "I have to go."

What?

"Did I say something wrong?"

"No. No, no. I just realized it's getting really late. I have to go before it gets too dark to ride home."

"Alright, well, it wa—"

She wouldn't even let me finish. My heart was pounding as she ran to her bike.

I shouted, "Sienna…wait!"

She waved frantically and took off like a bat out of hell. "Bye!"

I didn't know why it was so hard to let this girl go. It made no sense. But clearly, something freaked her out. I stood dazed, watching her long, black hair flailing in the wind until she disappeared.

As I continued my drive down the dirt road, I wondered if my tired mind had imagined her.

CHAPTER 5

EVANGELINE

By the end of the two-mile ride, my throat felt raw from gasping for air. Consumed by shock and humiliation, I had cried all the way to Adelaide's with tears streaming down my face.

Slamming the door behind me, it seemed impossible to catch my breath.

"Oh my word, Vangie. What on Earth has happened to you?" Adelaide had been cooking her famous beer and lentil soup on the stove and dropped the spoon down on the counter to rush toward me.

I shook my head repeatedly, unable to stop crying long enough to form words.

"Did someone hurt you?"

Wiping my nose on my sleeve, I shrieked, "No."

"Come here."

In Adelaide's arms, I let the remaining tears empty from me until I could find my voice again. As always, she smelled like a mixture of motor oil and patchouli.

"Sit down. I'm gonna make you some hot tea, and you're gonna tell me everything. Alright? *Everything.*"

Adelaide handed me the steaming hot cup of jasmine, and I took a sip. When I finally calmed down, I said, "I don't even know where to begin."

"Take your time."

"I was on my way here. I would have gotten here like an hour and a half ago, but I ran into this guy on the road."

She wrinkled her forehead. "Guy?"

"Yes."

"Alright…"

"I'd fallen off my bike, and he got out to help me. The second I laid eyes on him…it was just…something was there. He was so handsome. It was more than that, though. But God, he was…you know me…I don't find *anyone* attractive."

"I know. You rarely mention the opposite sex. I was starting to wonder if you were one of *my* kind. Just kidding, Vangie, but you know what I mean."

"Yes. I do. He was definitely great-looking, tall, black hair, mysterious eyes, big masculine hands. But see…it wasn't *just* his looks. It was more the way he looked at me, like he saw inside of me or something. There was a connection. It was indescribable. It was just this…"

"Chemistry." Adelaide nodded in understanding.

"Yes."

"Sometimes you can't really explain chemistry. It's just there from the get go. Keep talking. I'm just gonna go stir the soup," she said, walking over to the stove.

"Yeah. That's what it felt like, just this invisible charge or energy in the air. Anyway…at first, I didn't know how to handle what I was feeling. I just freaked out and left on my bike. But I could hear behind me that his truck wouldn't start, so I turned back around to help. You would have been so proud of me. I figured out what was wrong with it!"

"Son of a gun. Really?"

"It was one of those old Ford 100s with a flat V-8 engine? Two of the plug head wires came loose, so I reconnected them."

"That's my girl. Proud of ya, honey."

"Thanks. Anyway…after that…we talked for a while, got into some personal stuff, but we hadn't even exchanged names. He finally asked me for mine, and I told him it was Sienna."

"Sienna? Now, why would you go and do that?"

"You know I've never liked my name, Addy. I just wanted something pretty. And I honestly assumed I'd never see him again."

"I never understood why you feel that way about your name. Anyway…go on."

"He told me his name, too."

"What was it?"

Swallowing hard, I closed my eyes and said the word as it if were painful, "It was Sevin."

"Sevin…" Adelaide covered her mouth when she figured it out. "Sevin? THE Sevin? The guy who's coming here to court Elle? The guy who's moving onto your family's property? THAT guy? Oh no."

"Oh yes."

"Oh shit."

"I know." I buried my head in my hands and spoke through them, my voice muffled, "I know! I'm mortified."

"That's some crap luck and timing. Had you never seen a picture of him?"

"No. Elle never showed me an actual photo. She described him, but he was nothing like I pictured. She made him sound like a saint. But the guy I met was a little rougher around the edges. It was almost as though maybe she'd painted whatever picture she wanted to of him. I mean, they talk on the phone every day, and she's head over heels, but he was nothing like I imagined. He's not straight-laced at all, let's put it that way. He had this aura about him."

"Did you tell him who you were?"

"No. He still has no clue! That's the problem. As soon as he said his name was Sevin and I put two and two together, I got up and said I had to leave. I came straight here. I wasn't looking forward to him moving in *before* this, but can you imagine how I feel now? I can't go back there! I can't face him."

"You have to."

"I know." I stared down into my tea for a while then said, "He touched my face."

"What?"

"I had some grease. It was innocent. He rubbed it off with his finger. But when he touched me, it was like I felt it throughout my entire body. One simple touch. I'm so embarrassed."

"Don't be. That's a natural reaction to physical attraction."

"But I can't be physically attracted to my sister's soon-to-be husband."

"You didn't know, Vangie. It was an innocent mistake."

"I know, but how am I going to undo it now?"

"You may not be able to. You just have to be strong, accept this as one of life's freakish coincidences and face it head first."

"I'm so caught up in my own damn problem, I didn't even ask you how Lorraine is."

"Oh, honey, don't feel bad about that. She had a pretty crappy day, though. The meds are making her sick. But thank you for asking."

"Let me know if there's anything I can do, okay? Maybe pick up some more of the slack around the shop so you can be with her longer during the day."

"I appreciate that, but Marty and Jermaine are doing a good job. I'll let you know if things change. Tonight, though, you need to go home and face the music before it gets too dark to head back. You know I worry about you on that bike at night."

"Okay. I have no idea what I'm going to say or do."

"Don't overthink it. Just deal with each moment as it comes. I'll be here tomorrow if you need to talk again. And I'll save you some soup for lunch."

"Thanks, Addy. I don't know what I'd do without you."

"You won't ever have to find out."

I rode toward our house as if in a race against time with the fading sunset. As I passed the same grassy knoll where Sevin and I sat, guilt crept in. It wasn't because of what happened. I felt guilty because I knew that even if given the choice to go back and erase our moment in time, I wouldn't have changed a thing.

CHAPTER 6

SEVIN

When I pulled into the Sutton ranch, Lance, his wife, Olga, and Elle were all waiting for me on the farmer's porch. The sun cast a bright orange glow around their massive house that sat up on a hill. A few grazing horses were scattered about. It was hard to believe that this vast property was my home now.

Elle looked beautiful in a long, white dress with multi-colored flowers. She was beaming as she ran down the front steps toward me. It seemed strange not even being able to hug her after all this time. Lance's rules had been made very clear: Elle and I couldn't have any close physical contact until we were married. Since we were unofficially engaged, though, hand holding was allowed in a chaperoned environment.

Elle reached both hands out to me, and they were trembling a little. "You made it!"

"You nervous or something?" I asked.

"A little. I'm just super excited to finally have you here. I hope you like it."

"I'm happy to be here, Ellebell. There's nothing to be nervous about."

Lance came up behind her, causing me to instinctively let go of her hands. "How was the ride, son?"

"Long but uneventful."

Wow, it only took two minutes until my first lie.

"Glad to hear," he said.

Olga approached and gave me her hand. "The famous Sevin Montgomery. It's wonderful to meet you. I feel like I already know you with how much Elle talks about you."

"Likewise, ma'am."

"Please call me Olga."

I politely nodded. "Okay."

Olga wasted no time heading to the back of my truck. "Let's help move these things into the guesthouse."

Elle and I looked at each other and smiled.

A younger girl ran out to join us. "Number seven!" She looked like a little version of Elle with pig tails. Elle was the middle of three daughters. She'd mentioned that one of her sisters was a year older, while the other was much younger—about eleven.

"You must be Emily."

"How did you know?"

"Wild guess. Nice to meet you."

"Same." Emily looked over at her father. "Where's Evangeline? She should be here to meet Seven Heaven, too."

"Evangeline is off doing whatever it is Evangeline does," Olga answered as she pulled one of my smaller suitcases out of the truck. "She'd better be home soon, though."

Once we'd moved all of my things into the guesthouse, Lance and Olga left to go back to the main residence but asked Emily to stay with Elle and me. That was the protocol. Elle and I could be together as long as there was someone else with us.

"Take a look around the house. Do you like it?"

"It's cozy, but it's way more room than I've ever had to myself in my life."

The guesthouse was small but perfect for one person. There was a tiny kitchenette, a living room with a fireplace and one bedroom with a small adjacent bathroom. With dark wood and plaid décor, the house had a rustic log cabin feel. It already felt way more like home than Lillian's; that was for sure. More than anything, I was grateful to have my own space.

Emily was reading on the couch while Elle followed me into the bedroom where I started to hang up some of my clothes.

Glancing out the window, I noticed it was getting dark and couldn't help thinking about Sienna, hoping she arrived safely to wherever she was headed.

"What's next on the agenda tonight?" I asked.

"Dinner at the house in about a half-hour."

"Sounds good. I guess I should change out of this ratty t-shirt then, huh?"

Elle looked rattled when I suddenly lifted my shirt over my head to put on a button-down. I hadn't been using my brain and forgot that undressing in front of her was against the rules. She whipped her head to the side to look away from my bare chest, causing me to laugh inwardly.

"You can turn back around now."

Her cheeks pinked up. "You must work out a lot."

"I got a fair amount of exercise working at the stables. I'd do some weights and pull ups in my room back home, too, but I really like to run. That helps me burn off steam."

"My sister runs, too. I can't seem to do it for very long without having to stop."

"Well, we can do it together, start off slow if you want."

"I'd like that. They'll make Evangeline come with us, though. You know that, right?"

"Whatever. It won't be that way forever. As long as we can spend time together."

"Right." She smiled. "Hey…how did your brothers take your leaving?"

"They were pretty bummed when I drove off."

"And your stepmother?"

"Lillian was *real* devastated."

"She was?"

Elle knew that Lillian and I didn't get along. It surprised me that she didn't sense my sarcasm.

"Not because I was leaving. It's a long story." *One I didn't think Elle would appreciate.*

"I made you a little homecoming gift. Come see. It's on the couch."

Lifting a throw blanket, she opened it up to show me what was stitched on it. It was an S and an E.

I smiled. "Our initials."

"Yeah…I've been designing this logo that we could use for the wedding. I figured out how to stitch the design onto the blanket. Do you like it? The back says Montgomery."

"Sweet. It's really nice. Thank you. It'll keep me warm at night."

"Well…until we're married. Then, I can be the one to do that." She bit her lip and giggled.

That was the single most suggestive thing Elle had ever said to me. It was good to see her loosening up a little.

Before I could respond, Emily closed her book and said, "Yuck. I'm hungry. Can we go back to the house now?"

Poor kid, having to babysit two adults.

"Why don't you ladies go ahead, help your mother. I'll put away the last of my stuff and meet you up at the house in like ten minutes."

When Elle and Emily left, I retreated to my bedroom, locked the door and let out a sigh of relief. I was still tense from this afternoon, unable to shake what happened with Sienna from my mind. I needed to do something to relax before having to sit through my first dinner with the Suttons. I grabbed some lotion from the bathroom and lay back on my new bed. Unzipping my pants, I knew it wasn't going to take me long to finish. After squirting the white cream into my palm, I gripped my shaft, surprised at how fast I'd become hard as I pumped into my hand. Closing my eyes tightly, I tried to imagine Elle's petite body naked, what it would feel like to be with her. I wanted to visualize it so badly. All I could see was the curve of Sienna's ass through her long skirt, her messy black hair, her swollen lips wrapped around my cock. The image was clear as day and overpowering all other attempts by my feeble mind to envision anything else. I felt guilty but not enough to stop.

About halfway through, I decided to stop fighting the thoughts. To get the mysterious girl out of my system, I would allow myself to think about her just this once while she was still fresh in my mind. As the days passed, her image would slowly fade from my memory anyway. So, this would be the first and last time. Now, my imagination had her completely naked and riding me on the back of my truck as I pounded into her with all my might. My hand became her wet pussy wrapped around my cock. Tears nearly sprang to my eyes as I came so hard into my hand. Fuck. It felt so good to just let go.

The orgasm had knocked me onto my ass, and all I wanted to do was sleep. Deciding to take a shower to wake myself up, I washed my impurities away and reaffirmed my stance to never let that happen again.

***

"Hope you like chicken and dumplings," Olga said as I entered their spacious kitchen.

"That sounds awesome. I'm starving."

"Well, one thing we won't ever let you do is starve around here."

"Can I help with anything?"

"No." Olga smiled as she took a pan out of the oven. "The ladies have it covered. Just sit down and relax. You had a long drive."

Elle took notice of my wet hair. "You showered?"

"Yeah. I was in the truck for so long. I didn't want to gross you out on my very first night here."

"Elle's quite taken with you. I don't think that would be possible."

"Mama!" Elle whined, rolling her eyes and looking embarrassed.

One thing was for sure; they all made me feel very comfortable and wanted here. That wasn't something I was used to.

"What's your favorite meal in the whole world, Sevin?" Olga asked.

"You mean, besides chicken and dumplings?" I joked.

"Yes."

"Probably ribeye steak with garlic mashed potatoes."

"You hear that, Elle? You'll have to learn how to make it."

After helping them set the table in the dining room, we were just about ready to sit down to dinner when the front door slammed shut. Lance rushed down the hall, and I could hear him yelling.

"You've got some nerve coming home this late, Evangeline! Your mother and Elle could have used your help with dinner, you know."

"I'm sorry, Daddy. Please just don't yell. Not tonight. I had a mishap. It wasn't intentional."

"You have us worried sick that you're gonna get yourself killed riding that bike in the dark. Well, get on in here now and meet your sister's fiancé."

"I just need to use the bathroom. I'll be right there."

Elle, Emily and I were already seated when Lance came in and took his place at the head of the table. When Olga sat down, Lance said, "Sevin, you want to lead us in prayer?"

"Yes, sir." I closed my eyes and took Elle's hand. "Dear Lord, Heavenly Father, we thank you for this food. Feed our souls on the bread of life and help us to do our part in kind words and loving deeds. We ask in Jesus' name. Amen."

"Amen," they all said in unison.

When I opened my eyes, for a quick second, I seriously thought I was hallucinating. That was the only possible explanation because before I'd closed them, she wasn't there. Now, she was standing before me, looking exactly the way I'd left her, frazzled, disheveled and more beautiful if that were even possible. I blinked. She was still there. I blinked again.

What the fuck was going on?

My heart pounded out of my chest as I silently mouthed, "Sienna?"

She quickly shook her head frantically, a silent message for me not to say anything further.

Lance was the first to speak. "Sevin, this is our other daughter, Evangeline. She's very sorry she's late."

Her hand trembled as she reached it out to me. "Pleasure to meet you."

"Evangeline." It came out more like a question. I took her hand and squeezed it in an attempt to communicate my anger and confusion—a silent *what the fuck?* I wasn't even sure if I was angry at her or at the sick joke life was playing on me right now.

"Why are you so late?" Elle asked her.

Unable to look at her anymore, I stared down at my plate.

"A friend needed help," I heard Evangeline say.

My chest tightened. *Evangeline.* There was no Sienna. I was still processing everything, trying to figure out why she even lied about her name. At first, I wondered if maybe she did it because she knew who I was. But that made no sense because she'd freaked out when I told her my name was Sevin.

Emily was talking to Lance about some of the American history she learned in class. Elle and her mother were discussing a recipe. The sounds of their conversations, and the clanking of silverware all blended together. What was most deafening, though, was that which was unspoken. At one point, I looked up at her across the table from me, and we made eye contact before she looked down in shame.

The dinner went by in a blur. Managing to force myself to eat the chicken and dumplings, I wasn't able to stomach the lemon merengue pie for dessert. I mashed it up so that it looked eaten.

Unable to take any more of this, I needed to process it alone. My chair skidded against the wood floor as I got up. "I think I'd better turn in early tonight. Tomorrow is my first day at the plant, and I want to be alert."

"Looking forward to showing you around, Sevin," Lance said.

"Thank you so much for dinner."

Elle stood up. "Can I walk him back to the guesthouse?"

"Sure, honey," Olga said. "Evangeline, go on ahead with them."

She'd been looking down and lifted her head. "Excuse me?"

"Please accompany Elle and Sevin to the guesthouse."

"I'm really not feeling well. Can Emily go?"

"No. You've been extremely rude tonight. I think you need to go and apologize to them for your behavior while you're at it."

She looked humiliated, and my heart clenched. She reluctantly got up and followed us out the door. Elle grabbed my hand as Evangeline quietly walked alongside us.

Elle turned to her sister. "Did something happen to Lorraine? Is that why you're acting like this?"

"No. She's not doing well, but nothing's changed."

"Then, what is it?"

"It's nothing, okay? Please just drop it. I promise, nothing is wrong."

Feeling compelled to rescue her from an inquisition, I said, "People are allowed to have bad days, Elle."

Evangeline looked over at me for the first time since we started walking, and our eyes met briefly. Her expression softened as if to thank me for deterring any further prying.

We arrived at my doorstep, and I intentionally didn't invite them in because the walk itself was already too much stress for one night. "Thanks for walking me. I appreciate it."

Elle was still holding my hand and swung it playfully. "See you in the morning for breakfast."

"Alright. Good night." I stayed in my doorway watching them walk away. Elle ran ahead of her, and Evangeline surprised me when she briefly turned around to meet my stare.

Goodbye, Sienna.

CHAPTER 7

EVANGELINE

Three days had gone by, and I'd managed to avoid Sevin almost completely with the exception of dinnertime. It was like a sport—dodge Sevin—instead of dodgeball or something.

Luckily, Daddy had him in training a good chunk of the day. They usually didn't return from the plant until after seven-thirty at night. The most challenging part, though, had been attempting to act normal around Elle. Over the past several months, I'd listened intently as she boasted to me about the man courting her. I'd shared in her enthusiasm and participated in endless conversations about the wedding.

Elle and I both worked upstairs in the business offices of Sutton Provisions. While I would typically sneak over to Adelaide's after work, Elle would often ride her horse, Magdalene, in the late afternoons. But we were together almost all day until our shifts ended at three-thirty. Having to maintain the same attitude now was hard. Even harder was figuring out why I was making this so difficult. Nothing had really happened between Sevin and me. My attraction to him was my own issue. In reality, we'd just had an interesting conversation after I'd helped him with his car. Neither of us knew the other's identity at the time. It was all one big innocent misunderstanding. So, why did I feel so guilty?

It was early evening. Elle had gone with Daddy to pick up Mama's Aunt Imogene, who would be staying with us temporarily after being evicted from her apartment about an hour away.

I was in the kitchen when my mother emerged from the adjacent laundry room with some freshly-washed towels.

"Honey, I need you to take these over to Sevin's. Here's the key if he's not there."

I opened my mouth in an attempt to come up with an excuse, but honestly, I was going to have to face him at some point. The sooner this awkward phase ended, the better. Taking a deep breath, I grabbed the towels and headed across the open field to the guesthouse, secretly hoping he wasn't there.

The front door creaked as I slowly opened it. "Hello?"

There was no answer. He wasn't home. My heart rate immediately slowed. Unsure of where to put the towels, I walked through the bedroom to the small bathroom. There was no space in the cabinet under the sink, so I ended up placing them on the shelf at the top of the closet in his room. The smell of his woodsy cologne was everywhere. It immediately took me back to our first encounter on the road when the wind blew it in my direction. I grabbed the sleeve of one of his hanging shirts and sniffed it nice and slowly, closing my eyes to relish the scent.

"What do I smell like?"

I jumped.

Sevin removed his earbuds. He was shirtless. Sweat was dripping down his bare chest, slowly travelling down to the carved V of his abdomen. His breathing was ragged.

Dear Lord.

His body was so cut that it seemed almost obscene to be looking at it. But I couldn't look away.

Barely able to get the words out, I said, "I didn't hear you come in."

"I went out for a quick run. You left the front door open."

"I'm sorry…I was just…I brought you some towels. I don't know why I was smel—"

"It's alright, Evangeline." His eyes were intense. "I don't care if you smell my fucking shirt. Smell all of them if it means you'll stop pretending

I don't exist."

"Smelling your shirt was *not* okay. It was weird and—"

"You *are* a little weird, but it's what I like about you."

"Gee, thanks." I smiled.

"I was beginning to think I'd never see that smile again. I'm glad you're here."

"I've been avoiding you."

"Really? I hadn't noticed. I just thought you had really bad incontinence during dinner." He grabbed a towel to wipe his face then rubbed it over his chest. I was looking down at the floor to keep from staring at him when he asked, "Will you stay for a few minutes?"

"No. I really shouldn't be here." I walked past him toward the door to his room.

His voice stopped me in my tracks. "You think you're the only one who's freaked out? After you took off on your bike that day, it was impossible to get you out of my head, even though I was certain I'd never see you again. Then, I thought I was imagining you when you walked into the dining room that first night. But, of course, *you* already knew what you'd be walking in on."

I turned around to face him again. "I didn't want to come home. I was so embarrassed."

"Why did you run away when you figured out who I was? You could've just told me the truth. You could tell me anything. I thought we established that in the first hour we met."

When I laughed, the tense look on his face seemed to soften.

"I honestly don't know why I ran. It was a shock."

Sevin walked slowly toward me, his tanned chest still glistening. I could feel the heat of his body even though he wasn't touching me. "We didn't do anything wrong."

"I know," I said defensively.

"Why did you tell me your name was Sienna?"

"Honestly? I just don't like my name."

"Evangeline is a beautiful name. It fits you."

"Well, maybe I just don't like myself very much then."

"I love your name. You shouldn't lie about it."

"Thank you."

He looked up at the ceiling then back at me. "Let's try this again."

"What?"

"Hi, I'm Sevin," he said, holding out his hand.

I took it. "Evangeline."

"Hi, Evangeline."

"Hello."

We were still palm to palm. The sensation of his firm grip sent what felt like waves of energy and desire through the core of my body.

Why did hello feel like goodbye? Goodbye to the illusion of the man I met and hello to the reality of what our relationship would have to be moving forward.

"We're going to see each other every day. I'm going to be part of your family. So, we have to get used to this, Evangeline."

I let go of his hand, feeling sick at the thought. "I'll try, okay?"

"You'll stop pretending to be looking at yourself in the reflection of your plate at the dinner table?"

"Yes."

"You'll stop pretending you have to go to the bathroom every five minutes?"

"Yes."

"And you'll stop running the other way, tripping over people, when you see me at the plant?"

"Maybe."

"Good…because I hate it."

I nodded and looked at my watch. "I'd better get back."

"Okay. I'll see you later," he said without moving from his spot as he watched me walk backwards towards the door.

It was hard not to look down at his chest one last time before I turned around. If I thought I had a problem stopping my lustful thoughts about him before, it was going to be nearly impossible now.

***

Dinner that evening turned into an interesting experience for multiple reasons.

I'd been dressing a salad in the kitchen while Mama took a tray of kielbasa and potatoes out of the oven. Elle and Daddy hadn't returned yet from picking up Aunt Imogene. They were due back any minute.

Sevin walked into the kitchen. "Hey, Evangeline…Olga."

He'd showered after his run. His hair was wet, and he was wearing a form-fitting maroon pullover. His signature fragrance overrode the smell of the food. Sevin was suddenly all I could smell. It was dizzying.

"Will you please let me help with something, Olga?" he asked.

"You can help Evangeline set the table if you insist."

"I do. Thanks."

He quietly followed me into the dining room, carrying the flatware. The tension in the air was thick as he walked behind me around the oval table, setting down silverware after each plate I'd put down. It was like some weird game of musical chairs where awkward silence replaced the music. The hairs on my back stiffened. We weren't saying anything, but it was as if I could feel the weight of a thousand words along with the heat of his body so close behind me.

When I noticed he'd just put a fork where the spoon was supposed to go, I switched it. "The forks go on this side, actually." My hand was shaking. I couldn't believe how little control I had over myself.

Noticing my nerves, he suddenly placed his hand over mine and whispered, "Stop."

Chills ran through me. My heart started to beat faster. My nipples hardened. I hated my body for responding to him with equal amounts of fear and lust.

I turned to him, his hand still over my knuckles. It felt like I couldn't breathe as he just looked at me.

My mother's footsteps caused Sevin to move his hand off mine with lightning speed.

Mama entered, and we continued setting the table as if our stolen moment hadn't happened.

"So, while we're waiting for Daddy and Elle, I just thought I'd take the time to explain a little bit about my mother's sister, Imogene."

I cleared my throat. "Okay…"

"You met her a long time ago, Evangeline. She was well back then. The reason she's going to be living with us is because her mind is a little bit gone now. She has no children, so I'm her next of kin."

"Is it like dementia?" Sevin asked.

"Not entirely. I should clarify, Imogene hasn't really lost her mind as much as her filter over the years. She was in a car accident a few years ago and hasn't ever been the same. She says and does some inappropriate things, sometimes very sinful things. I have to believe that the Lord will forgive her for it because she's not well. You need to learn to ignore what she says or does. I just wanted to warn you while I had the chance."

About five minutes later, the front door opened.

My mother clasped her hands together and adorned a fake smile. "Imogene!" she said lovingly as she greeted her elderly aunt.

Imogene had long, white hair that was tied into a single braid. Her face was quite wrinkled, making her striking blue eyes stand out even more. When she smiled at Mama, I could see that all of her teeth were gone.

"It's wonderful to see you again, Aunt Imogene," I said.

"And you, dear." So far, she seemed like a normal old lady.

Elle walked over to Sevin and took his hand. "Imogene, I want you to meet my fiancé, Sevin Montgomery."

Sevin stuck out his hand. "Wonderful to meet you."

"My, my, you have big hands. Elle's going to be a lucky girl. If she's smart, she's already discovered what that means." She winked, flashing her toothless grin before my mother suddenly whisked her away to show her the bedroom where she'd be staying.

Once we were all sitting down at the table for dinner, I caught myself doing exactly what I promised I wouldn't; looking down at my reflection in the plate. Anything was better than staring across at Elle and Sevin's intertwined fingers.

Once the kielbasa links and potatoes were served, Daddy said grace, and we all dug in. It was a quieter dinner than usual. At one point, my mother suddenly asked Emily to come follow her into the kitchen. I happened to look at Sevin, and his eyes were practically bugging out of his head. Elle's face was red as a beet. Was I missing something? That was when I looked over at Imogene.

Oh my God.

I covered my mouth.

She was holding her fat kielbasa link upright in her palm and instead of eating it, seemed to be jerking it up and down, simulating a hand job. When she saw that I noticed, she did nothing but smile that toothless grin like everything was normal.

Sevin and I made eye contact. I could see he was about to lose it. Maintaining my composure might have been possible were it not for his expression. I buried my face in my hands and started to cry quiet tears of laughter, nearly peeing in my pants. I knew it was wrong to laugh at this, but I just couldn't help it.

My father was stoic and refused to speak. Elle just sat there in shock. Sevin slapped his cloth napkin down and left the room. I knew he was going to the bathroom to laugh in private. The whole situation was sick, yet after one of the toughest weeks of my life, I was grateful for the comic relief.

CHAPTER 8

SEVIN

Happy fucking birthday to me.

It was my twenty-first. That alone should have made it one of the happiest days of my life, but birthdays were never happy at all for me. This year was no exception. Even though I felt like drowning my sorrows in my first legal bottle of booze, I reminded myself of my vow to be a better person.

There was a knock on the door in a cheerful melodic rhythm. Elle and Emily were standing there with huge smiles on their faces.

"Happy birthday!" they said in unison.

"Thank you, sweetie pies."

This year, my birthday happened to fall on a Saturday, so Elle and I were supposed to be going into town for the day to celebrate. Emily was going to accompany us as our chaperone.

I hated that a part of me wished it were Evangeline.

But it was better that it wasn't. I couldn't think straight whenever that girl was merely in the same room, let alone joining us for an entire day. Today was one day I couldn't handle battling my attraction to her. Even though I'd told her that we needed to get used to being around each other, it seemed *I* was the one with the problem lately.

Determined to lose myself in Elle's company, I suggested she show me around Dodge City. We visited the Boot Hill Museum, the Dodge City

Zoo, and she took me to a couple of possible venues for the wedding reception. Elle managed to successfully help me forget about my problems for a while.

After a late lunch of burgers and milkshakes, we stopped at an arcade that Emily wanted to go to. It was the least we could do for her after she followed us around all day.

"Go on, Emily. Here's some money for the machine. We'll be right here." Elle seemed eager to have a moment alone with me, even though we weren't technically supposed to be alone at all.

Emily got sucked into a game at the far end of the crowded room. We were surrounded by flashing lights and arcade noises when Elle said, "I've been waiting to give you your birthday present."

She took my hand and startled me when she leaned in. Her lips were moving toward me. It was the last thing I expected. Elle brushed her lips gently over mine. When I moved my mouth over hers, I think she started to get scared I was going to slip her some tongue or do something else. She pulled away, stopping the kiss. It had been soft and felt innocent, even though I was sure it was a really big deal for her.

"Elle…you didn't have to do that. I could have waited."

"I know I'm not supposed to. But I wanted to. I have been *dying* to. I wish it could be more."

"It felt…really nice."

It did.

As she continued to smile up at me, I felt compelled to ask her a question.

"What do you want, Elle?"

"What do you mean?"

"I mean…out of life? What do you really want?"

"I want to be your wife."

"But aside from that, is there something you want to do but maybe feel like you can't? What are your dreams?"

"I don't know. Being a wife and—God willing—a mother…it's enough for me. Not every woman has to want more. Those things are really what I truly want."

"You're such a good person. Sometimes, I think you're too good for me."

"That's not true. You're everything to me."

Letting go of her hand, I ran my hand through my hair, trying to form my thoughts into words. "Don't get me wrong. I appreciate that so much, and no one has ever said that to me or even really felt that way about me. I guess, I just don't understand *why* you love me. Like, what have I done to earn that, and how do you know there isn't someone better for you out there than me—the guy your father chose for you?"

"First of all, my father didn't choose you. He introduced us, but I chose you. Life is short, Sevin. We're not even guaranteed tomorrow. Some people spend so much of their entire lives looking for that 'something more'…that they miss the gifts that God places right in front of them."

"I'm not perfect, Elle. I've done some bad things. Sometimes, I feel like if you knew about them, you—"

"I don't want to know. That doesn't matter to me. Loving someone means loving them despite their faults or mistakes. The Lord forgives you if you repent and accept Him."

While I felt that she truly believed that, our conversation still left me with more questions than answers. Namely, why I was suddenly overthinking the impending marriage when it was always supposed to be a business arrangement. I had accepted that. So, why was I suddenly questioning everything?

***

The candles flickered as wax dripped down off of them. I was twenty-one and staring down at my first ever fucking birthday cake. It was triple-layer chocolate and baked fresh by Olga. Growing up, before Lillian, Dad never celebrated my birthday, and Lillian didn't believe in birthday parties.

"Where's Aunt Imogene?" Emily asked.

Olga set the dessert plates down. "She won't be joining us for cake."

"Why not?"

"She's staying in her room for now," Lance said.

Imogene was odd; there was no doubt about that. But I found it kind of sad that they hadn't allowed her to sit with us at dinner at all anymore. I partly understood why they made that decision because of Emily, but it still didn't seem right. Elle or Evangeline would always just bring Imogene her dinner on a TV tray.

"Hey, Seven-Up, blow out your candles!" Emily shouted.

Staring into the flames, I extinguished them with one swift blow. Amidst the cheers and smiling faces, I couldn't help but notice the other person missing and wondered if she were intentionally avoiding my birthday celebration.

As if she could read my mind, Elle asked, "Where is Evangeline tonight?"

Olga passed her a piece of cake. "Lord knows. That girl keeps cutting it close on that bike at dusk. I just pray one of these nights, it's not a police officer knocking on our door instead of Evangeline."

My chest constricted at the thought of anything bad happening to her.

Elle put her hand on my shoulder. "You okay, birthday boy?"

"I'm fine. Why do you ask?"

"You just look a little down all of a sudden."

"I'm okay, Ellebell. If you want to know the truth, this was the best birthday I've ever had in my entire life." What I neglected to explain was how bad all of the other ones were. So, in truth, it wasn't much of a compliment.

I could hear the front door open, trying to ignore the sensations in my body that always seemed to erupt whenever I knew she was near. Something inside me always came alive, and despite my efforts to beat it down, it never ceased.

"Hi. Sorry I'm late."

"You missed Sevin's birthday party, Evangeline," Emily scolded.

"I'm sorry." She flashed me a fleeting glance. "Happy birthday."

Her eyes were red. She looked like she'd been crying.

"Are you okay?" I asked.

She didn't say anything, causing Elle to interject, "What's wrong? What happened?"

She shook her head as if she didn't want to talk about it then whispered to Elle, "It's Lorraine."

"Did she die?"

She shook her head. "No."

Olga entered the dining room. "My word, Evangeline. What is going on now?"

"I can't talk about it. You're gonna get mad at me, and I can't deal with this tonight."

Lance raised his voice, "Does this have to do with those lesbians?"

"Lance!" Olga turned to Emily. "Honey, please go to your room."

When Evangeline kept quiet, Lance repeated, "Well, what is it?"

"You don't really care. So, why do you want to know?"

Olga leaned in. "Honey, what's going on? You can tell us."

Speaking through tears, Evangeline said, "Lorraine is dying. She may not even make it through the night. The cancer has completely ravaged her. Adelaide is suffering. Lorraine's family is at the hospital and won't let Adelaide in the room. They've been together for twenty years. Lorraine is the love of her life, and Addy can't even be by her side when her partner takes her last breath. It's breaking my heart, and there is nothing I can do."

Everyone was silent. Watching her cry was causing me physical pain. I remembered the story she told me on that first day about having to sneak around to visit her friends, and the reasons behind her having to hide it were now even clearer.

"Evangeline, those women…they're sinners," Lance said. "What's happening is unfortunate, but the laws of the state and the laws of God are the same. The way they've been living is wrong."

"*You're* wrong, Daddy. Love is not wrong!"

"I beg to differ. It *is* wrong when it's between two members of the same gender. The Bible confirms that as well. I'm sorry. It's perverse. That poor dying woman is going to hell."

My fists tightened. I could feel my blood boiling as memories of Lillian and the hate she used to spew flooded my brain. I wanted to punch Lance in the face in that moment. The frustrating thing was that I knew he truly believed he was right.

Evangeline stormed out of the dining room. The front door slammed. I felt sick.

Lance and Olga retreated to the kitchen, leaving Elle and me alone at the table.

I turned to her. "What do you think about what your father just said?"

"What specifically?"

"That those women are going to hell for loving each other."

"I don't know, Sevin. There's a part of me that feels like it's wrong…you know, two women together. It's not what God intended. At the same time, I feel real badly for them and what they're going through."

That wasn't the answer I was hoping for out of her, and it only made me angrier. I'd had enough of this night. Needing to be alone, I got up from the table.

"Thank you again for today. I'm kind of tired. I'm gonna head over to the house."

"Can I walk you?"

"No. It's okay."

"Alright."

Stepping outside was a welcome escape. Smoke mixed with the cool night air; a neighbor must have been burning firewood. My heart felt heavy, and I couldn't even pinpoint the exact reason why anymore. I just wanted to get under my covers and shut off the world.

On my way to the guesthouse, I noticed a light coming from the small red barn on the property. Either that meant someone had accidentally left it on, or someone was in there. I needed to know if it was her.

She was huddled in a corner sitting on a mound of hay when I found her.

"Hey," I said.

She jumped and covered her chest with her hand. "You scared me," she said, sniffling.

"I'm sorry. I saw a light on and thought I'd come check on things."

"You shouldn't be here."

"I know." Instead of leaving, I walked toward her and sat down on the pile next to her. After several seconds of silence, I said, "You're right, you know."

"About what?"

"Your friends…they don't deserve what people are doing to them, keeping them apart. That's the real sin, and I truly believe those asshole family members are the ones going to hell."

She rolled her eyes. "Don't let my father hear you say that."

"Well, he almost did. I almost lost it. I should have said something."

"Don't. It's not worth it. He's too far set in his ways. It would be a waste of effort. I love my father, but I've just had to learn to agree to disagree."

"My brother is gay."

I'd blurted it out. It was the first time I'd ever admitted it aloud.

"What? Really?"

"Yep. No one knows, and I'm not sure he even realizes it himself a hundred percent." I chuckled. "But seriously, the attitude that people like Lance and my stepmother have makes me scared shitless for Luke and what the future holds."

"It must be such a horrible feeling to have to hide who you really are."

Lying further back onto the hay, I said, "I feel like I can relate to that myself a little lately."

"You mean here…with Elle?"

"Sometimes, yeah. I'm not perfect, and I really want this…my being here…to work out, but there are times when I feel like I can't be myself. But that's sort of how it's always been for me."

"You mean you can't show your inner pervert."

My stomach dropped.

She must have noticed the look on my face when she said, "Sevin, I'm just kidding. You confided in me about those drawings. It was just a bad joke. I don't think you're a pervert at all."

Throwing some hay in her direction, I said, "You're a little wiseass."

Her cheeks turned rosy. "Speaking of perverts...poor Imogene."

"Oh my God, Evangeline. That night...the two of us were the only ones losing it."

"You went to the bathroom to laugh, didn't you?"

"Yeah! I literally thought I was going to die from laughter. I don't think I've laughed that fucking hard in my life."

"I knew that's why you got up!" We both started to crack up, and when it faded, she said, "I'm sorry I missed your birthday."

"It's still my birthday." I smiled. "Anyway, you didn't miss anything. I've been in a real funk today."

"How come?"

"It's a long story."

"I have time," she said.

I threw some more hay at her in jest. "You just stole my line from the day we met." I hesitated. A part of me really wanted to tell her what was bothering me, but I didn't want to take away from her own problems. Instead, I changed the subject. "Do you come in here a lot to think?"

"Sometimes. How did you know I was in here anyway?"

"Like I said, I could see the light. Process of elimination."

"I would shut the lights off, but I'm deathly afraid of the dark."

"Really?"

"Yes. For some reason, it doesn't bother me so much being outside in the dark, but being in a pitch dark room makes me panic."

"That's a sucky feeling, but I'm the opposite. I like to sleep in total darkness."

"You're lucky you're marrying Elle and not me. We'd never be able to sleep in the same room."

"Yeah. Guess not, right?" There was a long silence before I looked over at her and asked, "Why *not* you?"

"Hmn?"

"If you're the older daughter, why did Lance want to marry Elle off first?"

"That's for him to explain. There are multiple reasons. But for one, I don't think he sees me as ready for marriage and for the responsibility that comes with it. So, you dodged a bullet." She winked.

God, she was beautiful. I needed to leave. Instead, I shook my head and asked, "What is it about you?"

"What do you mean?"

"What is it about you that makes me want to tell you all my secrets?"

"I feel kind of like that about you, too."

"You might think I'm strange for saying this…"

She interrupted me, "We're past that point. I've thought you were strange from the moment I met you, Sevin."

"Maybe that's why we get along so well. Freaks of a feather…" I joked.

She chuckled. "What were you going to say?"

"Something about you reminds me of what I imagined my mother was like."

"In what way?"

"Just a free spirit, someone who cared about people, who didn't discriminate, someone who was passionate and beautiful…inside and out."

Someone who would have loved me unconditionally.

"Wow. Thank you. She must have been something…"

"I don't really know. I never had a chance to meet her."

A look of shock washed over her face. "What?"

"I never met my mother."

"You mentioned that she passed away, but I don't understand. What happened?"

I couldn't believe what I was about to admit. It was the first time I uttered the words that were responsible for everything that was ever wrong with me. The words that defined me.

"I killed her."

CHAPTER 9

EVANGELINE

Sevin's eyes were watering when he'd said it. Shock and sadness ran through me, but I didn't say anything, knowing that he needed to find the words at his own pace.

My heart was racing. *He'd killed her.* What did that mean? He'd never met her, yet he'd killed her. Just as I started to figure it out, he resumed speaking.

"My mother died giving birth to me."

"Oh my God. I'm so sorry."

"I still don't know the details of exactly how it happened because my father always refused to talk about it. It was too painful for him."

"Does Elle know?"

"I'd told her my mother died when I was little, but we never discussed the details. That's partly my fault, because I always change the subject. I'm not sure if my father ever told Lance exactly what happened, either. If Elle didn't know, I suspect he didn't."

"You can't blame yourself for what happened."

"Deep down and logically, I know it wasn't my fault, but I spent most of my life wishing I were never born, wondering what she'd be like if I weren't here. It didn't help that my father was just a depressed shell for most of my early childhood. Then, he met Lillian and allowed her to basically kidnap his brain. In a weird way, he needed that. He needed direction, someone to take over, because he was just so lost. The one good thing Lillian ever did was save my father from the depths of despair. She just made everyone else miserable in the process."

"Your father loved you."

"I think he tried. He really did, but I never felt it. I look just like her. I can't imagine what it was like for him to look at me, a constant reminder of her, of the pain."

"She must have been really stunning."

I immediately felt embarrassed, realizing that my comment was basically an admission that I found *him* stunning.

Sevin's mouth spread into a smile as he also apparently drew the same conclusion. "Yeah, she was."

"What was her name?"

"Rose."

"That's so beautiful."

"My father loved her so much. That's the scary thing about loving someone like that, though. When they're gone, it feels like your entire life is over."

"I know. It's like what Adelaide is going through right now, but I know that she still would never trade her years with Lorraine to escape the current pain."

"Maybe one consolation is…I like to think my parents are finally together again now…where they belong."

"I definitely think they're together."

"Lillian and your parents would say with absolute certainty that they weren't in the same place. They'd say my mother was in hell because she wasn't a Christian."

"Well, I don't believe everything my parents say. In my heart, I know that things aren't as black and white as they've painted. There's got to be more to life than living in fear of punishment. It's such a shame. I just believe if you're a good person, God knows it. I don't think going to church every Sunday or saying you accept Christ makes a lick of difference in the end."

His next question startled me. "What do you want out of life, Evangeline?"

"That's a tough question."

"I know. I asked Elle the same one earlier."

"What did she say?"

"She said she wanted to be married to me, and that was enough for her."

"Elle is different than I am. Don't get me wrong, she's the best person I know, but we have different wants and needs. I truly believe she meant what she said to you."

"I do, too," he said.

"You believe what she said…or you have different wants and needs?"

"Both." His stare was penetrating. "So, answer my question."

"What do I want?"

"Yes."

"Too much."

"Too much?"

I sat up straighter and briefly closed my eyes to gather my thoughts before the words just seemed to pour out of me. "I want to be free, independent from my parents. I want to experience love, but I don't want to settle. I want to be loved back as much as I love someone, but I don't want that relationship to define me. I want to make a difference in the world, but I don't know how, and that frustrates me to no end. I want to be comfortable in my own skin. I want to make love in the rain someday and…skydive! I want to die knowing that I didn't live in fear but that I lived life to the fullest with no regrets. I don't want to feel guilty about being true to myself. I want too much, to the point where sometimes I feel like I'm gonna burst. It's overwhelming."

The weight of his stare was overpowering as he absorbed my words. He didn't say anything for the longest time before he simply whispered, "You're amazing."

Even though I'd never felt more connected to someone than I did to him in that moment, it felt like we were starting to cross a line. It compelled me to say, "Elle's gonna be a good wife. She'll make you really happy, Sevin." I swallowed the bitter taste of those words and suddenly got up, straightening my skirt. "I have to go back to the house before they come looking for me."

His tense expression from seconds earlier had transformed into one of surprise and disappointment at my sudden desire to leave. "Okay. Go on ahead." As I brushed hay off my skirt and started to walk away, he called out, "Evangeline…"

I turned around. "Yes?"

"Thank you for answering my question. I hope every single one of those things comes true."

***

Sleep was impossible that night between worrying about Lorraine and thinking about Sevin. When he asked me that question, I'd just blurted out all of the dreams kept hidden my entire life. I couldn't get over how he made me feel. For the first time, I truly sensed those feelings were definitely reciprocal. The way he looked at me confirmed that our connection wasn't all in my head. That was a dangerous realization.

This was the one man my mind knew it could never fall for, and yet my heart had other ideas. It had already fallen—hard and fast. As much as I tried, I couldn't stop thinking about him. I was desperate for a solution. Wanting someone you knew with absolute certainty you could never have was the very definition of agony.

When Elle walked into my bedroom the next morning, I could barely look her in the eyes.

"Are you okay?"

"Yes. Why?" I asked, playing with my hair as I always did when I was anxious.

"You haven't been yourself over the past couple of weeks. Everyone has noticed."

"Everything going on with Adelaide and Lorraine…it's taking a toll. I'll be okay. Don't worry about me. I'm sorry if I've seemed distant. How are you?"

"I didn't have a chance to talk to you yesterday, but something sort of major happened."

"What? Is everything okay?"

Elle smiled, her face turning red. "More than okay."

"Well, what is it?"

"I kissed him."

"You kissed Sevin?" My heart felt like it fell to my stomach.

She nodded. "You look shocked."

"I…I am. I thought you were waiting."

"I was. I don't know what came over me. It was his birthday, and I really wanted to show him how much he means to me. Mama and Daddy would kill me if they knew, but I don't regret it. Not one single bit."

"What did he do?"

"He kissed me back. It felt so good to kiss him. It just made me even more certain that he's the one."

The intensity of the jealousy I was experiencing was a wake-up call. Any other sister would have asked for details, but I was doing everything in my power not to think about them kissing. This was just a drop in the bucket compared to what would be coming as Sevin and Elle's relationship evolved. Getting rid of these feelings was not just an option but an urgent necessity.

Feigning happiness, I smiled. "Wow. That's great."

"I've been waiting for a moment to tell you, but you've been so busy."

"Well, I'm glad you told me."

She sat on the edge of my bed and crossed her legs. "I don't want us to grow apart."

"What do you mean? Why would that ever happen?"

"When Sevin and I get married. I don't want us to lose our connection. Even when I move away, I need to be able to talk to you about stuff…like sex. I'm not gonna know what I'm doing."

A wave of nausea and jealousy overwhelmed me. "I don't have any more experience than you do in that area."

"Are you kidding? You may not have real experience, but you've been studying it in your own way for as long as I can remember."

Elle was referring to the fact that I had always been more innately sexually curious than she was. I'd check out graphic romance novels from the library in secret, hiding them from my parents, sometimes forcing Elle to listen as I read some of the passages to her with a flashlight under the covers of the bed. So, while I hadn't had actual sex, I had definitely lived vicariously through fictional characters.

"I guess you have a point."

"The *real* point is that I don't want anything to change between us, Evangeline. Ever."

"It won't, Elle," I said, pulling her into a hug.

Taking in her sweet perfume that was just as delicate as she was, I closed my eyes tightly and silently vowed never to let anything come between us. My sister was more important than anything. That meant taking steps to ensure that whatever feelings I had for Sevin were eradicated immediately. There really was only one choice. I needed to find someone to take my mind off of him. If I wanted to continue living under my parents' roof, though, there was only one way to go about that. It would be their way or no way.

***

I knocked on the door to my mother's sewing room that afternoon after we'd all returned from Sunday service. "Do you have a minute?"

"Sure, honey. Come in. Is everything alright?"

"I've just been thinking about some stuff lately. I wanted to talk to you about it in private."

She'd been sewing a skirt on her black classic Singer machine and stopped what she was doing, placing the fabric to the side. "Alright."

I let out a deep breath and stared out the window at the rain falling outside. "With Elle and Sevin getting married, I've been pondering my future a lot. I know I told you I wasn't interested at all in being courted…"

"When you said you never wanted to get married, that was very upsetting to your father and me, you know. What does that mean for your future…turning into an old childless spinster? Look at your Aunt Imogene. She is a prime example of what can happen to people who lose their way in life and don't adhere to God's will."

I wasn't going to try to argue with my mother about poor Imogene, who had nothing to do with this. Imogene had issues, but I doubted they had anything to do with her never marrying.

"Well, at the time, when we last discussed this, I was strongly against arranged marriage. I'm still not a hundred percent sure, but I think I'd like to at least try seeing what my options are."

"You want to be courted? Because your father is not going to allow you to date traditionally without marriage as the ultimate goal and outcome."

"I know what his rules are. You don't have to explain it."

"Well, you know there are a lot of nice young men from our church around your age, Evangeline, but they're looking for wives, good homemakers who are ready to settle down. You have a very restless personality and are very hard to satisfy. Marriage is for life. Even though we want you to get married, you also have to be sure that it's what you want before entering into a courtship. It wouldn't be fair to the man if you didn't take it seriously."

I want love. But right now, what I really need is a distraction. I'll do anything for it even if it means going against everything that I believe.

"Like I said, I'm open to options. I have my hesitations about going this route, but I also don't want to be alone. I won't know if the courtship route will work for me if I don't try. But if I try and fail, I have a right to change my mind, don't I?"

"Daddy and I will talk about it, alright? You will always have a choice, but once you decide to pursue a courtship, it really needs to be taken seriously."

"I understand."

Mama and I continued talking until the rain cleared. Elle, Sevin and my father had taken a trip to a home improvement warehouse about an hour away. Sevin was supposed to be helping Daddy build a new shed the following weekend, so they were getting all of the supplies.

Opting to take advantage of the quiet, I decided to take a stroll around the perimeter of the ranch to clear my head until dinnertime. Veering off the property, I walked down the road to the nearest neighbor's estate. Amidst the fog and lingering drizzle, I came upon a beautiful rose bush, a striking cluster of red that stood out amidst a black and white day. I had never noticed it before.

Rose.

I couldn't help thinking of Sevin's mother, how he hadn't talked about the circumstances of her death with anyone but me. As much as this day had been about planning ways to move on from my infatuation, I never really stopped thinking about him.

Picking a long-stemmed rose off the bush, I looked behind my shoulders to make sure no one had seen. Smelling it, I decided that this would be a symbolic moment. I would take this rose and leave it on the doorstep to the guesthouse to let him know how much his sharing the story of his mother meant to me. I would then put it all behind me—everything that happened from the moment I met him to our encounter in the barn. The gesture would also symbolize my own vow to make peace with my sins and weaknesses, do the right thing and move on with my life.

CHAPTER 10

SEVIN

At first, I thought maybe it was a coincidence and that Elle was the one who left me that rose. When I called her later and asked her if she'd placed anything at my doorstep, she said she hadn't. Elle had also been with Lance and me all afternoon and had gone straight to the main house from the car, so it couldn't have been her anyway.

I didn't want to believe it was Evangeline. I'd already been trying so hard to control my thoughts about her after our talk. The fact that she'd been thinking about me, too—about my mother—reignited all of the feelings I'd been trying to fight.

The entire day out with Elle, I'd been rationalizing with myself and came to the conclusion that there was no way in hell that my attraction to Evangeline could ever be acted upon. So, the only choice was to find a way to stop it.

During a short reprieve before dinner that night, I attempted to sketch. Drawing was always my outlet to battle stress, but tonight it wasn't helping me. As I lay on my bed with my sketchpad in hand, all I wanted was to draw her: her curvy ass, the swell of her breasts, her silky black hair. *Those caramel brown eyes.* I wanted to recreate the passionate look in them when she answered my question with more honesty than I could have ever hoped for.

I looked down at the blank paper in front of me. The nudes I'd always sketched were typically of nameless, faceless women. I no longer had the desire to create them. It was like my hand was paralyzed when I tried to force myself to draw. The pencil wouldn't move. Chucking it across the room, I walked over to the mirror above my chest of drawers and ran my fingers through my hair as I stared at my reflection.

When Evangeline listed her hopes and dreams last night, something completely unfamiliar developed in my chest. It was like she was naming all of the things I never knew I wanted. I had always convinced myself that I didn't deserve certain things because of my role in Rose's death. But with each wish that came out of Evangeline's beautiful mouth, my heart beat faster and faster as if she were speaking directly into it. It was the first time I realized that maybe I did truly want more out of life. I may not have deserved it, but I wanted it.

I wanted her.

Fuck.

I continued to stare at myself in the mirror.

Evangeline wasn't an option, plain and simple. What was I supposed to tell Lance? That he made a mistake in the daughter he chose for me? That I'm more attracted in every way to Evangeline, even though I made a promise to his other daughter who truly believes she loves me? Where would that leave sweet Elle? She would be devastated, and I knew Evangeline would never betray her sister. In the end, I'd be out on the street—or worse—back in Oklahoma with Lillian. My plans were already set in stone. This was what my father wanted, for me to take over Lance's business. I owed it to his memory. It was the least I could do after years of fucking up. My bed was made, and I had to lie in it. What I wanted...*craved*...didn't matter. It was just unfortunate that the one woman who made me feel alive was the only person in the world I couldn't have.

You have to find a way to get past this, I thought to myself as I continued to examine my reflection.

The only thing that made sense was to try to get closer to Elle, to uncover some of the same things in her that drew me to Evangeline. I vowed that tonight was the night I would start the process of trying to fall in love with my soon-to-be wife.

***

"Evangeline won't be joining us for dinner tonight," Olga said as she placed a pork tenderloin down on the dining room table.

"Why not?" Elle asked.

"She just called to inform me that she would not be coming home at all tonight."

I suddenly lifted my head. "What?"

Jesus. Try to hide your interest a little, Sevin.

She looked at Elle. "Her friend...Lorraine...passed away about an hour ago. Evangeline took the keys to your father's car without asking and drove over to their house."

My heart suddenly felt heavy. *Shit. She must have been devastated.*

"She'll be duly punished for that when she gets back," Lance said.

I turned to him. "Don't you think that's a little harsh? It's not like she took it out for a joy ride. Someone died."

Elle seconded my sentiments. "Yeah, Daddy. You couldn't expect her to not be there for Adelaide at a time like this."

"Your sister knows how I feel about the company she keeps. What happened is unfortunate, but it doesn't change that. She had no right to steal the car without my permission. There is no excuse for that kind of behavior. Thou shalt not steal, Elle. Have you not learned anything from the Bible?"

The rest of that dinner was the quietest on record. After everyone helped Olga clean up the table, I pulled Elle aside.

"I need you to do me a favor."

"Anything." She smiled sweetly.

"After you go upstairs for the night and everyone is asleep, I want you to quietly sneak out and come to the guesthouse."

She looked behind her shoulder and whispered, "You know I can't do that."

"I realize it's against the rules, but I just think we really need to have some time alone. I promise you I'm not going to try anything. I just want to talk, Elle. I want to spend time with you without everyone breathing down our necks."

"Sevin…"

"Just think about it, okay?"

A look of extreme worry crossed her face. "Alright."

***

Shortly after midnight, just when I'd drawn the conclusion that Elle wasn't coming, there was a light knock at the door. When I opened it, my heart nearly stopped.

She was shivering, standing there with wet hair and tears in her eyes.

"Evangeline."

"Can I come in?"

"Sure." I swallowed and opened the door wide. "Please."

My heart was palpitating as she stood before me.

Her hair was dripping down onto her heaving breasts. "I don't know why I'm here, Sevin."

I stood there speechless, in total shock that she was in my house.

Fucking speak, Sevin.

"They said you were spending the night at Adelaide's."

"I was planning to, but I started to worry about Daddy's reaction. I didn't want the stress of dealing with his yelling tomorrow. I figured at least if I were sleeping in my bed in the morning, he might not punish me as hard. Your light was on. I know I'm not gonna be able to sleep. I didn't want to be alone up there with everyone sleeping. I just needed to talk to someone. I know I really shouldn't be here."

"No, you really shouldn't be here."

She started to back away. "I can go. I—"

"Let me finish. You really shouldn't have come here, but I'm really glad you did."

"Do you mind if I take off my jacket? It's kind of wet. I was standing

66

outside for the longest time contemplating whether I should knock on your door."

"Please." I took the coat from her. "Sit down. Relax. Can I make you something?"

She followed me into the kitchen and took a seat at the small counter. "Do you even have food here?"

"I dabble in making…" I hesitated and chuckled. "Pop Tarts."

Laughter replaced her crying as she wiped her eyes. "Pop Tarts! How gourmet of you."

"You want one?"

"I'd love a Pop Tart, actually."

I popped two frosted strawberry ones into the toaster. Winking, I said, "Only the best in my house."

When I handed her a plate, she took a bite of the pastry. "This is the best thing I've eaten all day. Is this what you do when you're alone? Sit around eating Pop Tarts?"

Pouring her a tall glass of milk and sliding it toward her, I smiled. "Sometimes."

"What else do you do when you come back here at night?"

Besides jerking off to thoughts of you? Well…

"Lately? I've just been listening to music, doing a lot of thinking."

Evangeline took a long sip of milk then said, "Even though you weren't happy back in Oklahoma, it must be strange starting an entirely new life."

"Yeah…it kind of is, but aside from my brothers, there really was nothing back there for me. I'm grateful for the opportunity your father's given me." Taking her empty plate, I said, "Enough about me. Tell me about tonight. What happened?"

"Adelaide called me crying to tell me that Lorraine had died. It wasn't a shock. We were all expecting it, but I still needed to be there for her. It was dark out, so biking it wasn't an option. I knew that Daddy would never willingly give me the car. So, I just felt like I had no choice but to take it."

"I respect you for that. You knew you'd have to suffer the repercussions of stealing the car, but you did what you had to for your friend."

"What other choice is there?"

"When he says he's gonna punish you, what does he mean?"

"Daddy's never hit me, if that's what you're asking."

"That's exactly what I wanted to know. I'm glad to hear that."

"He'll probably take away my bike for a while, which is actually going to be a problem since I need to help Adelaide around the repair shop over the next few days."

"I'll drive you if you need to get there."

"Thanks, but I don't want to make trouble for you, Sevin. I'll figure something out." She walked over to the old CD player in the corner of the room. "What kind of music do you listen to?"

"My taste varies."

I still had a lot of my father's CDs from when I was younger and before Lillian banned any non-Christian music. Evangeline lifted one of them. "Oh my God. I love The Smiths! I didn't think anyone else listened to this kind of music but me. Which album of theirs is your favorite?"

"Probably The Queen is Dead."

"No way. Hatful of Hollow."

"Wow. Impressive." I walked toward where she was standing. "I swear, Evangeline. I don't think I've ever met anyone like you in my life."

"Because I'm so weird?"

"When I say you're weird, I do *not* mean that in a bad way. You know that, right? You're just so different from other girls I've known."

"You must have known a lot of girls back in Oklahoma, I take it?"

"I've never had an actual girlfriend before Elle."

"How is that possible? You seem like the type that would have had many."

We stood staring at each other, and I got a sudden urge to open up to her. I wanted to tell her everything that was eating away at me even if I couldn't figure out why that was important. It just was for some reason. My heartbeat accelerated. "I've had sex…just not a serious relationship."

She looked down as if to process that information before meeting my gaze again. "I figured that you probably weren't a virgin. Does Elle know that?"

"I tried to start a conversation about all of that stuff one night. I told her that I'd done some bad things in my life, things she wouldn't agree with. I wanted her to know everything before we're married, to see if that mattered to her."

"She didn't let you tell her?"

"She said she didn't want to know, that God forgives me as long as I accept Him."

"She knows what she can handle. I think she might suspect that you've had sex, Sevin. It's not that bad of a thing anyway. I don't think Elle has the same expectations of you as those that are placed upon us by our parents. She just expects you to be a good husband to her once you're married."

"It wasn't just that I had sex."

"It's none of my business."

Then, I blurted out, "I slept with a married woman."

She stepped back a bit, looking a little shocked. "Oh."

"I'm not proud of it...at least not anymore. If I could go back in time now and erase it, I would."

Her face was flush, indicating that my revelation truly affected her. "You could have any girl you want, why take up with someone who's married?"

"For the sheer reason that it was wrong. It made me feel powerful somehow to go against the institution of marriage. It was a form of rebellion. I was very angry at life for not only how I came to be, but the way my stepmother sheltered me from the world. I never felt loved by my family. So, the sex with this person...it also allowed me to feel a false sense of love in the moment of the act without the responsibility after. I knew she wouldn't expect anything more from me. But it was the wrong way to go about it. I didn't have the respect for certain things that I should have. I see that now."

"Who was she?"

I swallowed. "She was our preacher's wife."

She covered her mouth. "Oh my God."

"I know." Running my hands through my hair, pulling on it in frustration, I paced a little. "Fuck. I don't understand why telling you all of this seems important. I can't explain it, but I want you to know who I am. Tell me what you're thinking."

She let a long breath out. "It's upsetting, but what you just told me doesn't define you. That's not who you are. You're not your mistakes."

"Thank you for saying that. I've never looked at it that way."

"Just the fact that you feel guilty about it proves that you're a good person. People screw up. Anyway, even though you were a willing participant, that bitch took advantage of you. She was older, I take it?"

"She was in her early thirties."

She nodded, looking down at the floor again to absorb everything. My body relaxed a little when she started to shake her head in slight laughter. "Wow. How did we get from talking about The Smiths to sex anyway?"

"Who the fuck knows? I feel like I could talk to you forever. One second we're eating Pop Tarts, the next I'm telling you my deepest, darkest secret."

"That was it? That was your deepest, darkest secret?"

"You want more than that? That was pretty fucking bad." My mind raced. I thought long and hard and realized that it really was probably the worst of my sins. "Yeah. I'm pretty sure that was it." My mouth spread into a smile. "So, it's only fair you tell me yours."

"My darkest secret?"

"Yeah." I said softly as I stared into her eyes.

She closed her eyes and when she opened them said, "Honestly? This. Right now. Being here…is my deepest, darkest secret."

I nodded in understanding and whispered, "Yeah."

"I really shouldn't stay much longer."

Please stay.

Then came a knock. Both of our heads turned in unison toward the front door.

Our shared panic was palpable as she asked, "Who is that?"

"It's Elle."

CHAPTER 11

EVANGELINE

My heartbeat accelerated. "Elle?" I ran to put my coat on.

"Just stay put. It's okay. I'll handle it."

Sevin opened the door. In his best casual voice, he said, "Hey…"

Elle immediately took notice of me standing in the middle of the living room. She squinted her eyes. "Evangeline?"

I lifted my hand somewhat awkwardly. "Hi."

"What are you doing here?"

Before I had a chance to respond, Sevin intervened. "Evangeline decided to bring your father's car back tonight so he'd have it in the morning. She thought she hit something on the road and wanted a second opinion on whether there was any noticeable damage done to the car. I was just about to grab my jacket and a flashlight to go take a look."

Upon hearing that surprisingly logical excuse, my nerves started to calm down. "That's right. I saw Sevin's light on and didn't want to wake Daddy. He's mad enough at me already." I looked briefly over at Sevin then back to Elle and asked a question I really had no right to. "What are *you* doing here?"

Jealousy was building up as it registered that Elle had snuck out to come see him. Had this happened before?

Elle looked panicked as she glanced over at Sevin.

Again, he intercepted. "I asked Elle to come by after everyone was

71

asleep. With everyone constantly watching us, I feel like she and I haven't really had the opportunity to get to know each other the way we should. We were just gonna have a talk. That's all."

Elle nodded and looked at me. "I know you won't say anything."

"Of course not."

Sevin got his jacket and a flashlight. He then walked out the door, pretending to go look at the car. As I looked over at Elle's sympathetic expression, feelings of guilt were now battling with the jealousy.

What was I thinking?

Elle walked over to hug me. "I'm so sorry about Lorraine."

Adrenaline was still pumping through me. I was so angry at my reaction. Let me get this straight; I was jealous over my sister sneaking out to see *her* boyfriend in the middle of the night. *Really smart.* That was just another indication that I needed to control this.

I really hadn't intended to come see him. But the day had been so painful, and I knew he would understand everything without judging me. I must have stood out in the rain for ten minutes before I finally garnered the courage to knock on his door. Elle showing up was a smack in the face and confirmed that my decision was a big mistake.

"I'd better get back to the house, Elle. I'll be quiet so they don't wake up."

"Daddy would kill me if he knew I was here."

Swallowing my pride, I gave the response that any good sister would. "Don't worry about it. You and Sevin should be getting to spend time together away from everyone's watchful eyes. This is the only way you can do it."

"I love you," she said.

My chest constricted. "I love you, too."

Sevin had his hands in his pockets as he stood near Daddy's car which was parked in the driveway. He was looking down at the ground when he said, "I didn't think she was going to show."

"*She* was the only one of us that had a right to be at your house in the middle of the night."

"I told her to come by because I really feel like I don't know her sometimes. I—"

"Please," I interrupted. "You don't need an explanation. You two are getting married. This was just the reality check I needed." I regretted that last admission as I abruptly started walking toward the main house.

"Evangeline..."

"I need to get going."

He called after me, "I never thanked you for the rose. That meant so much to me."

I stopped and turned around briefly. "Goodnight, Sevin."

***

Two days later, Lorraine was laid to rest. Mama had convinced Daddy to let me take my bike to the funeral.

After the service, I organized a lunch back at Adelaide's place for her family, friends and shop employees. Lorraine's parents had arranged a mercy meal at a restaurant for their own family and had forbidden Adelaide from attending. It was heartbreaking.

After everyone had left and I'd cleaned up all of the dishes, Adelaide and I were alone in her living room.

"Vangie, I can't thank you enough for handling all of this. You've risked so much to be there for me this past month. It means more than you know."

Pulling her into an embrace, I said, "It's the least I can do. Sometimes, I feel closer to you than my own family. You're my safe haven." I let go of her and got up from the couch. "I'm gonna make us both some tea, alright?"

"Tell me something new and exciting, Vangie. Anything to take this pain away."

"What do you want to talk about?"

"Tell me something funny. Make me laugh. Your perverted aunt pull anything new lately?"

Laughing, I accidentally spilled some of the tea water on my black dress.

"Mama and Daddy won't let her out of the room long enough to try."

"I've been putting off asking you about *you know who*. Figured you'd tell me if anything new came up."

"You can say his name."

"What's going on with Sevin?"

"What was the last thing I told you?"

"You told me about the rose you left at the door, which was very sweet. Honestly, though, it had me worried that maybe you were falling for him. That's dangerous."

"The bottom line is, you're right. It *is* dangerous. I've been playing with fire, and that will only end in my getting burned. I realized a couple of nights ago that I can't even be friends with him. My feelings are too strong. I need to step away and force myself to meet someone."

"You can't force love, sweetie."

"Something has to give, Addy. Right now, I'll trade love for a little bit of sanity." Steeping the teabag, I confessed, "I told Mama I'd be open to pursuing a courtship."

"Vangie, no."

"I promise I won't rush into anything that doesn't feel right. It's just something I think I should at least try. It might be good for me. It feels like the right time."

Adelaide knew me better than my own mother. She could see through my act.

"My God. What has that boy done to you?"

***

Later that week, I was asking myself that very same question.

Daddy and Sevin had taken Friday off to start building the shed on our property.

I'd just returned from helping out at Addy's shop when I parked my bike next to where they were working.

Sevin was wearing a baseball cap backwards and a plaid flannel shirt with the sleeves rolled up. When he turned around, I realized he had the shirt completely unbuttoned, showcasing his glistening bare chest.

When he noticed me standing there, he nodded and lifted his hand in a wave. I waved back before rushing inside.

From the kitchen window, I continued watching him work: the way his muscles moved as he banged the hammer hard, the way his jeans hugged his ass when he bent down to pick something up, the way his shirt would open further when he'd lift the back of his hand to wipe the sweat from his forehead. The muscles between my legs clenched as a painful desire pooled within my core.

My mother's voice startled me. "Evangeline, will you please take these waters out to them?"

"Where's Elle?"

"She drove Imogene to a doctor's appointment."

"Oh…okay."

Carrying two tall glasses of ice water, I walked over to where they were working.

Speaking over the noise, I shouted, "I have these waters. Where do you want me to put them?"

"Just put mine on the table over there," Daddy yelled amidst the sound of his drill.

Sevin dropped the piece of wood he'd been holding in a loud clank. He walked over to me. "I'll take mine now." My nipples tingled when his hand brushed against mine as he took the glass from me.

As he gulped down the water, I watched his Adam's apple moving up and down. I used the opportunity to glance over his sweaty body up close. The top of his underwear was sticking out of his jeans. The smell of him was intoxicating, a mix of cut wood, sweat and cologne. I thought about our talk the other night, how he'd confessed his sexual history. As much as it disturbed me, knowing he'd used that body to give a woman pleasure made me weak with desire. I could only imagine what that would feel like with him.

Elle would find out.

I was still looking down at his abs when he said, "Thank you." My eyes immediately shot up to meet his incendiary stare.

He'd caught me checking him out.

"You're welcome."

His mouth curved into a smile as he handed me back the glass. "How have you been? I haven't seen you much this week."

"Yeah. I've been busy."

"I have something for you," he blurted out in a way that indicated he was anxiously waiting to say it.

"For me?"

"Yeah. Wait here, okay?"

Sevin ran over to where his truck was parked and grabbed something out of the open window.

He returned to where I was standing and handed me a CD.

"What is it?"

"If you like the Smiths, you'll like some of the songs on here. I included a few Smiths songs—the ones from your favorite album, but there's also The Lemonheads, The Pixies...and Pulp."

"You made this?"

"Yeah. I made it for myself and burned you a copy."

"Thanks."

He looked me straight in the eyes and said, "Number ten is my favorite." Then, he walked away.

I immediately took it back to my room and dusted off my old portable CD player.

Lying down on my bed with the sun streaming in, I drowned out the world and listened to every song. When it got to number ten, I paid special attention, knowing he'd specifically called that one out.

The name of the song was *Like a Friend*. I later found out it was by Pulp. With each lyric, my eyes became heavier until they welled up in tears. The words described to a tee exactly how I'd been feeling about him. The singer was shouting out all his feelings about his friend, that she was everything he shouldn't want, everything that was bad for him, but yet he couldn't stop wanting her. He'd take what he could get even if that just meant being friends. Every single line spoke to me. It was the first time I realized that maybe I wasn't alone in my torment. This situation—whatever was happening between us—was taking a toll on him, too.

I must have listened to the song five times before I went over to the window and looked down at him. At one point, he finally looked up and noticed me. He squinted his eyes to see me through the glare of the sun. I still had my headphones on. He knew I had heard number ten. The look on his face when our eyes locked only confirmed that number ten wasn't *just* a song. It was his way of speaking to me.

***

The next morning, I was stretching outside of our front door, preparing to take my morning run. It was very foggy, but there was something so peaceful about running in that kind of opaque air before the world was even awake.

Hitting the gravelly pavement, I was about a quarter-mile into my route when I heard what seemed like the echo of my own footsteps. The sound got louder as it approached. My heart started to race.

Someone was running behind me.

I turned around to see a man wearing a black hoodie. Panic was starting to set in. As he got closer, the final recognition of his face slowed my breathing.

Sevin.

We said nothing to each other as we jogged side by side for the better part of a mile. When I finally turned to him, he glanced over at me. The black hood that was framing his face really accentuated the deep blue of his eyes. At one point, it became necessary for me to stop to catch my breath.

He unzipped his jacket and took a water bottle out, opening the cap and handing it to me. "You shouldn't run without water."

I took a small sip. "Thanks."

He lifted the bottle to his mouth. I watched the movement of his tongue through the clear plastic as he sucked the water out. When he pulled it from his lips, it made a noise from the loss of suction. He handed it to me, his voice gruff. "Drink some more."

This time when I drank from the bottle, I couldn't help but think about the fact that my tongue was now where his had just been. Chills ran through me as his eyes stayed glued to my mouth. I handed the empty bottle back to him.

We continued our run. With each stride, the tension in the air turned thicker than the fog. It was like a strange form of foreplay that couldn't be satisfied, so we'd run faster. When he looked at his watch and turned around to head back, I followed him.

We were almost back home. His breath was ragged when he suddenly said, "You always run this early by yourself?"

"Yeah. Why?"

"I don't like it. You saw how easily someone could come up behind you like I did. You shouldn't do it alone anymore." He looked over at me. "I'll run with you."

After that morning, it was a while before I ever had to run alone again.

CHAPTER 12

SEVIN

I lived for those runs.

Every morning, I'd wait at my window until she ran across the property toward the road. When she was out of sight, I'd head out my door to catch up with her. It was important that if someone happened to wake up and look out, that they didn't see us leaving together.

Even though we never talked about it, I knew she'd come to expect me, because she stopped looking behind her shoulder when she'd hear me approaching. She knew it was me. In the beginning, you could tell my being there was making her tense. With each day, though, comfortable silence replaced nerves as we ran together for miles.

Some mornings, we'd stop in the middle of the route and sit down on the grass just like we'd done when we first met. We'd just talk. We'd talk about anything and everything: our similar childhoods, music, my life back in Oklahoma, her hopes for the future. She wanted to eventually take over Adelaide's shop when her friend retired but knew the expectation was that she'd get married and be a homemaker, maybe work part-time for the family business at most. I'd also confessed to her all of my insecurities about being able to handle the responsibilities that would be expected of me someday at Sutton Provisions.

When we'd resume running and get to the last half-mile, I'd go ahead of her to make sure no one saw us together. I continued to convince myself that we were doing nothing wrong, that it was just innocent time spent with a friend. Yet, the second I returned to my house, I knew better because I'd be counting the minutes until the next morning.

Elle and I were sneaking more time alone together, but it wasn't helping me move on from my feelings for Evangeline. That was scaring the shit out of me. Conversations with Elle were different, never running that deep and always a bit contrived. I wanted so badly to develop stronger feelings for her, but it just wasn't happening naturally.

The running with Evangeline went on for about a month until one particular morning when midway through our trek, she suddenly stopped.

Her breathing was labored. "I can't do this anymore, Sevin."

I panicked, thinking she was in physical pain. "What's wrong? What happened? Are you having trouble breathing? Do you have a cramp?"

"No."

"What is it?"

"I can't do this with *you* anymore. It has to stop."

Even though I damn well knew the reason, I asked, "Why?"

"Because I fall asleep every night willing the morning to come quickly. Every day I want this time with you more and more. And one day soon, I'm going to turn around waiting for your footsteps, and they're not going to be there. I need to stop this before that day comes. I need you to stop running with me. Please." Her moist eyes were pleading.

My heart felt like it was being choked, because she'd just described exactly how I felt about these mornings. It finally clicked in that moment that her feelings for me were just as strong. I needed to protect her from getting hurt. From now on, that was going to be more important than my selfish need to be around her. I simply nodded then watched as she ran away into the distance.

Over the next couple of weeks, I barely saw Evangeline. Either she was working upstairs at the plant or helping Addy at the shop. We'd see each other at dinner; that was about it. Things were a lot like they'd been in the very beginning. I missed her something fierce, but I knew that this was for the best.

***

With Emily as our chaperone, Elle and I were out walking, holding hands one early evening before supper when she dropped more than one bomb on me.

"I have to ask you something."

I squeezed her hand. "Shoot."

"Are you busy August 17th?"

"What's August 17th?"

"The hall we wanted for the wedding had a cancellation. That date will work out perfectly with the availability of the church."

The fact that we hadn't been able to find an available venue to accommodate the size of the wedding was the main reason we hadn't set a date yet.

"That's in four months."

"Yes. Is that too long...too soon?"

Despite the unsettling feeling in my gut, I said, "No. It's good."

"So, we should book it?"

"Sure."

"Really?"

"Yeah."

"I'm so happy right now!" She hugged me. "I can't wait to tell Mama! I love you so much."

"I'm glad you're happy."

"Emily, are you ready to be a junior bridesmaid?"

"How come Evangeline gets to be the maid of honor?"

My stomach turned at the idea of Evangeline walking down the aisle at my wedding to Elle.

Elle playfully mussed up her sister's hair. "Because she's older, silly. Maybe by then, she'll be engaged herself."

We'd been swinging our arms, and I inadvertently stopped. "Why do you say that?"

"You know Callum Hughes?"

"That's your father's friend who invests in the business."

"Actually, it's his son, Callum Junior."

"What about him?"

"Evangeline and he have been talking over the phone."

My jaw stiffened. "Really…"

"Yeah. I think they're considering a courtship. He's actually coming to dinner tomorrow night."

***

Evangeline looked nervous as she carried items from the kitchen to the dining room. She refused to look at me, but that didn't stop my eyes from following her.

She was wearing a beautiful lavender dress, which was not her normal style. She'd wear skirts, but they were usually casual. She also had her hair styled into long curls. It was really hard to look away.

Elle sat next to me and took my hand in hers. "Why am *I* jittery?" she asked.

"I don't know. You tell me."

"I'm nervous for her. It reminds me of when I first met you. I was so scared when Daddy took me to your house in Oklahoma that first time, but then I took one look at you, and I just knew."

I know the feeling. That's how I felt when I first met your sister.

Apparently, Evangeline and Callum had been talking for a while, but this was the first time that they'd be face to face. He'd be coming with his parents. I wanted to meet him about as much as I wanted a hole in the head.

Lance went to the door, and the sounds of their voices got closer and closer to the dining room. To be respectful, I stood up when they entered.

"Sevin, this is my good friend, Callum Hughes Senior—I know you've heard me talk about him—his wife Barbara and Callum Junior."

With his blonde hair and brown eyes, their son Callum was physically the opposite of me. He looked like an older version of one of my brothers. I hated to discover that he was pretty built and good-looking.

Shaking Callum's hand especially hard and searching his eyes, I said nothing.

While no one would seem good enough for Evangeline, it was important to me that he was at least a good guy who would cherish and protect her.

Evangeline sat next to him while still refusing to look across the table at me for even a split second. Throughout dinner, their conversations seemed to flow easily. It was clear that they had been getting to know each other. The Suttons conversed with his parents the entire time. Trying to read her body language, I just watched Evangeline interact with Callum.

After dinner, we all retreated to the yard for dessert and coffee on the patio. Wind chimes blew in the brisk wind. The sun had completely set, so Olga had turned on the outside white Christmas lights. Evangeline and Elle were sitting on a bench swing together with their arms around each other. Their harmonious laughter was a beautiful sound, a reminder of why I was enduring this torture tonight. They were blood. I couldn't do anything to tear them apart no matter how strong my feelings for Evangeline were. I cared about them both too much to ruin that bond. One thing I admired about the Suttons was how strong a family unit they were. They had their disagreements, but overall, they were tight knit. They were *my* family now.

Callum was standing alone a few feet away from me and also seemed to be staring at the sisters. No one drank in the Sutton house, otherwise, I'd have definitely brought over one of the six-packs sitting in the fridge at my place. Something to take the edge off of this night would have been really nice.

Walking over to Callum, I forced myself to make conversation. "Nice night, huh?"

"Yeah. They have a really nice place. The last time I was here, I was too young to appreciate it."

"So, you used to know the girls when they were younger?"

"Yeah. We moved out of state, and I hadn't had a chance to reconnect with Evangeline until recently. I had the biggest crush on her even back then."

My body tensed as I gritted my teeth. "You don't say?"

"Yeah. Who would have known that I'd be courting her ten years later."

"I didn't realize it was official yet."

"I would say tonight is a good indication that it is, wouldn't you?"

"Well, what does *she* say about that?"

"We haven't made it formal if that's what you're asking."

I was coming across more like a lawyer interrogating someone on the stand rather than a casual brother-in-law. "So, whose idea was this pairing?"

"It was hers, actually. She told her parents that she was ready for this step in her life."

"So, *she* chose you?"

"The woman always has a choice. It's not like anyone is putting a gun to her head."

"But she didn't choose you. *They* did, and she agreed to it?"

He laughed. "No different than you and Elle. That's how it starts, right?"

"I suppose in this house." Glancing back over at the girls, I asked, "What do you like most about her?"

He gestured his hand toward the swing. "I mean…look at her. She's gorgeous. Those big eyes, those lips, that body. Those hips? She'll be popping out babies real easy."

Feeling a rush of adrenaline, my body seemed to be preparing to punch this guy out if necessary. "Is that right?"

"I hope so."

"Maybe she wants more out of life than just popping out some guy's babies. Has that ever crossed your mind?"

"We've spoken about it. She said she wants kids."

"Yes. But I guarantee you she doesn't mean right away."

"Have you discussed that with her or something?"

Actually, I have. I know her better than probably anyone.

"So, you think she's hot. What else?"

"She's sweet, funny…"

I interrupted him. "What is she afraid of?"

"What?"

"Name something she's afraid of."

"We never talked about it."

"Maybe you should ask her."

"There's plenty of time."

"I guess my point is, if you're gonna marry someone, you should really get to know everything about them. That's all."

"Well, once you marry Elle over the summer, I plan to do just that. I'm moving into the guesthouse."

***

Apparently, since they lived all the way in Missouri, the Hughes family planned to stay at the Sutton house for that entire weekend. Saturday night, Elle and I were supposed to be going on a double date with Evangeline and Callum.

I was still struggling with my emotions after hearing that Callum would eventually move into the house I now lived in. It felt like he was moving in on *everything*, and if I were being honest with myself, it wasn't really the house that was bothering me. By the time he planned to move here, Elle and I would supposedly have a house somewhere nearby that Lance would put up the money for initially. The plan was that we'd eventually pay him back.

I drove us to the steakhouse in my new truck. It still had that new car smell. I was making pretty good money now, so it had been time to replace the old Ford. After dinner, we were supposed to be going bowling.

Dinner was awkward as I forced myself to talk to him.

"So, Callum, I never asked, exactly what is it that you do?"

"I'm working a temporary contract job for an airline manufacturer back in Missouri."

"You said something about possibly moving into my guesthouse. What's gonna happen to your job?"

"Late summer or early fall will time out perfectly with the expiration of my contract. I spoke to Lance about taking a managerial position temporarily at Sutton Provisions."

"Temporarily?"

"Yes. If things work out between Evangeline and me, after we marry, she'll come with me back to Missouri. I'll eventually be taking over my father's business."

My eyes darted over to her. She was already looking at me, expecting me to react.

He was planning to take her away from her family and Addy.

And from me.

She couldn't have been okay with moving. That would have also meant shattering her dream of taking over Addy's shop someday.

Elle kept talking about the wedding plans. Callum pretended to care. Both Evangeline and I were quiet.

Callum reached over and grabbed Evangeline's hand. My eyes immediately landed on their interlocked fingers. He rubbed his thumb affectionately against her skin as he listened to Elle tell a story from across the table. It was my first real wakeup call that this was really happening. Evangeline was *with him.* As long as I was with Elle, I needed to learn to accept that.

I pried my eyes away from their hands long enough to notice that Evangeline had been watching me, too. Watching me watching her. We stayed looking at each other. For a moment, it was as if everyone else evaporated into thin air. I knew without a shadow of a doubt that I wished it were me on the other side of the table. Except, I didn't just want to hold her hand. I wanted to lean in and take her plump bottom lip into my mouth and suck on it slowly, run my tongue down her neck and chest in search of the nipples that were piercing through the fabric of her shirt right now. My mouth was watering, and it had nothing to do with steak. *Fuck.* The more I reminded myself I couldn't have her, the more I wanted her.

The waitress came by to serve our food, snapping us back to reality.

By the time we got to the bowling alley, I was ready to take out my frustration.

Pretending each pin was Callum, I kept hitting strike after strike. I had

86

never bowled in my freaking life.

At one point, Elle joked, "Gosh, Sevin. Maybe we have to find a bowling league for you or something."

Callum kept using excuses to touch Evangeline. He'd allegedly be showing her how to hold the bowling ball while practically wrapping his entire body around her in the process.

The one consolation was that he'd be heading back to Missouri soon.

The hardest part of the night had nothing to do with Callum, though. We were packed into my truck heading back home when Elle pressed a button and accidentally switched the music from radio to CD mode. I'd been listening to *Like a Friend* by Pulp earlier that day. Number ten on the CD I made for Evangeline said it all when it came to my feelings for her. When I was alone in my car, it was one of the rare times I could unwind. I liked playing that particular one on repeat. The song was a secret between us. And now, she knew I'd been listening to it.

Peeking through my rearview mirror, I could see Evangeline was looking straight at me. Not wanting to make her uncomfortable, I switched it.

"I liked that song," Elle said. "Why did you change it?"

"This one is better," I lied.

When I snuck another look at Evangeline, she was blankly staring out the window.

***

Two weeks later, Callum was long gone. Evangeline was still talking to him every day from what I heard. Elle was deep into our wedding plans. Everything was moving so fast, it was impossible to even absorb it. So, when Elle told me she'd be going out of town the following weekend with her parents, Emily and Imogene to visit some of Olga's cousins, I was grateful for the reprieve. They'd asked me to go with them, but I used the excuse of wanting to take that time to work on some much needed repairs to the kitchen at the guesthouse.

Evangeline also stayed behind. She was working every weekend at Adelaide's shop much to Lance's discontent. Even though he disapproved, he didn't do anything to stop her. Knowing that she and I would be the only two people on the property that weekend made me a little anxious, even though I had no plans to venture over to the main house.

Saturday started off exactly as planned. On my third can of beer, I'd put my drill down to take a break from installing one of the new cabinets. Deciding to make a sandwich, I turned on the TV. The local news had cut into whatever programming had been on. The words across the screen read: *Heavy Rains Moving Into Dodge City and Surrounding Areas This Afternoon and Evening.*

I'd been so immersed in my work, I hadn't noticed that the skies were unusually dark for the middle of the day. It almost looked like nighttime. When the rain started coming down, I ran over to the main house to check on things, make sure there weren't any open windows.

My stomach sank because Evangeline wasn't home. I hoped that she would be smart enough to stay put wherever she was. I didn't have her cell phone number because I never had a reason to call her. Concluding that Evangeline would probably just stay at Addy's, I decided against calling the Suttons for her number.

There was a small break in the rain, but by the time night fell, the torrential downpours returned in full force with even heavier winds.

The next time I turned on the TV, the caption read: *Tornado Warning for Dodge City and Surrounding Areas.*

My heart started to race. *Fuck.* I needed to find out where she was. Before I had a chance to digest that thought, everything went black.

CHAPTER 13

EVANGELINE

Thank God I decided to take advantage of that small break in the rain. Addy tried to convince me to stay, but I might have never gotten home if I hadn't made a break for it. I wanted to sleep in my own bed tonight.

I tried not to think about the fact that Sevin was at the guesthouse. This was the first time we were ever alone together on the property. If I played my cards right, I wouldn't have to see him at all.

My cell phone buzzed. It was Callum.

"Hello?"

"Hey, baby. I'm just checking on you. I heard there were some serious storms passing through there."

"I'm home. I'm safe. No need to worry. I think I'm gonna try to watch some TV to get my mind off the thunder and lightning, though."

"That's a good idea. I miss you. I can't wait for when I come visit again soon."

"I'm looking forward to that."

"Check in with me in a couple of hours, okay?"

"Okay."

After we hung up, I went downstairs and turned on the TV, hoping for something light to watch. Instead, my heart dropped upon seeing the words splayed across the screen: *Tornado Warning. Hundreds of Power Outages Reported.*

89

I looked outside unable to see past the heavy bands of rain. It dawned on me that I needed to get away from the window. I immediately ransacked the kitchen in search of candles or a flashlight. Having no idea where my mother kept those things, I started to panic. Sevin didn't have a landline phone at the guesthouse, and I didn't have his cell phone number. I was afraid to go outside. That was the last thing they say you should do if a tornado hits. Just as I went in search of my phone to call Daddy, the lights went out.

Oh no. No, no, no.

My only real phobia was total darkness.

My breathing intensified as I felt around me to see where I was. I managed to return to the living room and sat on the couch in a fetal position. Tears started to sting my eyes. I knew I should probably go to the basement, but I was terrified to be down there alone. The howl of the winds intensified, prompting me to get up once again and feel my way to the basement door. I opened it and carefully walked down each step.

Shaking, I held my head in my hands. A huge bang coming from upstairs shook me to my core. I was sure a window had blown, or maybe something collapsed—until I heard his voice.

"Evangeline!"

I got up from the ground, overwhelmed by an immediate sense of relief.

"Sevin! Oh my God. Sevin. I'm down here. In the basement!"

The rush of his footsteps approached. A flash of light hit me in the eyes as the basement door opened, and he flew down the stairs. Within seconds, my face was pressed against his bare chest. His heart was beating so fast. Tears from my eyes poured onto his skin. We were completely quiet as he held me tightly into him, his heart thundering against my ear. It was the first time any man had ever held me like this.

"It's okay. I'm here."

Hearing him say that made me cry even harder, not only because I was so happy not to be alone but because being in his arms made all of the feelings I'd been trying to bury rise to the surface.

When he let go, cold air replaced the warmth of his body. "Thank God

I thought to check on you again."

"Again?"

"I came earlier, and you weren't home. I assumed you stayed at Addy's. When the lights went out, I knew I needed to get over here just in case there was a chance you came back. I found my flashlight and ran. I know how scared you are of the dark. I also wanted to make sure you knew to go to the basement. I never expected to actually find you."

"I'm so happy you're here."

His cologne and the scent of his damp skin masked the mustiness of the lower level. Sevin was wearing a shirt, but it was open at the front. He was probably working on the house like that before booking it over here when the lights went out.

He cupped my face in his hands and gently wiped my tears with his thumbs. In the dim light afforded by his flashlight, the dark blue of his eyes was penetrating through the darkness. He shocked me when he said, "I've missed you so fucking much."

The raw emotion of his words seemed to cut through all of my resolve. I released the hold on my thoughts. "This has been really hard."

We'd been fighting a battle together against our feelings, one that only the two of us knew about.

The wind outside shook a small basement window. Sevin wouldn't let go of my cheeks. Worn down by months of pent up desire, my entire body felt weak as he touched me. I prayed that he didn't try to kiss me because I knew that I wouldn't have been able to resist him.

He slowly slid his hands down and placed them away from me by his side. While my mind was relieved, my body was screaming for the return of his touch. Even without the physical contact, I still indirectly felt him as he continued to stare me down.

"Look around, Evangeline. There is no one else here. It's just you and me."

Swallowing, I replied nervously, "I'm aware of that."

"We've talked about a lot of things since we've met, things we fear, things we're passionate about. But never...not once...have we talked about this, what's been happening between us." When I looked down, he placed his hands on my face again, forcing my eyes upward. "We *need* to talk about it."

I closed my eyes, nodding in agreement, feeling a weight slowly lifting off of me. Keeping everything inside had been arduous. "Okay. Let's talk about it."

His eyes held an intensity that almost scared me. "I'll start," he said before pausing. He blinked repeatedly, clearly trying to figure out how to articulate what he was thinking. "Sometimes, I feel like my whole life has been a lie, whether I was pretending to be something I wasn't or just the bullshit people fed me. From the moment I met you, before I even knew your fucking name, it felt like you were somehow a reflection of the real me. When I'm around you, I never want to be anyone else but myself. That's never happened to me before. No more bullshit. I need you to be honest with me. Can you do that?"

Even though I was scared, not entirely sure of what I was agreeing to, I nodded. "Yes."

"I'm gonna ask you some questions. I don't want you to think about the repercussions of your answers or what you think you should say. I just need your truth."

"My truth?"

"Yes. No lies to protect anyone, just the unbridled truth. Can you do that for me, even if just for tonight?"

A teardrop fell down my cheek as I whispered, "Yes."

He stepped back away from me a bit. He was breathtaking with his broad chest exposed in that open plaid shirt. His inky black hair was wet from the rain. My insides were bustling with need. Unable to control my body's reaction to him, being here alone with Sevin felt like a very dangerous predicament. I couldn't help wanting to touch him, and that scared me.

His voice startled me. "First question. Are you really planning to marry him?"

After hesitating, I said, "I think so."

"That's not really an answer. Give me a yes or no."

"That's the truth. I'm planning to, but I'm not a hundred percent sure I can follow through with it."

"Because you don't really want it."

"I want to get married."

"You don't want him." He moved in closer, his voice more demanding. "Tell me the goddamn truth."

Reminding myself of my vow not to lie, I admitted, "I don't really want him. But I need him."

"Why?"

"Because it's going to hurt me to stay here. And he's my ticket out."

Now that was *definitely* the truth.

He took two more steps toward me, causing goosebumps to form on my arms. "When we were in the barn that night and you listed your hopes and dreams, you told me that you wanted to experience love."

I nodded and whispered, "Yes."

"I thought I was incapable of that." He paused. "But I think I might be experiencing something very close to it…with you."

What he'd just admitted was a total shock. Even though he remained silent, Sevin seemed overcome with emotion. He expected those words no more than I did.

He continued, "Tell me I'm not crazy, because I think you feel the same way."

I do.

I finally spoke, "You're not crazy. That's why I have to leave. These feelings aren't going away, so *I* have to go away…because I can't have you."

"Look at me. Can't you fucking see that you already do?"

"What?"

"You have me, Evangeline. You. No one else. From the moment we met, it's been you."

"We can't be together."

"I don't want to hurt Elle, either. That's the last thing I want, but I can't control this."

"I don't think you understand, Sevin. That doesn't matter. You and I will never have a future. Number one, my father...he'd kill you. There is nothing in this world more precious to him than Elle, and if you hurt her, he'd destroy you. But more than that, I can't betray my sister. She loves you so much."

"She *thinks* she loves me. She doesn't know me, not like you do. I know I made a promise to her and your father that I fully intended to keep, but I am so confused. The only thing I'm sure of anymore is that I can't shake my feelings for you. Lord knows, I've tried."

"Try harder. Please. We have to. I refuse to hurt her."

"I refuse to hurt *you*," he snapped. "My being with her is hurting you."

"Don't worry about me."

"Don't worry about you? You're gonna let him take you back to Missouri, away from Addy, away from your family, all because you're running away from me. I should be the one leaving town if that's the case."

"Don't you say that, Sevin. This is your home. This is your future. You deserve this opportunity."

"I've seriously thought about leaving and going back to Oklahoma."

The thought of him disappearing altogether and my never seeing him again was even more upsetting than the thought of him marrying Elle. Knowing he'd be part of my family forever was a bittersweet solace. It was really screwed up, but it was true.

"Do you want me, Evangeline? Forget about how you think you should respond to that question. Please. I need to hear you say it." My face was burning up as he moved in closer. "Please."

"I want you."

He closed his eyes and opened them. "I want you more than I've ever wanted anything."

"Not everything we want is good for us."

"Don't you dare try to say that you wouldn't be good for me. If our life circumstances were different, you'd be fucking perfect for me, and you know it."

"Where is this conversation going? What are you asking of me, Sevin?"

"I don't know. Right now…nothing. I just needed to know the truth. I'm so sick and tired of pretending…trying to hide this."

"Well, I told you my truth. It just doesn't change anything."

"You want to know my truth?"

"Yes."

His eyes were burning into mine. "You're my truth. Everything else is a lie."

The winds intensified, shaking the basement walls. The sounds of metal and debris flying around outside put me on edge. Something hit the basement window hard, and I instinctively jumped into Sevin's arms. He held me there for a while. Breathing in his smell, the physical need for him felt unbearable.

The warmth of his breath against my ear caused my nipples to harden when he said, "It feels so good to hold you."

"It's wrong."

"Then why haven't you pulled away?"

I couldn't answer that. In my head, I had somehow justified allowing it because of the storm. But even when the winds eventually calmed down, that didn't stop me from staying nestled in his arms, telling myself that this was the first and only time I would ever experience it.

That was the first of many lies I would tell myself when it came to justifying my actions with Sevin.

***

The next morning, my family returned to the house. Daddy apparently packed their car and drove everyone back early as soon as the rain stopped so that he could assess the damage. The tornado never made a direct hit on us, but there were countless downed trees and power lines. Much to his dismay, there was also some damage to the new shed that he and Sevin had only just built.

"Thank the good Lord you're okay, Evangeline," Mama said, pulling me into her.

"I really panicked when the lights went out. You know how I am about the dark. Thankfully, Sevin came to check on me and stayed until the storm passed."

Elle's eyes held an inquisitive yet upsettingly serious look. "You were with Sevin?" Tilting her head, she said, "He didn't mention that when I called him from the road."

My stomach dropped. *Why hadn't he said anything?*

Thinking quickly, I said, "Sevin was really helpful. He helped me stay calm when the blackout happened. I don't know that I would have survived it otherwise."

I prayed I didn't look as guilty as I felt. I hoped the expression on my face didn't say, *"Yeah, he held me tightly until the storm passed. I had to beg him to go back to his place before morning because I was afraid I wouldn't be able to resist kissing him."*

"That's a good man you have there, Elle," Mama interjected.

"He is. I'm glad he was here so that you didn't have to go through that alone."

"Yeah, me too."

Sensing that something was still bothering Elle, I asked, "Is everything okay?"

"Everything is fine," she replied quickly.

Maybe it was just my own paranoia causing me to wonder whether Elle was bothered by the fact that Sevin never mentioned to her that we were together during the storm.

***

Later that afternoon, there was a knock on my bedroom door. Elle entered before I told her it was okay to come in.

"You got a minute?" she asked.

"Of course. What's going on?"

"I need to talk to you about Sevin."

My heart was palpitating. "What about him?"

"Something isn't right between us, and I need to fix it."

Inwardly freaking out and patting the bed, I scooted over. "Come sit next to me."

Elle hopped on my bed and slid closer to me as she leaned her back against my upholstered headboard. "I think that Sevin might be having some doubts about the marriage."

"What makes you say that?"

"For one, he hasn't given me a ring."

"The wedding date has been set. Maybe he's just waiting to give it to you that day?"

"I don't know. I remember before he moved to Dodge City when we were doing the long distance thing, he said something about planning to buy me a ring once he got out here, but he hasn't followed through or even mentioned it."

"I think you're overthinking it. I mean, a date has been set. I'm sure he is going to get a ring."

"I know what his hesitation is."

Dread was starting to set in. I braced myself. "What?"

"Why would you marry someone if you haven't tried the goods?"

"What are you talking about?"

"People assume I'm so naïve. As much as I try to be good, I'm not stupid. Look at him. I know he's not a virgin. I know he's been with girls. I think he even tried to confess it to me one time, but I honestly don't want to know."

"What are you getting at?"

"I really think that he's just not used to having to wait like this. To be honest, I'm really starting to grow impatient, too. We're engaged. We should be able to do certain things."

"What exactly are you saying?"

"I'm saying I want to give myself to him."

My heart started to race. "Don't you think you're rushing into things? You're getting married in a few months. What's the difference?"

"The difference is…I'm not sure Sevin is fully comfortable committing to me without knowing whether we connect well in that area. I don't think anyone has ever made him wait like this, and I think it's taking a toll on him and making him doubt us."

"So, you're going to start having sex with him?"

"Well, maybe not instantly. But I want to let him know that I'm open to letting him try things, giving up control of my body to him."

A rush of adrenaline hit me. "Have you tried anything up until now?"

"Not aside from the kiss."

Relief.

"You feel like you're ready for this?"

"What's the difference? I'm going to be marrying him soon anyway. Mama and Daddy would kill me if they knew I was considering breaking the rules, but what they don't know won't hurt them. It's more important for me to keep Sevin happy at this point. That has to be my number one priority. I don't want to lose him."

A battle between good and evil ensued within me: the good sister versus the jealous sister. "I don't know what to say. I wasn't expecting this from you. You've been so diligent about sticking to the rules. This is just a little bit of a shock."

"I just want your support and honesty. Do you think it's a bad idea?"

Breathing in and out, I said, "I think you need to do what you feel you have to."

"Are you going to stick to the rules with Callum?"

"I haven't thought about it. It's too soon."

"He's a really nice guy, Evangeline."

"Yeah. He is."

"Just think...this time next year, you and I will both be married. Who knows, maybe even a baby on the way."

"Who? Me?"

"Or me." She smiled.

I felt sick.

"You want kids that soon?"

Elle looked truly surprised. "You don't?"

"No. I feel like I'd need more time to enjoy married life first. Kids are a big responsibility, and once you have them, that's it; there's no going back."

"I can't wait to be pregnant with his baby. Our kids are gonna be beautiful if they look anything like him with that bone structure, olive skin and dark hair."

Unable to listen to any more of this, I suddenly got up.

"Are you okay?" she asked.

"Yeah. I'm fine. All this talk of marriage and babies…I'm just not there yet, Elle."

"I didn't mean to scare you. I'm sure Callum will understand if you want to take things slowly."

"I hope so."

"Anyway, I just wanted to tell you about my decision."

***

I never joined my family for dinner that night. Making up a fake illness, I stayed in my room and ruminated in my intense state of jealousy. I didn't know what came over me. Sevin and Elle's imminent marriage meant that their having sex was inevitable. Deep down, I'd known that but had apparently been in denial.

The hope was always that I'd be able to get myself out of this obsession with Sevin before the wedding. Now that Elle was planning to take things to another level with him sooner—at any given moment—I would have no time to adjust, no time to get over my feelings before that happened.

The mere idea of them having sex made me sick. It was starting to really become clear that this reaction wasn't going to just magically go away in a matter of months. Panic started to set in. My first thought was that I needed to stop things between them from happening. I was so disappointed in myself for even thinking so selfishly.

The entire night, I tossed and turned, attempting to block out unwanted images of them naked together. My time alone with Sevin in the basement kept replaying in my mind, too. He'd laid everything out on the line.

He'd told me he thought he might be falling in love with me.

This situation had become more serious than I ever imagined.

I needed to talk to someone, and there was only one person I could trust.

***

The next day, I snuck out of work and rode my bike to Addy's. She was in the garage in the middle of rotating a set of tires when I walked in. The smell of grease was always oddly like home to me.

She wiped her hands on her navy mechanic's jumpsuit. "Vangie, I didn't know you were coming by so early in the day."

"I'm supposed to be working at the plant. I have to get back soon, but I really needed to talk to you."

"It's almost lunchtime anyway. Let's head inside the house."

Addy made us sandwiches. We ate together as I recalled everything from what happened during the storm to my conversation with Elle.

"I'd always worried that it was gonna come to this," she said, taking our plates away.

"Tell me what you mean."

"From the moment you walked in here after first meeting him on the road, I was afraid this connection you two have would turn out to be stronger than either of you could handle under the circumstances."

"I thought I could control it."

She returned to the table and grabbed both of my hands in hers. There was a long pause while she looked me straight in the eyes. "You love him."

Letting go of her and burying my face in my palms, I said, "I don't know."

"You love him, Vangie."

"How do you know?"

"Because you would never choose this pain in a million years if you didn't. It's just like my being gay. Why would a woman choose to put herself in a situation that might mean being ostracized? You would never want to hurt your sister or be disowned by your family. The fact that you can't shake this despite that is the very proof that you love him."

What she said made so much sense.

100

"I would never choose this."

"You can't choose love. It chooses you, and once that happens, it doesn't let go. You can pretend it's not there, but when you try, it only fights harder…louder…until you finally get the message and give in."

My lips were trembling. "Please tell me what to do."

"I can't tell you what to do, honey. What I *can* tell you is that you need to pick a side and stick with it. This middle ground purgatory you're in right now has to end. You need to make a decision to either come clean to Elle about Sevin, tell her what's been going on and be prepared to suffer the consequences, or you stay away from him altogether. You can't keep living this way."

"When you say stay away from him…you mean move away?"

"As much as I don't ever want to see you go, I do agree that given the situation, you won't be able to live here if he marries your sister. I don't believe your feelings are going to change. I know you, Vangie. That scenario would be pure torture. I don't want you to have to suffer, seeing her with him every day. There's a reason for the old saying 'out of sight, out of mind.'"

"I'm so afraid."

"What are you afraid of most?"

"Hurting my sister."

"Then maybe that's a hint as to which direction you need to go. You shouldn't make this decision alone."

"You think I need to talk to Sevin?"

"Yes. I do. I don't think it should wait."

***

I couldn't sleep at all. In the middle of the night, I got up and peeked into Elle's room to make sure she was fast asleep. I couldn't risk this being one of the nights that she planned to sneak over to Sevin's, too.

When I was sure everyone was out like a light, I quietly tiptoed out of the main house. Still in my nightgown, my entire body was shaking because at that moment, I had no idea what was going to happen. I just knew it was necessary to take Addy's advice and settle this thing with Sevin once and for all.

Unlike the only other night I showed up at his door this late, there were no lights on at the guesthouse this time. He must have been sleeping. I wasn't sure how to wake him up. I grabbed a small rock and threw it at his window. The main house was far enough so that the noise wouldn't wake anyone there.

On the second try, a light went on in his bedroom. He appeared, looking painfully handsome. He was shirtless, and his hair was unruly from sleep. "Evangeline?" he asked groggily.

I spoke up into his window. "We need to talk."

He disappeared without a word. Seconds later, the front door opened.

"Come in," he said.

"Thank you. I'm sorry if I woke you."

"I wasn't sleeping…trying to, but I couldn't. What's going on?"

"I came to talk to you."

When he looked at me, I saw something in his eyes that I'd never seen before: fear.

His irises were dark, his face sullen. "I know why you're here."

"Are you okay, Sevin?"

Everything was still, except for the tick of a clock as we stood facing each other in the middle of his living room. He reached for my hand and placed it over his heart, which was beating so fast. His voice was strained. "No, I'm not, Evangeline. I'm really not fucking okay."

I kept my hand over his heart for a while. My own heart was competing with his rampant beat. A revelation hit me in that moment. I cared for Sevin at a level that I hadn't felt for anyone before. As much as I loved Elle and wanted to protect her from this, I loved Sevin equally and wanted to protect him, too. It was tragic, because that meant that either way, someone I loved was going to get hurt.

"Why do you think I'm here?" I asked.

"Elle and I had a talk out in your parents' yard after dinner tonight. I know she mentioned to you what she was going to talk to me about. I also know that you encouraged her."

"I guess I did in a roundabout way but—"

"She also told me something else."

"What?"

"She overheard you on the phone this afternoon asking Callum if he thought your parents and his parents would allow you to move to Missouri now instead of later, rather than him moving here. So, yeah…I can put two and two together as to what you came to tell me."

I couldn't believe Elle had been listening to my conversation with Callum. She must have thought Sevin would take it as good gossip. She had no clue it would actually devastate him to know what I was considering.

After I'd gotten home from Addy's earlier, I was desperate for a solution. I kept thinking about her advice and concluded that the only way out of my dilemma was to leave town immediately. So, I decided to put some feelers out about moving into the Hughes' guesthouse and possibly working for the chain of supermarkets they owned.

It wasn't until I walked into Sevin's tonight and saw the fear in his eyes that I started to doubt that I could go through with it. Feeling his heart beating that way made me forget everything I'd decided upon. It put me back at square one.

"You think you know what I came here for? How could you possibly know what I'm gonna say when I don't? I'm so confused. Every time I think I've made a decision, I look into your eyes, and you're all I see."

"You came here to tell me you're leaving. Am I right?"

"I don't want to leave."

"You *can't* leave. You can remove yourself from Dodge City, but can't you see that you can't really erase me? I'm still gonna be here. So is your sister. When you tell me to forget about you, to keep with the original plan and marry Elle, sometimes I don't know if you realize what you're *really* asking of me. It's not just a wedding. Marriage is a life sentence. It means being her man, having sex with her, sharing my life with her and only her. If I marry Elle, I'd be vowing to do all of those things and following through with them for the rest of our lives. Is that what you want? You want me to make babies with Elle? I don't thi—"

I screamed, "No! It's not what I want! It's not what I want! I'm so scared of that." My hands were on each side of my head as I tugged at my hair in anger.

"You scare the hell out of me, too, Evangeline."

"I'm trying to do the right thing, but I want you so badly it hurts. When she told me what she was planning to offer you, I got so jealous that I haven't been able to eat or sleep. This feels like an impossible situation. You're right...I came here tonight to try to tell you that I was leaving. But the second I'm in front of you, the way you make me feel...all I want to do is stay. Why couldn't I have found you under different circumstances?"

He pulled me into a hug and spoke into my shoulder. "Don't go back there tonight. Please. I promise I won't try anything if you stay here."

"There are seriously moments that I feel like I could die from this. Sometimes, it's so bad that I hate you." A slight laugh escaped me for having admitted that.

He smiled. "No, you don't. You wish you did."

"My staying here tonight is not fair to her. That's crossing a line."

"You don't think we've already crossed it?" He grabbed my face. "Wanna talk fair? I don't think you can say that it's fair for me to marry her when all I want, all I fucking dream about is you. Elle is a sweet, wonderful God-fearing person. She calms me down and makes me feel good inside. But you..." He moved his face in closer. "You light a fire in me, Evangeline, one I can't put out, one I don't want to. I wish I could show you how I feel."

Fire. That was a good word to describe the level of burning desire coursing through me at the thought of what he'd do to my body if he could. He had experience. As much as it made me jealous to think about him with other women, the thought of experiencing something like that with him thrilled me. I knew I wasn't going to give in to my physical needs, but my mind needed to be satisfied if my body couldn't.

I'd often fantasized about the nude pictures he confessed to drawing. I wanted so badly to see the objects of his creativity.

"I want to see your drawings."

"The women?"

"Are there other drawings?"

"No."

"Will you show them to me?"

"You're gonna think I'm twisted."

"You already told me the story behind them. I promise I won't."

The mood was extremely tense as he led me to his room. A small lamp provided just a little bit of light. He took out a medium-sized black box from the back of his closet. "I've never shown these to anyone before. My stepmother accidentally found them when I was moving out, but that doesn't really count. You're the first person I'm ever willingly showing them to."

Leaving the box on his bed, Sevin walked over to the opposite side of the room and leaned against the wall. He crossed his arms and watched me as I opened the box.

My eyes widened. I didn't know what I was expecting, but the reality was absolutely shocking and breathtaking all at once. Beautiful women of all shapes and sizes. Body parts were clearly and graphically recreated to perfection with fine details like pubic hair and beauty marks. The faces were mostly turned to the side or looking down. Some had their eyes closed. Some were more sexually provocative than others, but they were all tasteful.

"These...are amazing. You don't use real models?"

"Yeah, right. I had loads of naked women stashed away in my old bedroom back home." He pointed to his head with his index finger. "No, it's all from up here. None of them are real people."

"How do you do it?"

He gestured with his hands and my eyes followed their movement as he spoke. "I start off with a bunch of angles, one for her head, one for her middle and one for her hips and legs. I call that the framework. Then, once that base is drawn, I start drawing the actual shapes of her body. It's hard to explain. I just do what I see in my head."

"You're incredible."

"I'm gonna tell you a secret," he said.

"Wouldn't be the first."

His mouth curved into a smile. "I haven't drawn a single one since moving here."

"Why not?"

"I've tried."

"You just can't?"

"You're gonna think I'm crazy."

"Too late for that." I grinned.

"In order for me to draw one, I have to visualize the person. They're not real people, but I have a clear picture of *her* in my mind. But ever since the day we met, I can't see any other woman in my head except you."

"Have you ever tried?"

"Tried what?"

"To draw me."

"No."

"Why not?"

"I honestly think it would be too much for me. Too real. And to be honest, I'm not sure I could replicate you."

I didn't really know what came over me. Seeing the dozens of beautiful images he'd created left me with an overpowering need. I was already drawn to him in so many ways already, and then to discover this amazing talent was overwhelming. I wanted to be every one of these women, the objects of his desire and passion. I wanted to see him create.

I knew why he was standing away from me. Because all of this—our confessions, his showing me his most intimate creations—ignited emotions that were too powerful. Tonight further solidified the fact that it was even more important to stick to my original plan to leave town. This attraction between us would continue to simmer until it exploded, destroying everything in its path in order to be satisfied.

If I couldn't stand to hurt Elle, if I was going to be selfless and leave, then I at least wanted to take one piece of him with me.

I stood up from the bed. "I need you to draw me."

CHAPTER 14

SEVIN

I stood there dumfounded and honestly didn't know how to respond.

It wasn't because I didn't want to do it. It was because I wanted it so much that I worried about the aftermath. A feeling in my bones told me she was going to make the decision to run away from all of this, to leave home. Whether I said yes or no to drawing her tonight, either way, I would probably regret it.

More than anything, I was confused about what she expected drawing her to entail.

Still keeping my distance as I leaned against the wall, I repeated her statement, "You need me to draw you…"

"Yes."

"Why?"

"I think they're beautiful, and I want to see how you see me."

The look of melancholy on her face was killing me. There wasn't a trace of humor or even happiness in her request; she was dead serious. She wanted me to draw her, yet at the same time, something about that was making her sad.

"I told you. I don't normally draw real people. The images in my head are self-created. I don't know that how I imagine you would translate well enough onto paper."

She shocked me when she said, "I could take off my nightgown."

Never in a million years did I expect her to suggest that. "Why would you want to do that?"

"I don't have to. I just thought maybe that would make it easier for you to draw me."

How could she think that would be safe? Did she have no clue what she did to me? "No. No way." I snapped, "Why are you doing this?"

She looked surprised and mortified upon my adamant refusal. "I'm sorry. I can't believe I even suggested it. Forget I said anything. This was a mistake. I have to go."

She rushed out of the room heading in the direction of the front door.

Grabbing her wrist from behind her, I said, "Stop."

She turned back toward me, closing her eyes but said nothing.

"Open your eyes." When she obliged, I said, "Don't ever be ashamed to tell me what you want. I'm sorry I overreacted. The truth is that I want to draw you so badly right now that it's scaring the fuck out of me. I just don't think it's a good idea, so I'm gonna say no. But please don't leave. Stay with me."

After a long pause, Evangeline nodded and followed me back into the living room. She sat on the couch, clutching a pillow. "Do you have anything to drink?"

"What are you in the mood for? I have soda, water, coffee…"

"I meant a *drink* drink."

"I have that, but I didn't think you drank."

She laughed. "I don't. But I never needed one more than now."

Smiling in understanding, I said, "All I have is beer. Is that okay?"

"Yes."

Cracking open a can of Bud Light, I glanced over at her. She looked beautiful in her white nightgown as she curled into my couch.

This.

This was what I wanted every night.

I poured the beer into two glasses and brought them over to her.

As we sat drinking, she said, "I feel like we need to eat something with this. Do you have any Pop Tarts?"

"What do you take me for? Of course, I do." Grinning, I got up and put two of them into the toaster and waited before carrying her over a plate.

Her mouth was full. "These are so good."

"I make sure to have them on hand now in case you happen to show up randomly in the middle of the night."

"Are you serious?"

"I wish I weren't."

We spent the next hour playing music, going through all of my CDs one by one. She picked out songs that she wanted me to burn for her.

Sitting on the floor with her legs crossed, she sifted through my father's old CDs and broke out in laughter. "Being here…drinking beer. There are just so many reasons why I'd be crucified for this."

"Everyone needs a night off from that world once in a while."

"There are way worse ways to sin than with beer, Pop Tarts and music, I suppose."

I chuckled. "If those are your worst sins, I'd say you're doing pretty well."

"I only sin when I'm with you, Sevin. What does that say?"

"That I'm a bad influence. Everyone always said my mother was a sinner and a bad influence on my dad. I guess I inherited that gene from her."

"She would be really proud of you."

"Because I'm a sinner or a bad influence?"

"Neither. Because you're a good, non-judgmental person like she was, and you're a hard worker. I see you at the plant. Daddy's always bragging about you, too. But you also show me a side of you that no one else gets to see. I'm lucky that you've trusted me. I've gotten to see your passion and your vulnerability…your need to be loved."

"I'm pretty sure I killed the one person who would have loved me unconditionally despite my faults."

"Is that what you believe? That you're not capable of being loved by anyone else?"

"Unfortunately, sometimes I do believe that, Evangeline."

"I can assure you that's not true." She closed her eyes, looking like she wanted to say so much more. Her voice was barely audible when she opened them and looked up at me. "When I asked you to draw me, it was because I wanted something from you that's just mine. I can see now how beautiful your art is. I just wanted to be a part of it, experience it with you—experience something passionate with you. I know it's wrong, but it's something I could keep forever."

"You want a keepsake. Because you're leaving…"

She didn't say anything. She didn't have to.

In all those years of drawing the women, it was almost as if through practice, I'd been trying to create the perfect one to no avail. From almost the first moment that Evangeline came into my life, there was no need to imagine it anymore. Nothing that my mind could ever conjure up compared to her.

A mix of anger and selfish desire consumed me. "I changed my mind. I want to draw you."

She could see the seriousness in my expression before she quietly followed me back to my room.

Opening the drawer, I nervously fumbled for my supplies. It somehow felt like all of my experience drawing until now had been leading up to this moment. I used two different kinds of pencils, one for outlining and one for shading. I stuck one of them behind my ear. Sitting on my bed with my legs crossed, I stared at her as she stood against the wall. Her chest was rising and falling.

"Don't be nervous."

I was telling her not to be nervous when I had to keep my own body from shaking.

"I'll try," she said, her voice trembling.

"Stay where you are, okay? Don't come any closer to me."

She nodded. "Alright."

Since I only had one lamp, my room was dim. Lighting a match, I lit three candles and placed them on the bureau next to where she was standing. The light from the flames cast a glow on the wall, causing a shadow behind her.

I wasn't going to tell her to disrobe. Instead, I'd try to draw how I imagined her, hoping that she wasn't disappointed in my interpretation.

Hesitant to start, I rubbed my fingertips along the thick paper of my sketchpad and closed my eyes for a moment to grab my bearings.

When I opened them, my heart skipped a beat before pounding out of control. Her arms were slowly lifting the cotton white nightgown she'd been wearing up and over her head. She'd completely closed her eyes so that she didn't have to witness what she was doing.

My conscience was screaming for her to stop, but I said nothing because I wanted this more than I ever wanted anything.

I couldn't believe she was letting me do this.

Evangeline reached around to her back and unsnapped her bra, which fell to the ground. I swallowed hard as I took her in, but there didn't seem to be any saliva left in my mouth.

Her breasts were so full, so heavy and perfectly symmetrical. Her nipples were darker than I imagined—a beautiful mauve—and a little larger than half-dollars. Yearning to suck on them, I licked my lips. My dick hardened. I needed to adjust myself but wouldn't dare in case she opened her eyes at that exact moment. Thank God her eyes were closed because I couldn't help the painful arousal now straining through my pants.

She was ten times more perfect than I could have ever imagined. Her eyes were still closed as she slowly slid her white panties down her legs. My heart was pumping faster than it ever had before. Remembering how my father died, I wondered if I were genetically at risk for a heart attack.

Evangeline stood before me completely bare—meaning her pussy was just that. I didn't know what I was expecting, but I never expected that she shaved it. Knowing that I was the first man to ever see her like this meant more to me than she could have ever possibly known.

But this was more than just physical.

She was baring herself to me because she trusted me. She knew that I felt as strongly about her when my eyes were closed or when we weren't even together as I did with her naked in front of me.

Feelings of pride and possession overtook me. I knew with absolute certainty that I couldn't possibly share this with anyone else. This was sacred to me. *She was sacred to me.* It was the purest thing I had ever experienced, and I wanted it all to myself. All of her. Evangeline didn't know it, but that was the exact moment I vowed to do whatever it took to fight for her; even if that meant giving everything else up and suffering whatever consequences resulted.

Her eyes were still shut as she shifted her head to the other side, causing her wild black tresses to slightly cover one of her breasts. I would draw her exactly that way.

It took everything in me to muster enough energy to start the first stroke. I much preferred staring at her and marveling at her natural beauty without having to think about anything else aside from what it would feel like to be inside of her. I forced the movement of the pencil.

Once I started, I couldn't stop, so incredibly focused on the precision of the angles and depicting her proportions accurately. All of my practice runs prepared me for this. The way she was standing, I couldn't make out her chest as clearly as I needed to. I had to know if she had any beauty marks, too.

As much as it was a risk, I stood up from the bed and slowly walked over to her. "Keep your eyes closed."

Her breathing intensified, but she did as I told her. Holding the pencil in my hand, I used it to lightly trace the shape of her breasts one at a time. When she flinched and opened her eyes, I whispered, "It's okay. I'm just tracing them to get a feel for the shape. I promise I won't do anything else."

She nodded, but now her eyes were open and following the movement of my hand. Her breathing was labored.

"Do you want me to stop?"

"No," she breathed out.

I tried to burn the fine details of her body into memory: the pear shape of her breasts, the small brown beauty mark on the inner skin of her right one. Her beautiful bare pussy…it took everything in me not to kneel down and devour it. When I'd gotten what I needed, I forced myself to step back.

She looked up at me when I stopped touching her with the pencil. Our eyes locked. As erotic as it all was, I couldn't take it any further.

I knew she was turned on. There were obvious signs, like the way her nipples puckered and the way she kept shifting her legs. But more than that, *I felt it.* In fact, her resistance was weaker than I ever expected. I would have been willing to bet anything that she was as wet as I was hard. The mere thought of that was making me insane. But as much as my body craved her, this wasn't the right time to consider anything more than what we were doing. I wasn't going to take advantage of the gift she'd given me tonight.

So, I returned to my bed and vowed to stay there until I finished the sketch.

***

It was almost morning by the time Evangeline got dressed and returned to the main house.

Seeming to really love it, she'd gasped when I showed her the drawing. I had to admit, it was truly my best work. I hadn't ever realized how much easier it was to create an accurate depiction when you had an actual live model.

Before leaving, Evangeline hid the picture inside a large Ansel Adams photography book that I'd let her borrow. She'd better have found a damn good hiding place for it.

Left in a state of excruciating need, I immediately retreated to the bathroom and jerked off to thoughts of all the things I wanted to do to her but hadn't. Now that almost every corner of her body was crystal clear in my mind, the fantasies were unbearably vivid. I came hard three times in a row...in the bathroom standing, in the shower and again in my bed. I'd considered taking a day off from work just to masturbate but stopped myself when I thought about how ridiculous that was.

At breakfast that morning, I could barely look Elle in the eyes.

"Sevin, are you feeling okay?"

"Yeah. I'm just a little tired. I wasn't able to sleep last night."

As I looked into her sweet eyes, for the first time, my guilt felt like it was completely transparent. The one consolation was that Evangeline was apparently still upstairs sleeping.

When Elle had recently suggested we take things to a physical level, I'd somehow managed to convince her that it was best to continue waiting.

When Olga was out of earshot, Elle whispered to me, "I want to come see you tonight."

"Okay. Sure." I didn't know how to respond. I knew for certain that I wasn't going to lay a finger on her, but being alone with her lately still made me uncomfortable. She seemed desperate to connect with me while I just became more distant.

With each day that passed, it seemed less likely that the wedding to Elle was ever going to come to fruition. The chances of my moving back to Oklahoma, however, seemed greater than my ending up with Evangeline.

"Callum is coming to visit this weekend. I told Evangeline the four of us should go out again."

It felt like everything was closing in on me. Evangeline had all but told me outright that she was leaving town with her "boyfriend." Meanwhile, the wedding plans were ongoing. I felt like I needed to do something drastic and soon.

***

Callum had driven down from Missouri, and the Suttons had stuck him in my guesthouse. So, I had a very unwanted roommate for the weekend.

The night I drew Evangeline was a game changer. There was no way I was able to tolerate the idea of this guy so much as touching her, let alone marrying her.

The alone time with Callum, though, was my opportunity to play dumb and get as much information about Evangeline's plans as possible.

We were outside working on rebuilding the shed that was damaged during the storm. It was a clear afternoon, and the sun was beating down on us. Elle and Evangeline went to town to the farmer's market to buy produce for dinner. Lance and Olga had gone to a church function with

Emily. So, aside from Imogene, it was just Callum and me on the property.

What started out as a routine afternoon of work turned out to be anything but ordinary.

I banged down with my hammer onto a piece of plywood and removed the nail that I'd been holding between my teeth. "So…Evangeline says she's now planning to move to Missouri?"

"Yeah…it was her idea."

"What's the rush all of a sudden?"

"I have my theories."

"Oh, yeah? What are those?"

"Well, you know. This environment here isn't exactly conducive to having a relationship. My parents aren't nearly as strict as the Suttons. They believe in traditional roles and all, but their courtship rules are different."

"So, you think Evangeline wants to move to Missouri so she can fuck around with you?"

"Partly, yes."

"And when you say, 'traditional roles,' what exactly are you talking about?"

"That means multiple things. For one, once we get married, Evangeline will stay home and raise our kids while I work outside of the home."

"I thought part of the reason she's supposedly moving is to work for your parents' company."

"Well, that'll be okay for a while, but Evangeline's not gonna be able to have a career once we have babies."

"Does she know that?"

"It's understood."

"So, you've discussed it…"

"Yes."

"Bullshit. No you haven't."

"Excuse me?"

"Evangeline would never go for that. She's way too ambitious."

"That's nice and all, but once we're married, she's going to do what's best for our family and therefore best for her. That's how it works."

"What's best for her is whatever makes her happy."

"So, you're telling me that Elle is going to continue working once you have kids?"

"Elle can do whatever the hell she wants to do, whether that's staying home with her children or working. It's not my place to tell her how to live her life."

"Sorry, but that's not how I was raised. A wife doesn't have a choice in the matter."

"I didn't realize you were raised by a tribe of fucking hyenas."

He lifted his arms up. "Dude, what the fuck is your problem?"

"My problem is your archaic thinking and the fact that you don't know diddly squat about the woman you're supposedly marrying."

"And *you* do?"

"A heck of a lot better than you, apparently."

"What is it with you and Evangeline anyway? Why are you always in our business? You wish you were marrying her instead? Why don't you stick to worrying about Elle. Go fuck her or something. Stay out of Evangeline's and my affairs."

"Evangeline is my family, just as much as Elle. She is my business."

"Well, not for long."

"If you think she's gonna marry you and agree to lose her identity, you have another thing coming."

"She's gonna do whatever the fuck I tell her to do as her husband."

"I suppose you think she also should fuck you whenever you tell her to, right?"

"Actually, yes. As my wife, whether she wants to or not, she *will* submit to me wherever and whenever I tell her to."

I really didn't mean to practically knock out his teeth. But as soon as that sentence exited his mouth, my arm took on a mind of its own. The next thing I knew, Callum was on the ground, and his mouth was a bloody mess. It all happened so fast.

There were no witnesses in sight—or so I thought. It would be his word against mine as to how the fight happened.

"You nearly fucking knocked out my tooth, you bastard!"

"You say shit like that about people I care about again, and I will make sure you don't have one single tooth left next time."

I didn't know how I was going to explain this to the Suttons. Callum would definitely make me out to be the bad guy.

As if this shit show couldn't have gotten any worse, Callum and I looked up into the window above at the same exact time. It seemed we had a witness to our fight. Imogene was standing there smiling down on us with her toothless grin. She'd been watching us like a spectator sport. I hadn't seen her in weeks, since the Suttons did such a good job of keeping the poor thing hidden.

Pervert that she was, she must have been ogling Callum and me as we both worked shirtless in the sun. That wasn't the worst part. When she noticed that we spotted her, she lifted up her shirt, exposing her long saggy tits. She started shaking them around.

What in the hell?

Callum and I were speechless. That marked the end of our fight as we both returned to the guesthouse in shock and silence.

CHAPTER 15

EVANGELINE

Callum had a fat lip. He wouldn't tell me the truth about what happened, but I had a sinking feeling Sevin had something to do with it.

At dinner that night, I noticed that Sevin had a bruise on his hand, so it wasn't hard to put two and two together.

When I confronted Callum about it later, he made up a story that the two of them were drinking too much and ended up wrestling. He said things got out of hand. The whole thing sounded bogus.

I'd been intentionally avoiding Sevin completely, so asking him wasn't an option. I knew he would tell me the truth, but I wasn't sure I wanted to know. The one time he was able to get me alone in the kitchen after dinner Saturday night, he said he needed to talk to me about something important. Perhaps it had to do with what happened with Callum. Elle had walked in seconds later, and that was the end of it. Now that my decision about leaving had been made, there was no point in making things worse by spending any more time with Sevin. After that night, I stopped showing up for dinner.

Sunday evening, Callum had just left to go back to Missouri. His next trip to Dodge City in two weeks would be to pick me up and bring me back with him. Although Mama and Daddy had given me their blessing to move in with the Hughes family, I hadn't yet told anyone exactly how quickly I was planning to leave. I was waiting until the last minute so that it didn't get back to Sevin. That also meant keeping it from Elle.

I was in my room discreetly packing some of my small items in preparation for the move when Elle walked in. I tried hard to look casual so that my packing up wouldn't seem so obvious.

She smiled. "Hey, sis. What are you up to?"

"Just organizing some of my things."

She plopped down on my bed. "So, you're really planning to eventually move to Missouri?"

Letting out a deep breath, I said, "That's the plan."

"There's nothing I can do to change your mind?"

"Don't make me cry. It's not that far away. We can still visit each other."

She sighed. "I know. I just always envisioned us raising our babies together, walking them around the property every day in their strollers while we visited Mama. I understand that Callum has to take over his father's company and all, but I never imagined that you'd move away. It makes me sad. I can't help it."

Tears that came out of nowhere were starting to form in my eyes. "I'm really sorry, Elle."

Sorry for my weakness, which screwed up your dreams for us.

Sorry for falling in love with your fiancé.

Sorry for everything.

I was truly sorry.

Elle got up from the bed to hug me. "Don't worry about me. It's okay as long as this is what's going to make you happy."

Your happiness is more important.

Elle really had no clue how unhappy I was. I thought that maybe after all this time, Sevin or I might have given off some kind of vibe, but it truly amazed me that Elle didn't sense that something was off with either one of us. My misery felt like it should have been written all over my face.

"By the way, is Callum okay?" she asked.

"What do you mean?"

"His lip…"

"Sevin didn't say anything to you?"

"No. I asked him if he knew what happened, and he said it was nothing. He wouldn't go into details."

"The way Callum explained it, apparently they were drinking while working on the shed and were horsing around, and Callum cut his lip."

"That sounds really weird."

"I know."

She smiled and shrugged her shoulders. "Boys will be boys, I guess."

"Right."

I breathed out a sigh of relief when she left to go downstairs. It was so hard not to tell her how soon I was planning to leave. But once it got back to Sevin, I knew he would try to stop me. I couldn't risk anything happening between us that might deter me.

After the night that he drew me in his room, I knew I couldn't allow myself to lose my inhibitions like that ever again. I'd wanted him to draw me as a form of closure, but it had an opposite effect on me, one so strong that it solidified the need to leave as soon as possible.

I couldn't close my eyes at night without remembering the feel of his pencil tracing my breasts—the look of desire in his eyes when he did it.

He'd been so intensely focused, drawing me as he sat on the bed with his legs crossed, that pencil tucked in the crook of his ear.

I will never forget one single second of that night. The sensations that had pulsed through me were ones I didn't think my body was even capable of.

The ache for him was now more unbearable than ever. Forcing myself to stay away from him made it even worse.

I missed him so much but could no longer trust myself around him. This was the way it had to be. All he'd have to do was touch me one more time, and I was afraid I might lose it. And losing *it* would mean losing my sister and being responsible for Sevin's downfall all at once.

***

One week before my scheduled departure, the feelings of emptiness and longing hadn't waned; they'd only intensified. In a fruitless attempt to shake them off, I decided to do something that I hadn't done in weeks.

Lacing up my sneakers, I prepared to go out for what would likely be my final early morning run here, since the rest of the week's forecast called for rain. There was less fog than usual, and the sun was fighting to peek through the morning clouds.

As my feet hit the dirt of the grounds outside the ranch, the enormity of my leaving really started to sink in. I ran faster to fight the feelings of despair. The cold morning air attempted to dry the tears that were streaming down my face.

I didn't want to leave.

The symbolism of my running was not lost on me. That was exactly what I would be doing, running away from everything here. I didn't know if that made me a hero or a coward.

About three minutes into my run, it felt like my heart was beating out of my chest in synch with my feet. I could have sworn I heard it pounding outside of me but soon realized it wasn't my heart at all. It was the sound of footsteps pounding the pavement behind me.

I didn't have to turn around. I knew it was him. I sped up. By the time he made his way to my side, it felt like I'd lost a race against time.

He could see the tears falling down my cheeks, the redness in my eyes. He must have known I was crying long before he ever showed up.

Sevin's gray hood covered his head. His beautiful dark blue eyes were piercing from beneath it. He looked tormented, devastated...stunningly beautiful—a clear reminder of exactly why I'd been staying away from him.

He wasn't saying anything. The faster I ran, the faster he would go to keep up with me. You'd think we were being chased by something when in fact the only thing we were running from was each other.

I was losing my breath. It felt like I was going to drop, and he sensed it.

He grabbed my arm, forcing me to a halt. "Fuck! Stop, Evangeline."

Wrapping his hands around my cheeks, he pulled my face close to his. We were just inches apart and both gasping for air. The air that escaped his mouth and entered mine made me weaker and weaker. I wanted to consume each and every one of his breaths. This moment was different from all of the others we'd shared. The intensity in his eyes wasn't anything like the focused stare he normally displayed when looking at me. It was wild, uninhibited and held no control at all.

Sensing that something was going to happen, I cried, "We can't do this. We'll go to hell, Sevin."

He spoke over my lips, "Don't you know I'd burn in hell for a single taste of you?"

That was the last thing he said before I felt my lips completely disappear into his mouth. If everything before this had been a controlled burn, then this was the explosion. Pulling him deeper into me, I opened for his tongue, letting him take full possession of my mouth. The heat of his kiss, the warmth of his body pressing into mine eclipsed all else around me. I could see nothing. Hear nothing. I could only *feel* him. Reaching up, I ran my fingers under his hood, grasping at his hair to pull him closer. It never seemed close enough. It wouldn't ever be. Because I needed him inside of me. The way he swirled his tongue in hard and controlled movements inside my mouth mimicked what I knew he would do to other parts of me. I was throbbing between my legs, so incredibly wet with desire. My awakened body was ready to take on more. So much more. Knowing that I could never be satisfied until he was inside of me was a dangerous realization.

This was so dangerous.

When I attempted to pull back, Sevin spoke into my mouth, "Please don't tell me to stop."

It felt like I *couldn't* stop, like nothing else mattered anymore. Maybe that was what happened when you finally surrendered fully to the person that was meant for you. *Nothing else mattered.* I lost any ability to speak when he started to kiss down my neck. My head was bent back as far as it could while he kissed, sucked and gently bit on the skin there.

We were in the middle of the desolate road with no sound but our breathing and the morning call of the birds. Suddenly, the sound of a car approaching ripped our bodies apart.

Panting, we moved to the side of the road as a sheriff's deputy whizzed by us. It could have been someone who knew us. Worse, it could have been Daddy leaving early for work. That rarely happened, but it was possible.

We were both trying to catch our breath, still in shock, looking down at the concrete. When I looked up into his lust-filled eyes, it took all of the strength in me to move back and say, "Please don't touch me again."

"That will make it easier for you to go back to pretending I don't exist?"

"You think that's easy for me?"

"No, in fact, I think it's impossible."

"You're right. The more I try, the harder it is."

"You can physically stay away from me, Evangeline. Sure. You can even move hundreds of miles away. But can't you see I'll still be with you?" He patted his chest. "I'll be right here…in your heart, in your dreams, under your skin. That's how it's always been for me with you. The more we're apart, the more I long for you. Sometimes, the harder we fight something, the more it shows its power over us."

"Please, just let me go."

"I fucking wish I knew how. The only time I've ever prayed in my entire life was to ask God to show me how to let you go. But He's not helping, because we aren't meant to be apart." He looked down at the ground, shaking his head in frustration. "Listen to me and listen good. You can stay away from me all you want, but please…*please*…don't marry him. He's not the one for you."

"You don't really know him."

"He wants to trap you, make you be his fucking slave. You should hear the way he talks when you're not around. Traditional roles bullshit, how once the two of you are married, you're gonna just do whatever he says…fuck him whenever he wants…be barefoot and pregnant. I've been trying to warn you, but you won't give me the opportunity to get you alone. I've been freaking the fuck out trying to talk to you about this. I wanted to kill him."

"You hit him."

"Yes, I fucking hit him. Was that not obvious?"

"How Elle hasn't figured it out is beyond me, between the bruise on your hand and his mouth."

"Imogene saw the whole thing."

"Imogene?"

"Yes. Right before she flashed us her tits from the window."

My eyes widened in disbelief. "What? Are you serious?"

He nodded. "True story."

We burst into much needed laughter. Tears were falling from my eyes again, and I couldn't be sure whether they were tears of sadness or laughter or both.

When the laughter faded, I looked down at his hand and said, "I'm sorry about your bruise."

He stretched his fingers out, looking down at his knuckles. "This is nothing compared to what I fucking feel inside, Evangeline. Anyway, it really was nothing. I'd do anything to protect you."

I love you, Sevin. I love you so much.

He looked so vulnerable and desperate, like he'd do anything to make me stay. His hair was messed up from my fingers having raked through it. He looked so incredibly sexy—hungry. I wanted nothing more than for him to ravage me on the grass. My body was tingling, throbbing, aching all over like never before.

He walked toward me. "You were crying when I caught up with you. You're not happy. Please let *me* make you happy."

"At the expense of what? I don't love Callum, okay? You know that. But he's the only option I have at the moment for a fresh start. I don't know that I'm even gonna go through with marrying him. Right now, the only thing I need is another place to live for the time being. My staying will only destroy my sister and ruin your future."

"I don't want a future without you in it."

"I have to go."

"Don't run away from me again."

"I have to."

Taking off without another word, I ran like hell toward the ranch, leaving Sevin behind in the middle of the road. But he was right. I could run all I wanted from him, but he was still with me. Needing him with all of my heart and soul may have been a sin, but it was the truth. He *was* my truth. Even if that made me a sinner. Very soon, my truth and my sins would catch up with me faster than I was ready for.

CHAPTER 16

SEVIN

Dear Sevin,

I'm writing to let you know that I will be leaving at the end of this weekend for Missouri. I know this is going to come as a shock because it's sooner than anyone ever expected, but it's for the best.

There is something I need to tell you before I go.

I debated for a long time whether I should write to you. I feel safer communicating with you this way because for obvious reasons, I no longer trust myself to be physically around you.

Anyway, back to the point of this letter. You said once, in regards to your mother dying, that you felt that you killed the one person who would ever love you. You were wrong. You are capable of being loved. I'm proof of that. Because I love you. Unconditionally. I wish I didn't.

I love your passion. I love your art. I love how you appreciate my oddities. I love your music and how you use it to express yourself to me. I love the way you look at me. I love how you make me feel. I love who I am—myself—when I'm around you. I love YOU. I love you, Sevin. No matter what happens, I need you to know that.

My feelings are too strong for me to handle. Through my weakness, I've put myself in situations with you that tested both of us. Even though I don't regret any of the secret time we spent together, it doesn't change the fact that it was wrong. Sometimes, love also means putting the needs of those you love ahead of your own. Elle doesn't deserve a big sister betraying her behind her back. If you love me, then please take care of her. The only thing worse than the hurt I'm feeling now, is imagining Elle experiencing the same if she were to ever find out about us.

I don't want you to worry about me. I have a good head on my shoulders. If things between Callum and me don't feel right, I promise I won't marry him. I'm going to be making more money at Hughes Foods than I do at Sutton. I plan to save every penny until I can figure out a plan for myself.

Maybe someday I'll get over you, and then I can come back. Until then, this is what I have to do.

I will never forget that kiss for as long as I live.

Love always, Evangeline

P.S. Please destroy this letter as I can't risk anyone finding it.

Holding the letter in my hand, it felt like a death. For the first time in my life, it was almost possible to imagine what my father felt like when he lost my mother. In some ways, the fact that Evangeline would still be alive and moving on with her life seemed like it would be harder to handle. It would have been easier if she just disappeared into thin air.

Opening my cabinet, I took out a small bottle of Jack Daniels that had been harbored away for some time. I returned to my bed, downing the alcohol in one long sip as I continued staring down at her meticulous handwriting.

There was a knock at the door.

Shit.

Shoving the letter under my bed, I walked over to answer it. It was Elle and Emily.

Elle walked past me while Emily turned on the television in my living room.

"So, I have some news," Elle said, looking sad.

"What's that?"

"Evangeline is leaving for Missouri this weekend. She's moving in with the Hughes family. I thought it wouldn't be for another few months, but it's happening now."

Swallowing, I said, "Really…"

"Yeah. The next time we see her will be the wedding."

Feeling numb, I didn't know how to feign surprise. How the fuck could I pretend that the news of Evangeline leaving hadn't already shattered my world just a few moments ago?

Elle continued, "I don't understand why she has to leave so soon. The wedding is only weeks away. I was really hoping she'd at least stay until then."

The second mention of our impending wedding sent waves of nausea through me.

She approached. "Sevin, are you okay?"

I stood there speechless, feeling like I was about to blow.

"Have you been drinking?"

"Just a little."

Despite the smell of alcohol, my angst had to have been written all over my face. I looked into her sweet eyes, and reality just hit me like a ton of bricks. Everything seemed so clear in that moment. It was funny how stress could fog your brain for months on end. Then all of a sudden, clarity could just come out of nowhere.

I couldn't go through with it.

I couldn't marry her.

I needed to end it.

When Lance first proposed this arrangement, it seemed to make sense. So much had changed since then. I had changed. What I wanted changed. What I needed changed. And even if Evangeline never allowed herself to be with me, Elle would always remind me of her sister. And if I couldn't have Evangeline, I couldn't be reminded of her every day for the rest of my life.

It wasn't fair to put Elle in that predicament, either. She deserved better than to marry a man who was secretly desperately in love with her sister.

I needed to buy myself some time. Breaking this news to the Suttons was going to have to be handled very carefully. It would devastate them, but better now than ten years down the line. There would still be time for Lance to find a replacement to take over the business.

Finally answering her, I said, "Actually, things aren't okay. I have to go back to Oklahoma for a while."

"What?" Her eyes widened. "Why?"

I lied, "My brother is going through some stuff. He needs me. I'll be gone for a few days at the very least."

"When did you find out about this?"

"Today."

"Well, okay. Um…when do you leave?"

"Tonight."

It was hard to believe it was actually coming to this. Deep down, from almost the very beginning of my time here, I knew that going through with the wedding was wrong. I still always believed I'd go along with it.

I really needed the advice of someone older and wiser. Times like these were when I really wished my father were still here.

***

Driving around Dodge City aimlessly later that afternoon, it was unclear where I was headed. With my small suitcase in the back of my truck, I had no real intention of actually driving the several hours to Lillian's house in Oklahoma.

I finally decided to look for a hotel about an hour out of town. I just needed a quiet place where I could think straight and come up with a plan about how to approach things with the Suttons. The thought of that conversation made me ill.

As much as I knew it was wrong, one final stop would be necessary before getting out of Dodge.

Elle had mentioned that Evangeline was working a final shift at Addy's car repair shop. Since I was leaving town for a few days, she would be gone to Missouri by the time I returned.

It felt like I needed to see her more than I needed my next breath. It was the only thing I was sure of as I drove around lost in my thoughts. I didn't know what the months ahead would mean for me or where I'd end up. I just knew I couldn't leave town without one last moment with her.

She would be pissed at me, but I didn't give a fuck. If I was about to give up everything because I loved her, she was going to have to face me one last time.

Say goodbye to my face.

I'd never been over to Adelaide's. When I parked my truck across the gravelly road from her property, I hesitated before going inside. I took everything in, thinking about how this was the place that Evangeline seemed to love most in the entire world.

Addy's small gray house stood adjacent to the shop, which was a bigger structure with three large garage bays. The sounds of metal clanking and laughing could be heard from inside.

A husky female voice startled me. "Can I help you?"

"Hi. I'm—"

"Sevin," she answered. "I know who you are."

"You do?"

"I do." She looked me up and down. "Wow."

"I take it, you're Addy."

"Jesus H. Christ, Vangie wasn't kidding."

"What's that?"

"She said you were handsome. She didn't say you were the kind of handsome that might just turn an old lesbo like me straight."

Addy made me smile, which wasn't an easy task. I could totally see why Evangeline was drawn to this woman.

"Well, thanks."

"I know why you're here."

"You do…"

"You're here for her." She smiled. "Vangie is in the garage working on a tune-up." She nudged her head toward the house. "You want to come inside…chat with me for a bit?"

The firm look in her eyes told me she wasn't asking me to come in; she was telling me. She was a big woman, not someone to mess with. Even stronger was her personality. It felt like I could feel her spirit if that were possible. This felt no different to me than meeting Evangeline's mother for the first time. Addy probably knew more about her than anyone.

She led me inside the house, gesturing for me to have a seat at her kitchen table. Something garlicky was cooking on the stove.

Addy stirred the pot then wiped her hands on an apron and sat across from me. "I'm not gonna beat around the bush here. It's not my style."

"Alright…"

"You kids have gotten yourself into some deep shit."

Finally, someone who spoke my language.

"How much do you know?"

"Everything, Picasso."

Shit.

"Wow."

"Don't worry. You can trust me, okay?"

Looking straight into Addy's eyes, my tone was almost frantic. "I love her. Tell me what to do, Addy. Just tell me what to do." Being able to talk to another person about what was happening to me felt like a huge weight lifted off of my chest. It wasn't normal to have carried all of this around alone for so long.

"I know you love her."

It felt so fucking good to talk about this with someone.

Raking my hands through my hair, I let out a deep breath. "She's really planning to leave town tomorrow?"

"Yes. Working on that damn car was what she wanted to do on her last day here, can you believe it? But that's partly because she needs to keep herself busy, otherwise she'll crack, and she knows it. By the way, I love that girl to death, too."

"She won't ever be with me because she'll never hurt Elle. I just don't see a solution."

"I need to confess, I recently encouraged her to make a decision one way or the other. Seems she took my advice. Here's the thing…I'm not so sure that was the right idea anymore. I feel like I should have tried to skew her decision, but I wanted it to be her own choice. If I tell her to do one thing, and she ends up getting hurt from it, I'm not sure I could forgive myself."

"Are you saying you think we should find a way to be together? That's what I want. Even if we have to keep it a secret. I don't care."

"Listen, I spent my life being persecuted for loving someone who everyone told me was forbidden. That love of my life just died. She's gone. Forever. In a weird way, losing her made me appreciate all of our struggles even more. I couldn't imagine her leaving this Earth without our having had the chance to fully express that love to each other. I just couldn't fathom that. Not having that regret is the only reason I sleep at night now. My nightmare is that Vangie is going to regret running away. Regret is a horrible curse. I don't want that for either one of you."

"I can see why Evangeline loves coming here."

"I know we just met, Sevin, but I care about you, because *she* cares about you. I want you to know if either one of you ever needs a safe haven, you're always welcome here. I'll give you work and a roof over your head. Vangie's like the daughter I never had."

"I can't tell you how much that means to me. I don't have parents. I don't have anyone."

"You do now."

"Thank you."

"I know it seems impossible, but don't give up on her."

"I need to see her."

"Go on. She's in the garage."

She hadn't noticed me standing there for the longest time. Looking almost exactly like the day we first met, Evangeline had grease on her face, and her wild black hair was all over the place. A beautiful mess.

She'd been worried about going to hell for our kiss. Hell to me was life on Earth without her. Time was running out fast, but I had a lot of fight left in me. The one area where I'd been holding back was also her biggest area of weakness. I knew she couldn't resist me sexually. She would literally run from me to avoid giving into the strong physical pull between us. Needing to try everything to get her to stay, I knew that holding back wasn't an option anymore. I wasn't going to let her run straight into the arms of another man just because she was afraid of the consequences of loving me. Over my dead body. She was mine.

I needed to claim what was mine.

I called out, "Evangeline."

She jumped and placed her hand over her chest. "What are you doing here, Sevin?"

"It's raining. I came to pick you up."

CHAPTER 17

EVANGELINE

Hiding out at Adelaide's, I'd been crying inside most of the day. When I saw him standing there, as much as I'd prayed he'd stay away, my heart leapt for joy. I should have known better than to think Sevin was going to take that letter as closure. I didn't even try to ask him to leave because the look in his eyes told me he wasn't going anywhere. It also told me I was screwed.

I cleared my throat. "I'm almost done."

Sevin crossed his arms and leaned against the wall. "I'll wait." The heat of his stare was overpowering as he watched every moment of my hands as I tightened the distributor.

When I finished, I said, "I'm just gonna go wash up."

He was standing in the same spot when I returned from the wash room. He looked amazing in a black hoodie that hugged his chest snugly. His hair was still damp from the rain. But it was the self-assured look on his face that really made my knees weak.

"Let me just get my coat."

"Do you need to say goodbye to Addy?"

I shook my head. "I'm stopping by tomorrow before…I leave."

His jaw clenched at the mention of my impending departure, his eyes telling me that I wasn't going anywhere.

"Let me help you with that." Sevin pulled the coat from my grasp and opened it up for me. His palms lingered on my shoulders, igniting a warm current of energy down my spine.

I turned around to meet his eyes, his face too close for comfort.

"Let's get going then," he said as he stared into me.

It was dark outside, and the earlier rain had turned into a drizzle. Sevin opened the passenger side door to his truck and waited until I was seated before shutting it.

His smell saturated the inside. It was enough to make me drunk off of him. His eyes darted to the side, and he looked at me briefly before starting the car.

Neither of us was saying anything as he kept driving fast down the long dark road in the opposite direction from our ranch.

I was looking out the window which was covered in raindrops when his warm hand landed on mine, prompting me to look at him. The intensity in his eyes made my heart beat faster.

After several minutes of driving in silence, he pulled over into a desolate open field. My stomach dropped. Sevin turned off the ignition and leaned his head back before looking over at me.

"If you're leaving, so am I."

What?

Panic set in. "No."

"You were just gonna leave without saying goodbye, leave me with a fucking 'dear John' letter?"

"You know why I couldn't see you."

His face was turning red. "Because you're weak? Because you can't trust yourself not to let me fuck you?"

"No," I lied.

"Yes. You're weak. So am I. So fucking weak." Gently brushing the side of my cheek, he said, "Let go, Evangeline. Let...the fuck...go." Sevin wrapped his hand gently around my neck as he rubbed over my throat with his thumb. "I promise it will feel so good to let go."

My breathing was ragged. I tried to say something, but the words wouldn't come out. All I wanted was for him to keep touching me. It was all I could think about.

His mouth curved into a wry smile. "Look how you react to me. Just a simple touch. You think we can stop this? Neither one of us can resist each other."

No. We can't.

Unleashing an unintelligible sound, I closed my eyes as his calloused thumb continued to stroke my neck. The simple movement was causing my entire body to buzz with arousal.

He lightly squeezed my neck. "If you're gonna say goodbye to me, say it when I'm touching you," he said gruffly. "Say it to my face. You can't. You can't even fucking speak. I love this, how you react to me. I'm so fucking hard right now."

Tears began to fall down my cheeks. He was right. I couldn't say goodbye to his face, and it was impossible to resist him. I was afraid to even look at him.

Still, I made one last attempt to run from the powerful feelings that had overtaken me. Opening the door, I slammed it behind me.

Struggling to breathe, I sucked in the misty air. Walking to the back of the truck, I crossed my arms over my chest. Light rain was starting to fall again. It was pitch dark except for the illumination of the moon and the light from his pickup. Sevin's door slammed shut.

I couldn't let this happen.

I couldn't let this happen.

I couldn't let this happen.

As I closed my eyes, I felt him pull me into his arms. I knew in that moment that I'd lost the race. I was done. I was his. People were going to get hurt.

"We'll figure it out," he whispered over my face as if he could read the racing thoughts in my head. He touched his forehead to mine. "Together. As long as we have each other, we'll figure out how to deal with this."

When I opened my eyes, they were met with his intense stare. I could feel his love for me pouring out of those eyes, his body and his soul. I wanted nothing more than to spend my life loving this beautiful broken boy, to prove to him that the way he came into the world wasn't in vain. Sometimes, words weren't necessary. Sometimes, all it took was a certain look. He must have seen that same look in my eyes, the look that told him my body was all in. I was giving in.

He released a breath that sounded like he'd been holding it in forever before pulling me in tighter. Allowing myself to release the pent up tension, my body relaxed into him. He kissed my head while he traced his fingers along my back. I could feel his erection against my stomach. I'd never felt a man hard before. It stunned me how big and warm it felt against me. Wetness and weakness developed between my legs.

Sevin pulled back and held my face in his hands. "I have so much love inside of me that's all yours, and it's been trapped inside. I need to give it to you, because holding it in is killing me. I know your heart belongs to me. But I'm selfish. I want all of you. I want your body before you run away from me again. Because I promise you, once we're connected, you're gonna know that we were meant for each other. Unless you tell me not to, I'm gonna take you. Right here. Right now, Evangeline."

His words alone made my body quiver.

I'm gonna take you.

Trying to bury my guilt in him, I drew his body into me.

Take me.

Bending my head back, I closed my eyes and silently willed him to do what he pleased. I'd dreamt for so long about what it would feel like to fully surrender to him.

"I don't know what I'm doing."

"I'll show you everything. I'll tell you what to do."

He started to kiss my neck, and with each movement of his mouth, the pressure was progressively harder. He started sucking on the base of my neck and on my chest to the point of pain. My back was pressed against the cold metal of the truck. I often wondered what Sevin would be like sexually. He had experience, and I had none. It didn't take long for me to realize that there was nothing gentle about him. But it didn't scare me; I wanted more.

His strong hands gripped the material of my shirt as he kissed over my breasts. Fumbling with the buttons, he grew impatient and ripped my blouse open. He unclasped my bra then threw it into the back of the truck behind me.

Sevin spoke over my skin, in between licking and sucking my breasts. "You have no idea how hard it was not to touch you that night in my room. I don't have any resistance left in me." Pushing my breasts together, he squeezed them and licked slowly down the middle before nipping on my nipple.

No man had ever touched me like that before. To have my first experience be so rough and primal was unexpected. He worked my body like he owned me. I didn't want it to cease for even a second. Any guilt became completely overshadowed by need. My conscience was no longer powerful enough to stop this from happening.

Sevin kissed me harder before kneeling down on the wet grass to pull down my skirt. More wetness trickled down my inner thighs. He slipped his fingers into the sides of my underwear and took his time sliding them down my legs. A deep breath released from me when I felt him slip two of his fingers inside of me.

"Does that feel good?" he asked as he finger fucked me.

"Yes," I breathed.

Moving his hand in and out, he looked into my eyes.

"You want me to do it harder?"

"Uh-huh."

His fingers were deep inside of me while his thumb circled my clit.

He stood up. "Touch me, Evangeline."

"Where?"

"Wherever you want."

Rubbing my palm along his jeans, I felt his hot erection bursting through the seams.

"You feel that?"

"Yes."

"I've never been this hard in my life."

I rubbed my hand up and down over his crotch while he fingered me. I could feel him throbbing through the material. When he pulled his fingers out, he licked them slowly, never taking his eyes off me. The muscles in between my legs clenched at the sight of that.

"I've been waiting so long to taste you. I dreamt about this on the very first day we met."

"What do I taste like?"

Instead of answering me, he pulled me into a kiss, thrashing his tongue against mine and allowing me to taste myself. I couldn't get enough as I pulled his hair. While he was still fully clothed, we continued to kiss as I stood completely bare against him in the middle of the field.

When he stopped the kiss, he slid his hand down the length of my body and began to slowly run it over my mound.

"I can't believe you shave it. I nearly died when I was drawing you. So amazingly hot. I could eat you up."

"You could, or you will?"

"I'm about to."

He suddenly knelt down. I gasped when I felt Sevin's wet mouth between my legs. It was a feeling so unbelievably foreign in an amazing way. Grabbing the back of his head, I pushed him into my swollen clit, guiding his movements.

"That's it. Move my face however you want. Show me how you want me to fuck you with my mouth."

With every dirty word that escaped him, the muscles between my legs pulsated against him. His moaning vibrated through me. My own sounds seemed to egg him on as he devoured me faster and harder. I'd given myself orgasms before, but I never imagined that the build up to one could feel this good. Nothing had ever felt as good as his wet tongue pressing against my folds.

He couldn't seem to get enough of me. He abruptly stopped and crawled up onto the back of the truck with the finesse of a tiger, pulling me up with him. He lay down on his back and positioned my body over his mouth. "Ride my face."

My sex throbbed at his words. Hesitant to take control, I didn't move.

He grabbed my hips and guided them over his mouth as he devoured me. With my weight on top of him, the sensations were even more powerful. It didn't take long before my muscles began to contract. He felt it.

"Let go. Come against my mouth, Evangeline. I want to taste it."

I was so wet. He massaged his tongue into my throbbing clit harder. My orgasm came on suddenly and fierce. My hips were bucking, my body writhing over his mouth. His tongue lapped harder. He kept his lips on me until he knew I'd completely calmed down from it. Then, he softly twirled his tongue over my sex and kissed it until the quivering stopped. "I want to do that to you again," he said, his soft voice vibrating between my legs. Even though I'd just come, it felt like I needed to come again.

He slid me off of him and scooted up, pulling my mouth into his. His lips were covered in my come, and it turned me on to no end.

"I want to taste you, too."

"You will, but I need to be inside of you before I explode."

He flipped me around, pinning me down under him with one arm on each side of me. He looked into my eyes before lowering himself to kiss me again. My tongue searched desperately for his as I pulled on his wet hair. Licking, tasting, needing more, never enough. He suddenly stopped. "Look at me. Tell me you want this for real. Because once I'm inside you, I don't know if I could stop."

"I'm scared, but I want it so badly."

"It's gonna hurt at first."

"I know."

"I'm gonna go slow. You're gonna guide me in. Alright?"

"Okay."

"Tell me if it gets to be too much."

"I will."

"Don't be nervous. I love you, Evangeline. I won't do anything to hurt you. I promise. I just want to show you with my body how much I love you."

"I love you, too."

"We could go somewhere else if you want."

"No. I want it to be right here."

Letting out a slight laugh, he said, "Thank God."

He slowly unzipped his damp hoodie, throwing it aside. After he lifted his shirt off his head, I rubbed my hands across his broad chest and could feel his heart pounding just as hard as mine. It was hard to believe that I was touching him freely, feeling all of the ripples and muscles that I'd only been able to admire from afar.

"I've always wanted to touch you," I whispered.

He grabbed one of my hands and placed it on the bulge straining through his pants. "You're gonna be doing a lot more than touching me."

He was even harder than before as I massaged him through his jeans.

"Take it out," he demanded.

I slowly unzipped his jeans and stuck my hand inside his pants. His erection sprung forward as I lowered his boxer briefs. The skin of his cock was like warm silk wrapped around a thick bone. I couldn't help marveling at how phenomenal it felt. His tip was beautiful, like a sprouted mushroom covered in his wet arousal. Going down on a man was never something I'd ever fantasized about, but there was nothing more I wanted than to take him into my mouth and run my tongue along the line that ran across his crown, sucking every ounce of the cum off of it. I didn't have the guts to do it yet, but my urges definitely surprised me.

As he jerked himself off slowly, I let him direct me. He repositioned my hand over his cock as he spread my legs open wide. His voice sounded different, thick with desire. "Touch me to you. Put me where it feels good."

So incredibly wet, I gripped his shaft and slid the head slowly up and down over my opening. He hissed, letting out a shaky breath and for the first time, seemed to exhibit a slight loss of control as he looked down at his cock rubbing against me. "God, that feels...so good. So fucking good. It's taking everything in me not to come all over you right now. I can't imagine what it will feel like inside you."

Sevin took back control and rubbed the length of his cock across my slit over and over. Slow. Back and forth. Back and forth. The rhythm of his breathing matched each stroke. It was hypnotic. I looked up at the starry night sky for a moment, thinking that this all felt like a dream. It was surreal being out in the middle of nowhere with no sounds except our breathing.

"I love just feeling you like this," he said.

The extent of my need was surprising. I shocked myself when I said, "I want you inside of me."

"Not yet. I need you to be ready for me."

He continued rubbing his cock against me for several minutes. My legs were quivering with need, and I was soaking wet.

"Slide back."

He placed his hoodie underneath my ass and positioned himself over me, holding his body up with both arms at each side of me. His pants were still halfway down his legs, so he pushed them off.

"Put me inside of you."

Wrapping my hand around his cock, I led him into my opening. He barely made it halfway in when I gasped. It was definitely more painful than I anticipated.

"Are you okay?"

"Yes."

"No, you're not. We need to take it slow."

"Okay."

He hovered over my body while we kissed as he pushed slowly into me. His mouth never left mine as he kissed me deeply with each movement. Inch by inch, I felt the slow burn of him entering me.

Sevin let out a loud moan of pleasure once inside me, his voice echoing in the night. No one was within earshot. Hearing him lose control made all of the pain worth it. With each slow and steady thrust, he entered me more easily until eventually he was balls deep.

Grabbing his ass, I pushed him into me harder. "It's okay. Give me more."

"You're sure?"

When I nodded, Sevin wrapped my legs around his back and fucked me harder. His hips were moving in a swift circular motion as he filled me over and over. Our bodies rocked together rhythmically, shaking the truck. The harder he pumped into me, the more turned on I was. I never imagined I would want it rough, but I loved him hard, and so it only made sense that our lovemaking reflect that intensity.

The rain started to fall harder over us as I dug my nails into his back. My muscles began to contract, and my orgasm came on strong and unexpectedly. Sevin could feel it.

"Come, Evangeline. Come. Come all over me. God…you feel…so amazing." When he sensed I was done, he pulled out of me and jerked himself hard as he bent his head back. I watched in amazement as endless streams of his hot cum shot out onto my stomach. Out of everything we'd done, nothing had turned me on more than seeing him come.

Even though I was sore, I wanted to go another round just so I could see him orgasm again. It truly fascinated me.

Sevin planted himself on top of me. His hard chest pressed against my breasts as he kissed me deeply before pulling back. "That night in the barn, you said you dreamt about making love in the rain. I'll never forget that. I wished so hard that I could be the one to do that with you, thinking it would never be possible. No matter what happens, I'll never forget this, the best night of my life."

***

We lay together for an indeterminate amount of time before Sevin led me into the truck. We sat in silence for many minutes until he turned to me. That was when the mood darkened. "Do you know how it felt to know that the next time I was supposed to see your face was when you were walking down the aisle at my wedding to your sister? How fucked up is that?"

"I'm sorry. I thought you'd understand."

"I do understand. Too well. That's the problem. You love me. I love you. It's actually quite fucking simple."

"Simple?"

"I love you so much, Evangeline. To me, it was crystal clear what needed to happen, and it didn't involve either one of us marrying other people."

"You made a promise to my sister who loves you. I was trying to make it easier for you."

"You know what? In a way, you did make it easier for me. You helped me see that I couldn't marry Elle."

"What happens now?"

"I'm not going to go through with any of it. I'm leaving. I can't pretend to love someone else, not when I'm hopelessly in love with you. That's not ever going to change. Even if you didn't exist, it's not fair to marry someone whose love you can't return. I see that now that I know how powerful real love is. I'd also be keeping her from experiencing being on the receiving end of that."

"Do you understand what you're saying? Daddy will ruin you. He'll run you out of town if you do this after all of the investment he put into your future."

"Did you not hear me say I was leaving? I understand the repercussions."

"You're going to ruin your life. You won't have a job, a roof over your head…nothing. That doesn't matter to you?"

"It matters in the sense that I don't want to hurt Elle. But the other stuff is not important to me. There is nothing that matters to me more than you. I won't let you marry him just to get away from me. And I won't make you watch me marry your sister when I know in my heart it would hurt you beyond belief. No career in the world is worth knowing you're suffering because of me."

"Where will you go?"

"Anywhere but here."

Grabbing his hand, I looked out at the rain pelting the window. "This is a shock."

"Is it really, though? This day was always going to come. You couldn't feel it looming? I knew in my bones that it would be impossible to stay away from you. I think I knew that from the very first time I saw you sitting across from me at that dining room table the day we first met. What we have is too strong."

On the verge of tears, I asked, "What are we going to do? Daddy's going to make your life a living hell. I don't want you hurt, either."

"The only thing that can possibly hurt me is losing you."

"Where does Elle think you are right now?"

"I told her I was going back to Oklahoma for a few days. I lied. I made up a story about my brother needing me. I had to get away to figure out how I'm gonna tell her."

"She's going to be devastated."

"Would you rather me do it in two years after Elle and I are married with a kid?"

Just the mention of his having a child with Elle made me nauseous.

He continued, "My mother didn't die giving birth to me so I could spend my life living a lie. She wouldn't want that. I want to live the truth. And you're my truth."

"I want us to be together. But how? How can I possibly do this to my sister?"

"I'll love you in secret if I have to."

"In secret?"

"If you can't break her heart, no one has to know."

"But how?"

"I don't have the exact answers yet. Maybe I can build a life somewhere out of town but close by. We can be together there until we can figure things out. Maybe someday things will be different. Elle will find someone who truly loves her. We can tell them someday what happened."

"Promise me you won't say anything to Elle about leaving until we've thought this through."

"I'm going away to a hotel for a couple of days to think. I'll come back to the ranch, and when the moment is right, I'll tell everyone I'm leaving."

"I can't believe it's come to this."

"From the moment we met, it was supposed to happen this way. We were meant for each other, Evangeline. It's why God led me here. Not to find her…to find you. It was fate."

Deep down, I knew he was right. We were meant to be together. But fate didn't always come without detours and twists. Sometimes, fate could be fatal. We'd soon learn that the hard way.

CHAPTER 18

SEVIN

After I returned to the Sutton ranch, Evangeline and I decided to wait a week before my announcement. Talking to Elle would be the first priority. I would let her know that my feelings about the marriage had changed. That was going to be the most painful part. Then, I'd sit down with Lance to give him my formal resignation, profusely apologize for wasting his time and hurting his daughter, hoping he didn't take his shotgun out. It was going to be a nightmare, but it had to be done.

The plan was for me to hide out at Addy's until I could get a job. Evangeline would eventually figure out a way to come with me wherever I was. At least, that was what she was telling me and what I was banking on. Despite our consummating everything in the open field and professing our love, a lingering feeling that she wouldn't be able to go through with it was haunting me.

Evangeline snuck into the guesthouse almost every night that week. Her signature rock would hit my window, and I'd come around to let her in. She was completely riddled with guilt, but we still couldn't resist each other. My body ached when she wasn't around. We were completely addicted to the sex. After we'd finish, I'd always just hold her because I knew she felt sick about giving into me while Elle still thought there was going to be a wedding. But even that didn't matter enough; we couldn't stay away from each other. Now that we'd gotten a taste of it, it was simply impossible to stop. Like a druggie, I was addicted to her smell, her taste, the feel of being inside of her. When she wasn't around, it felt like I was missing an appendage. She was a part of me now.

I wished I paid more attention to every last detail of our time together that last night. Wednesday night. The last night we made love before everything changed. The last night we both had a little bit of hope for the future. The same night I stared at my mother's engagement ring while Evangeline slept in my bed. I knew I was going to give it to her and wondered how soon after everything went down she would allow herself to accept it. The feeling of elation was still overshadowed by an inexplicable uneasiness in my gut.

Thursday afternoon, the source of my dread revealed itself.

Everything changed in an instant.

They say when a traumatic event occurs, you always remember where you were and what you were doing. I happened to be at Sutton Provisions slowly cleaning out my desk area in the event that Lance didn't allow me access back into the building once I broke off my engagement to Elle.

One of the beef processing managers walked in. "Sevin, something's happened. Lance just got called home and rushed out. You'd better leave. I think something went down at the ranch with one of his daughters. I don't have any other information."

Flying out the door, I ran to the truck and drove home as fast as I could, praying that everything was okay.

Several emergency vehicles were parked outside the property when I pulled in. Flashbacks of my father's death tormented me as I ran toward the flashing lights.

Evangeline ran to me, her eyes were swollen and red. She was sobbing and unable to speak clearly.

My heart was pounding out of control. "What happened?"

"It's Elle. They're taking her to the hospital."

"What?"

"She was out riding one of the horses. Emily says the horse went ballistic and threw Elle to the ground. She was unconscious for a while. I don't know what's happening now."

The scene was chaotic. Olga stepped into the back of the ambulance. The door shut, and it took off.

Lance was pacing before he spotted me. "Sevin, take Evangeline and Emily and follow me to the hospital in your truck."

The ride to the hospital seemed to take forever. The sisters were huddled together in the backseat. Evangeline was comforting Emily who'd apparently witnessed Elle getting thrown from the horse.

I looked in the rearview mirror. "Emily, tell me what you can."

Emily wiped her eyes. Several seconds went by before she would answer me. "After Elle got home from work, she went out riding like she normally does. I was watching her on Magdalene. She was mounted, doing her usual jumps. Things were fine. Then, I went inside for a second to get a drink. When I came out, the horse was going crazy. Elle got tossed off. I ran to her, and she wouldn't wake up." Emily's sobs grew louder. "Everything changed...just like that."

Evangeline held her tighter. "It's okay, baby."

Despite the silence for the remainder of the ride, the fear among the three of us was loud and tangible.

The long wait at the hospital for information was excruciating. Even Olga was told to stay outside in the waiting room.

A doctor finally came out after about an hour. "Elle is awake."

We all seemed to let out sighs of relief in unison.

"Is she going to be okay?" Olga asked, tears falling from her eyes.

"There is something you need to know." He paused. "As of right now, Elle is experiencing a total loss of feeling in her lower extremities. We are running some tests to determine the extent of the paralysis and whether it's temporary."

"She's paralyzed?" Lance cried.

"We don't know that it's permanent," the doctor said.

It wasn't setting in. This seemed unreal. As the doctor babbled on, all I kept thinking about was the actor Christopher Reeve and hoping that whatever happened to Elle wasn't anything like that. The doctor didn't seem to know yet.

"So, the good news is, she's alert and able to recall what happened. There doesn't seem to be any permanent brain damage, but we are still assessing the level of spinal cord injury."

"Can we see her?"

"She asked for a Sevin. Is that her husband?"

"That's her fiancé," Olga said.

Out of everyone, she wanted to see me.

Crushing guilt consumed me, knowing that tomorrow was supposed to be the day I broke her heart. Today was so much worse than tomorrow could have ever been.

"Go on, Sevin," Evangeline said.

Walking down the hall to her room, selfish worries were instinctually clamoring at me. I needed to push away all thoughts of what this predicament was going to mean for Evangeline and me. Elle needed to come first right now.

The door slowly creaked as I opened it. Elle was lying on the bed with her eyes closed.

"Ellebell?"

She opened her eyes and turned to me, reaching out her hand. "Sevin."

"You're gonna be okay."

She was shivering. "I can't feel my legs."

Gently rubbing my hands down her thighs, I asked, "You can't feel this?"

"No. I'm so scared."

"Listen to me, Elle. We'll get through this. The whole family is here. The doctor is gonna figure out how to help you. They're running some tests."

She started to cry. "I don't know what happened to Magdalene. One second, I was riding her like normal, the next she just lost her mind. I got thrown."

"I'm so sorry."

"What about the wedding?"

Her question felt like a bullet in my heart.

"What about it?"

"We have to postpone it. We'll lose all that money."

"Don't worry about that stuff right now. It's not important. You getting better is the only thing that matters."

"What if I don't ever get the feeling back?"

"You will. You will, Ellebell. You have to believe that."

I really wanted to believe that too, but the truth was I had no clue how serious this was.

Over the next few days, Elle's doctors ran a series of tests. A neurological assessment determined that her injury was what they called "complete," which was more serious, often resulting in permanent paralysis. Elle's MRI, CAT scans and X-rays also confirmed significant damage to her spinal cord.

It went without saying that my plans to break up with her were put on indefinite hold. Life in general was also put on hold as the entire family forged together.

Each day became about making Elle comfortable and helping her to feel safe. Evangeline and Emily cared for her every need after we brought Elle home. I played the part of the supportive boyfriend, holding her hand, telling her everything was going to be okay. Whatever it took, we had to do it. Elle was all that mattered for the time being.

At the same time, there was a massive disconnect developing between Evangeline and me. It was killing me. I knew she somehow felt responsible for what happened, even though she had nothing to do with Elle's injury. Whatever guilt she held before the accident was ten times worse. She handled it by staying away from me and throwing all of her energy into helping Elle. I couldn't say I blamed her, but it hurt like hell.

Even though I had accepted the new normal, I still hadn't given up on us. As each day passed, it got harder and harder to believe that Evangeline and I would ever get back to the place we were, that she would ever come back fully to me. We were physically around each other all day, but she'd closed herself off.

We were all traumatized. The shock and sadness I felt toward Elle's situation was the only thing keeping me from focusing solely on the heartache of Evangeline slipping away from me.

Over time, it started to feel like this was more of a permanent life change as opposed to a temporary rough patch. Caring for Elle got a little bit easier with each day, though. She started to go to physical therapy. They'd teach her ways to control her bladder and bowel function. An occupational therapist would come to the house to try to teach us how to make the environment more conducive to Elle's disability. She'd also teach Elle ways to care for herself.

Elle's doctor also put her on an anti-depressant. She'd been struggling with her emotions and the loss of the future that she envisioned for herself. The doctor had indicated that while some people with spinal cord injuries could get pregnant, that wouldn't be an option in her case. Not being able to have children was by far the biggest blow, since she placed almost all of her self-worth on becoming a wife and mother someday.

Days turned into weeks. Imogene was eventually sent to live with another relative because the family couldn't handle any additional responsibility besides caring for Elle.

Evangeline ended her courtship with Callum using the same excuse that I was going to pull on Elle before all of this happened; that she had a change of heart. Evangeline and I hadn't talked about our situation. There seemed to be a silent understanding between us that it wasn't the right time to focus on anything but Elle.

***

When I felt the rock hit my window one night, I could hardly believe it. Knowing that it could only be one person, I jumped out of bed, flew to the door and opened it.

Evangeline was standing there in her nightgown with tears pouring from her eyes. She looked like half angel, half witch with that gorgeous dark hair.

"I need you, Sevin."

Pulling her close, I whispered, "I've been waiting for you to come back to me." I buried my nose in her hair and took a deep breath in of her scent.

"This has been so hard."

She pressed her body into me, her soft breasts were plastered against my chest. "Don't say anything, okay? I can't handle talking about any of it. I just need you to make me forget for one night. Please. I'm begging you. Just make love to me hard like you've never made love to anyone before."

"I've only ever made love to you."

"I need to feel you tomorrow. And the next day. Please…"

I knew I could give her what she wanted, but the fact that she'd gone for weeks without so much as touching me to now wanting me to fuck her hard confused me.

"I'll give you whatever you want, baby, as long as you stay the night. Don't run away again."

She didn't make any promises as she walked past me. When we got to my room, Evangeline took my face in her hands and started kissing me like I was her last meal. My lips were hot and sore from the intensity of the suction. So starved for her, I wasted no time lifting her nightgown over her head. She had no bra or underwear on. So desperate to feel the inside of her again, my pants weren't even all the way down when I lifted her over my cock. Her back was against the wall. We'd never done it standing up before.

"Fuck me hard," she breathed. "Until it hurts."

I didn't understand where her sudden need for painful sex was coming from. It seemed like she was looking for it as some sort of punishment. Even though it turned me on beyond belief, something wasn't sitting right with me. Too weak to resist her begging, I gave her everything she asked for.

My hand was around the back of her head to protect it. I was pumping into her so hard, taking all of my frustrations from the past several weeks out on her body. I kept having to remind myself it was what she wanted as I let go of all inhibitions and fucked her in the rawest way imaginable. Her pussy felt so tight wrapped around my engorged cock.

Nothing seemed to be enough for her. "Please, Sevin. Harder."

It was easier to fuck her mercilessly when I focused my thoughts on her alienating me these past several weeks. As much as I understood why, it still pissed me off and made me desperate for her all at once.

Thrusting into her over and over, I spoke into her ear, "You think you can just pretend that we never happened? You'll never be able to forget me now. Is this hard enough for you? Huh? You want more?"

She gripped my ass and pushed me into her even deeper. "Yes."

My orgasm suddenly came on fast and hard as I felt her muscles spasm around my cock. I always knew exactly when she was coming, but this time was the most intense. It was the most earth shattering orgasm of my life, my load shooting into her in a seemingly endless flow.

Her legs stayed wrapped around my waist. Her body was limp. It was the roughest sex I'd ever had. When I looked up into her eyes, they were dark. Instead of some kind of post-coital bliss, Evangeline just looked tormented as if she'd been hoping that the sex would take care of something that was bothering her.

"Come on, lie down with me."

"I really should go back."

"Lie down with me, Evangeline," I demanded.

I held her tightly, afraid to fall asleep and find her gone, or worse, discover that the beautiful angel-witch who appeared in my room was just a dream.

I eventually nodded off. It was noontime by the time I woke up. My instincts were apparently correct, because while Evangeline was nowhere to be found, in her place was a note.

You'll always be my truth. But sometimes, the truth hurts too much.
I love you.

The paper shook a little in my hands. A feeling of intense fear and dread overtook me as I tried to interpret her words.

Getting dressed as fast as possible, I ran to the main house to try to find her. Lance and Olga were on the phone, yelling at someone. Something was going down. Elle was sitting in her wheelchair in the kitchen, her face buried in her hands.

"Elle? What the hell is going on?"

"Something horrible has happened," she said.

Adrenaline started to rush through me. "Is someone hurt? What?"

"Evangeline is gone."

My head was spinning. "What are you talking about?"

"She left a note this morning. She ran away. Apparently, she'd been seeing some guy behind all of our backs, someone that my parents wouldn't approve of. No one knew about this. It's all in the letter, but she basically says she needs to go find herself away from us, that she's really sorry but that she needed to go away for a while and that she's not sure when she's coming back."

Too shocked and dazed to form a sentence, I simply said, "What?"

"I think she left because of me."

Still processing everything, I repeated, "What?" Elle must have thought I was going deaf.

"I said I think she left because of me, Sevin. I think she can't handle what happened to me. I know it in my heart. She couldn't stand to be around me anymore."

I was too devastated to comfort her and address her last statement. "Where's the letter?"

"It's on the counter."

My hands hadn't stopped trembling since reading the note she left earlier. Now, they were full on shaking as I picked up the letter written on paper ripped from a yellow legal pad.

The explanation was exactly what Elle described, a bullshit story concocted by Evangeline about having connected with someone who was not a God-fearing man, someone she wasn't supposed to love but couldn't help wanting to be with. Evangeline's lies continued as she went on about needing to find a purpose in life and how she didn't feel badly about leaving Elle because she knew her sister had me to take care of her. It was all a crock of shit. If I wasn't so goddamned heartbroken, I could have killed someone.

Seeing as though I couldn't remember the moment that my mother died, her death didn't impact me the way it did my father. So, it was pretty safe to say that this moment, standing in the kitchen knowing that the woman I loved had abandoned not only me but her entire family was the single worst moment of my life.

Elle continued to talk. Unable to process anything but the vivid images in my head from the night before, I simply wasn't hearing her. The terrified look in Evangeline's eyes as she asked me to ravage her now made sense. Last night was a goodbye fuck meant to numb the pain of what only she knew would be happening today.

One thing was clear: wherever she went, she was hurting badly. A frantic desperation to find her consumed me. The only person whom she might have told was Addy. I needed to go to her house and grill her for information.

***

My knock was loud and abrupt.

"Addy! Addy, let me in."

The door swung open. "Sevin? What's wrong?"

Letting myself in, I huffed, "Don't act like you don't know."

"What in heaven's name are you talking about?"

"Evangeline and her disappearing act. Where did she really go?" I frantically searched the house. "Wait…is she here?" Things were falling all over the place as I weaved in and out of the rooms.

"Stop ransacking my house! Vangie's not here, Sevin."

"Then she told you where she was going."

"Calm down. Tell me what's going on. The last time I talked to Evangeline was two nights ago. She didn't say anything to me about going anywhere."

"You're serious?"

"I wouldn't lie to you about something like this."

"She left a letter with some hokey story about running away with some guy and needing to find herself away from Dodge City. You and I know that's bullshit. You're the only one who knows about us."

"Where could she have gone?"

"I have no idea. She doesn't have a pot to piss in."

"Did you try her cell phone?"

"Yes. The number was disconnected."

"What are the Suttons doing about it?"

"What can they do? She's twenty-one. Lance was talking to the police, but they won't take action because she left on her own accord. Olga talked Lance out of searching for her any further, saying Evangeline needed to learn from her mistakes."

"She seemed particularly upset the last time she was here. I just assumed it was the usual stress of Elle's situation and the effect it's had on you two."

"Swear you're not lying to me, Addy. Swear you really don't know where she is."

"Boy…can't you see that this is shaking me up just as much as you?"

"What the fuck am I going to do?"

"You'll wait until she comes back to you. Mark my words. She will be back. Vangie loves you too much."

"If she doesn't come to her senses soon, I don't know what's going to be left of me when she comes back. I was losing it as it was. Ever since Elle's accident…it's hard on all of us. Evangeline's presence on a daily basis was the only thing getting me through."

"If there are days where you feel like you can't go on, you come to me. I'm your sounding board. Don't do anything stupid."

"Thank you, Addy. Really…thank you."

***

Addy was right about one thing; Evangeline would eventually come back. What Addy couldn't have predicted, though, was that it would be five years later. By that time, it was too late to undo the damage that had been done.

Just over a year after Evangeline initially disappeared, Elle and I got married. It was either that or give up my job and the only home I had. Without Evangeline in the equation, those things that were simply necessary for survival became more important again. At that point, I truly believed Evangeline was gone for good. Not one word from her in a full year. Each day was like dying a slow death.

Aside from my own inner struggle, it was impossible to abandon Elle in her condition. She needed a provider and caretaker. To be honest, with each passing week, the love that belonged to Evangeline inside of me slowly festered into what felt like hate. I couldn't understand how she could just walk away.

Marrying Elle was a way of putting a nail in the coffin of my dreams for Evangeline and me. Elle needed me. Even though I wasn't in love with her, I decided to keep my original promise. My primary reason for not wanting to marry Elle had always been about how it would affect Evangeline. After a full year of waiting, it didn't matter anymore whether or not one of my choices resulted in Evangeline suffering. In fact, anything I could have done to hurt her half as much as she'd hurt me seemed only fair.

Playing the role of the good husband to Elle wasn't an easy task. It was a serious responsibility. After long days at the plant, I'd come home and do nothing but tend to her. I'd help her move around to avoid body sores and help her change her catheter.

It was also my responsibility to make her feel loved. I'd rub her shoulders, tell her she was beautiful to me and kiss her. Sometimes, that led to other things. Elle couldn't have intercourse, but I did what I had to do as her husband to keep her satisfied. Nothing Elle and I did physically came even close to what I had with Evangeline. Guilt would try to creep in, and I'd have to remind myself that Evangeline was the one who abandoned me, not vice versa.

Even though I still kept some of my belongings at the guesthouse, Elle and I ended up living full time at the main house. It was easier because we'd made it handicap accessible. Lance had a ramp put in and arranged for some other modifications. It was just as well because the guesthouse was where the ghost of Evangeline lived. Every corner of that place reminded me of her, particularly the wall of my bedroom that served as the backdrop to both the night I drew her and the last night we were together when we fucked like animals against it.

My passions and desires took a backseat to my obligations as a husband to Elle. It was a tremendous amount of responsibility. I took care of her every single day for five years.

Until the day she died.

PART TWO

AFTER ELLE

CHAPTER 19

EVANGELINE

This was truly worse than my worst nightmare. Facing Sevin after five years was one thing. Having to see Elle lying in a coffin just a few feet away was another. That made facing him seem like a walk in the park.

As cowardly as my running away had been, nothing could keep me from one last look at my beautiful sister. At the same time, it was the ultimate punishment for my sins. After this experience, nothing would be able to hurt me anymore.

I felt the weight of Sevin's stare as I walked over to Elle's lifeless body.

"You've got some nerve," Daddy seethed as I passed by him. I didn't care. I just needed to get to my sister.

Collapsing over her, a pool of tears emptied from my eyes and onto the silk white dress she was wearing. Everyone was staring at me in shock. Mama was the only one who knew I was coming today. I couldn't bear to look at Sevin again. The death stare he'd given me when I walked in was enough to tell me everything I needed to know regarding how he felt about my showing up. There wasn't an ounce of shock on his face—just pure anger.

This whole experience was surreal.

I'll never forget receiving that phone call from Mama. She was the only person who knew my whereabouts all these years. She told me that Elle developed an infection that spread throughout her body and poisoned her blood. Septicemia she called it. It took her fast.

Apparently, Mama didn't tell them I might be showing up, because the rest of my family truly looked like they'd seen a ghost.

The funeral director had to pry me off of her body. I just couldn't leave her. They needed to move her light blue coffin for the procession out of the church. Sevin was one of the pallbearers along with Daddy and some of the guys from Sutton Provisions.

Everyone followed the casket out except for me. Instead, I just stared vacantly at the empty pews.

My little sister Emily startled me. "Evangeline…"

Not so little anymore. I hadn't even noticed her when I walked in. Emily looked like a grown woman. She was going on seventeen now and resembled Elle more than the little girl I remembered leaving behind.

"Hi, sis." We hugged and cried in silence for several minutes.

She sniffled. "How did you find out?"

"Mama told me."

"She knew where you were?"

"Yes, but please don't tell anyone."

"Where have you been all this time?"

"I've been living in Wichita."

"That's only a few hours away. Are you kidding? Is that where the guy you ran away with lives?"

Even though I hadn't met Dean until after running away, it was easier to stick to my lie. "Yes."

I wouldn't let Dean come with me to the service. There was no way I needed that extra pressure today. He wasn't happy about having to let me out of his sights on my turf, but by some miracle, he let it go.

"What's the name of the person who's so important that you had to leave your family?"

"His name is Dean."

"We needed you. You left us when we needed you most for…some guy? How could you do that to us?"

"Em, someday I'll tell you everything. Just know that I didn't feel like I had a choice at the time, okay? Leaving you was the last thing I really wanted."

"I'm confused."

"I know."

"Elle is dead, Evangeline! She's dead."

Covering my mouth at the realization again, I wept and whispered into my palm, "I know."

Emily and I held each other for about a minute before she pulled back. "We'd better go. There's a car waiting to take us to the burial grounds."

"Go ahead without me. I'll follow."

I was left alone in the church. I had no intention of going to the gravesite and watching as they lowered her into the ground. I just needed to see her one more time, and I had that chance. I didn't want to make things even harder on Sevin.

Dropping to my knees, I prayed at the altar amidst the scent of burning votive candles. Nightmares about Elle had been haunting me every night. I knew they were only going to get worse after facing reality today.

Please, God. Give me the strength to face this.

***

Afraid to face Daddy's wrath, instead of stopping at the house, I drove straight back to Wichita. Seeing nothing but flashes of Sevin's angry stare, the ride back was a complete blur. The man who had my heart to this day probably wished I were the one that died. I really wished it were me, too.

The closer I got to our house, the more it felt like my insides were rotting. Rehashing this day to Dean was the last thing I felt like doing tonight. I just wanted to go straight to bed.

Dean was sitting on the couch watching television. "Evie, it took you long enough to come home. I'm starving."

"Why didn't you make yourself something?"

"You know I can't cook for shit."

"I just came back from my sister's goddamn funeral. You think I want to spend the rest of tonight cooking a meal for you?"

"You hadn't seen your sister in five years. If she hadn't died, you wouldn't have even gone back."

"That means I'm not supposed to be devastated?"

All this time, Dean thought I was estranged from my family by choice. He didn't really know the whole truth about the pain of my past and my reasons for leaving Dodge City. He couldn't imagine how much I truly loved Elle. He definitely couldn't imagine how much I loved Sevin.

Sevin.

God, even the thought of his name caused shooting pains to run through me. It was as if I could feel all of the hatred and anger he felt toward me within my chest. That, coupled with my own self-loathing, was now too much to carry within me.

Dean must have noticed that something was seriously off with me, because he softened, which was rare. "Sorry, babe. I didn't mean to upset you. Go make us some dinner, huh?"

It was easier to just give in to him than start an argument. I never won those with Dean. He would just make the rest of my night miserable until he forced me to screw him, calling it makeup sex.

Retreating to the kitchen, I cracked some eggs into a bowl and whisked them around. I'd make cheese omelets and frozen waffles. Breakfast for dinner. Done.

"What's taking so long?" Dean yelled from the living room.

"Just putting some finishing touches on it!" I doused the eggs with extra pepper, twisting the peppermill in an exaggerated way.

Dean watched the television from the kitchen table while we ate. There was never any dinner conversation with Dean. After our meal, I was washing dishes when my cell phone rang.

It was Mama.

"It's my mother. I need to take it," I said, taking the phone to the bedroom and closing the door.

"Mama?"

"Evangeline, you need to come back."

"Why?"

"Daddy is really angry at me. He wanted to know how you found out about Elle. I told him I only recently discovered your whereabouts. He's irate with me for keeping it from him. It's too much stress on him right now, but he wants to talk to you. Emily needs you, too."

"I can't go back, Mama."

"You told Emily you were living in Wichita. You're her only sister left. It's time. It's time to face everything. You can't keep pretending that we don't exist, not now that everyone knows where you are."

"Dean is not going to give me the car to go back right now."

"We'll come get you. Besides, what kind of a man would keep his wife from her family at a time like this?"

The possessive crazy kind that I married, who does nothing but smoke weed all day and has no regard for anyone but himself.

"I'll tell him that I'm going next week. If he won't give me the car, then you might have to come get me."

"Okay. I'm going to hold you to that."

"Mama?"

"Yes."

"Is Sevin okay?"

There was a long pause. "He's in a very bad way."

***

One week later, the meeting with Daddy went smoother than I thought. I'd half expected him to take me over his knee with a belt. Instead, he just took me in his arms and cried. I guess losing a child makes you much more forgiving towards the children you have left.

After he eventually got his anger out, he made me tell him where I'd been all this time. So, I gave him a story that was half-full of lies, telling him that Dean was the reason I ran away. The true parts were that I'd worked as a waitress and that Dean and I got married.

"Evangeline, if this were a few years back, I might not have let you back in this house. You're a grown woman now, responsible for your own decisions. I don't agree with your running away or the non-Christian life you're living. But that doesn't change the fact that you're my daughter. I will always love you."

His forgiveness meant everything to me. Emily and Mama were in tears, both also surprised at Daddy's reaction to my return.

We agreed that I would come back to visit again soon. He wanted to meet Dean. I would deal with that when the time came. There was no way I was going to bring my husband back here. My father would probably send the authorities to come collect him.

Sevin apparently lived back at the guesthouse again. One of the conditions of my coming to see my parents was that it be done in the middle of the day when he was working. It was a cowardly move, but I just couldn't handle seeing him. Daddy had left the plant early to meet with me.

When I got in my car to leave the property, I looked around, overcome by an immense feeling of nostalgia mixed with sadness. Everything looked the same, yet so much had changed. For a moment, it felt like no time had passed.

I became overtaken by an overwhelming need to see Addy despite being ashamed to face her. What I'd done to her was no different than my actions toward Sevin.

***

My heart sank when I pulled up to her house. The shop looked abandoned. Tears filled my eyes out of fear of what I was going to find when I knocked on that door.

The person who answered the door was not who I expected.

"Can I help you?" a handsome blond boy asked.

"Hi. I'm Evangeline, an old friend of Addy's. Is she here?"

"You're Evangeline?"

"Yes."

He blinked a few times and seemed to be examining my face. "Wow. Um...she went to town to go food shopping."

"Who are you?"

"I'm Luke. Sevin's brother."

"Sevin's brother?"

"Yes. I live here."

"I don't understand."

"I was going through some stuff. I left home. Sevin told me I could come to him if I ever needed him, and I took him up on the offer. Adelaide found out I was here and offered me her spare room. I take care of everything around here for her in exchange for room and board."

"Are she and Sevin close?"

"Yes. He's like a son to her. So am I."

The reality of how much I'd missed was difficult to swallow. "What happened to the shop?"

"It shut down. Two of the guys left for better jobs, and Addy couldn't keep up with the demand. She lost a lot of regulars. She still does odd fixes here and there, mostly word of mouth."

"I'm sorry to hear that."

"Did she know you were coming over?"

"No. She has no clue."

"She talks about you all of the time. She was heartbroken when you left."

"What about Sevin? Did he ever mention me?"

"No. Anything I know of you came from Adelaide. Sevin won't talk about you."

"Yeah…" I nodded in understanding while my eyes felt heavier. "Can I wait here?"

"Sure."

I sat on the couch and looked around. Everything was the same. The kettle was still at the same spot on the stove. The house still smelled like patchouli. A rush of emotions pummeled through me because this place was the real home I'd abandoned.

The door opened, and I immediately stood up.

Addy was carrying a paper shopping bag and froze. Her lips were trembling as she mindlessly placed the bag down on the table.

I stood there speechless as the tears I'd been holding fell freely.

She shook her head in disbelief and suddenly rushed toward me, pulling me into a warm embrace. Her shoulders were shaking up and down. I'd never seen Addy cry like that, not even after Lorraine died. It was a testament to how much she loved me. Luke left the room to give us some privacy.

After holding me for several minutes, she pulled back. "I didn't know if you were dead or alive."

"Sevin never mentioned that he saw me at the funeral?"

"No."

I didn't know where to begin. "Addy…"

"You know what I'm gonna ask, Vangie. And don't you dare lie to me. Where the hell—"

"I've been living in Wichita."

"Wichita? She repeated louder, "Wichita?"

"Yes."

"All this time, and you've been right here in Kansas, just a few hours away?"

"I know you want an explanation, but I'm afraid I can't give it to you. All I can say is that leaving you was one of the worst parts for me."

"I know you felt like you had no choice, but Sevin…" She stopped speaking and looked down at the ground.

"What?"

"It completely wrecked him, Vangie. He's not the same person." Hearing that felt like a stab through my heart.

"I know. I could sense that. Not that I expected any different, but it's hard to see it for myself."

"Who are you living with?"

"I'm married."

Her eyes widened. "Married? To who?"

"His name is Dean. I met him after I left. Daddy thinks I ran away to be with him, but you know that's not true. I was on my own for a while, and then he sort of took me in."

"Took you in? Were you homeless?"

"It never came to that, but it was close."

"Vangie, listen. You know I love you. You may not be ready to tell me everything, but I expect a full explanation of why you did what you did to us. Leaving town is one thing, but leaving the way you did without telling us where you were…"

"I promise, Addy. Someday, I'll tell you everything that happened while I was away. I just can't right now. I can't handle it all yet, okay? Please just know that I love you and never meant to hurt you. You have to believe that."

"You know I'm a strong person, and you know I love you. You could have stayed away for twenty years, come back, and I'd welcome you with open arms. I'm not the one you owe an explanation to. I'm not the one who was completely destroyed. You need to face him."

"He doesn't want to see me."

"Doesn't matter. You still need to face him."

"He hates me."

"You really believe that? Let me tell you something. That boy looked everywhere for you. I was there. I saw how much he suffered after you left. That doesn't mean he hates you; he's angry, yes. But it's not hate. You know what else happened while you were gone? That boy became a man. He owned up to his responsibilities, took care of your sister every day until she died. Even though you'd left him completely shattered, he found his inner strength. Love gone wrong can disguise itself as hate. Let me define Sevin's hatred for you. It's a self-protective mechanism for a love that hurts so bad he has to fight it every day. At the very least, he deserves an explanation."

She was right, but it wasn't going to happen today. Looking down at my watch, I knew if I didn't get the car back by a certain time, Dean was going to kill me. "I have to go, Addy. I promise I'll be back again soon."

Addy made me give her my address. I didn't want her to know where I lived because she'd probably be horrified at what she found, but I was done hiding. I couldn't hurt the people I loved any more than I already had.

***

It was two weeks later before Dean would let me take the truck to Dodge City again. I kept telling myself that I didn't have to go through with it, that I could change my mind at any time. That was the only way I was able to conjure up enough bravery to face Sevin.

It was late on a Sunday afternoon, cloudy and overcast. Bypassing my parents' property, I parked Dean's Dodge Ram in front of the guesthouse. Heart pounding, hands shaking, I stayed in the driver's seat for the longest time before finally forcing myself out. Breathing heavily, I just stood there taking in the scenery. It was eerily quiet, the only sound my mother's wind chimes in the distance. There were two cars parked outside, a truck I assumed was Sevin's and a Toyota sedan.

The front door opened before I had a chance to knock.

"You just let me know if there's anything else you need," an attractive redheaded woman around my age said to Sevin as she exited the house.

Who was that?

I froze when his eyes landed on me with the same angry, vacant look he'd given me at Elle's funeral.

"Who are you?" she asked. "Can we help you?"

We?

A long, uncomfortable silence ensued as Sevin and I just stared at each other.

I finally looked back at her. "I'm Evangeline."

"My sister-in-law," he scoffed bitterly.

"Oh, I'm sorry. I didn't realize. Anyway, I'll call you later to check on you, Sevin," she said as she got into her Toyota and drove off, leaving a trail of dust behind.

He remained in the doorway giving me the same icy glare. My heartbeat was out of control as I really took him in for the first time. Sevin was bigger, more muscular. His hair had grown out some, and his face was framed by a five o'clock shadow. He was truly a man now in every way. And even though everything about us was shattered—there was no us—my broken heart felt more whole than it had in all the years I'd been gone simply because he was near. The electric energy that always existed between us was still there. It just manifested itself in a different way now.

After an indeterminate amount of time passed, he was the first to speak. "What are you doing here?"

Swallowing, I said, "I needed to see you."

"All of a sudden you need to see me?" He shook his head in disbelief but didn't say anything else.

A roll of thunder rang out in the distance, a fitting addition to this ominous reception. It was starting to rain.

"Can I come in?"

"No." His answer was abrupt. His body was rigid, and his hands balled into fists.

Nodding, I looked down at my feet, feeling ashamed for even coming.

"I'm sorry. I should have known you wouldn't see me."

"I don't really understand why you're here." He sounded tired, like he barely had the energy to say those words.

Why was I here?

"Because I can't live like this anymore. I need to explain some things to you."

My nerves were shot, but I walked closer to him anyway. His familiar smell sent shockwaves of nostalgia, desire and pain through me. All of the feelings I'd harbored away began to awaken. I just wanted to throw myself into his arms. As if he could see inside my head, Sevin took two steps back away from me and into the house.

"Get the fuck out of here, Evangeline."

His words were like a punch in the gut.

"Please. I don't get the car very often. I need to talk to you. I—"

The slam of the door in my face caused me to shudder.

I closed my eyes tightly as tears began to fall down my cheeks. So much had changed in our lives, but at that moment, I was simply the same Evangeline who loved Sevin with all of my heart and soul.

Walking around to the side of the house, I peeked into the window.

Sevin was sitting on the couch with his head down by his knees. A bottle of Jack Daniels was open on the table. He didn't see me. It was impossible for me to look away. That vision epitomized all of the damage I'd caused. Seeing firsthand how badly I'd hurt him was so hard to take.

I deserved every bit of the horrible existence I was left with now.

Returning to the truck, I started the engine and took off down the long, gravelly road leading out of my parents' property. I wasn't worthy of his forgiveness. I deserved my punishment, which was my life with Dean. I continued back to Wichita, vowing never to return to Dodge City again.

CHAPTER 20

SEVIN

It took me nearly an hour to get up off the couch that day. I was so damn angry at myself. After everything she'd done, I should have wanted to kill her. Instead, I had to slam the door in her face because of the fucked up feelings rocketing through me. When the urge came on to grab her and hold her, I worried that I was insane. How was it possible to hate someone and love them at the same time?

My judgement was clearly fogged, which necessitated getting rid of her before I did something I would regret. Still emotionally weak from the trauma of Elle's death, there was no way I could let Evangeline in and allow myself to become manipulated by her. I could never trust her again, but it was all too easy to get sucked in. Over my dead body would my weakness for her erase the past five years. She wasn't going to get my forgiveness. There was no excuse for leaving me the way she did—leaving Elle in that condition. I needed to stand my ground.

But closing that door did nothing to rid my heart of her. She lived inside of me, always had, constantly haunting me even when she wasn't physically present. I was going to have to try harder to fight this.

For days after her visit, I couldn't eat or sleep and did nothing but drink. A battle was being waged inside of me. On one hand, I wanted to protect myself from the truth of where she'd been this whole time. On the other, the curiosity was killing me.

I knew I needed to talk to Addy. We'd spoken on the phone after Evangeline first showed up at her house, but she didn't know Evangeline had now come to see me. Addy was my voice of reason all of these years, the only person who kept me sane through the worst of everything. Bonding in our misery over Evangeline's abandonment, we'd been there for each other every day. When Luke ran away from Oklahoma and moved to Dodge City, the three of us became like a family. The two of them were a piece of normal in the midst of my life, which otherwise had consisted mostly of work and my obligations at home with Elle up until she died. Addy and Luke were my strength and my solace. At the same time, Addy's was a place where I could just kick back with a beer and be myself.

She and Luke were playing cards when I showed up for the first time since Evangeline's appearance at my door.

"You look like you got run over by a truck, son," Addy said. "What's going on?"

Taking a seat at the table, I put my feet up on the chair opposite me. I let out a deep breath and rubbed my tired eyes. "She came to see me."

Addy placed her deck of cards down and got up to grab me a beer from the fridge. "I figured she would. I told her to."

"*You* told her to?"

Half smiling, she placed the bottle firmly down in front of me. "Sure did."

"Why?"

"Because the sooner you get the inevitable over with, the better. Tell me what happened."

"I slammed the door in her face."

Addy and Luke looked at each other and started to laugh.

Looking between them, I asked, "What exactly about this is funny?"

Addy shook her head and crossed her arms. "You can't do that, Sevin. You can't run from her."

"Why the hell not?"

"Because now that you know where she is, you won't be able to ignore it."

"I don't know where she is."

"You do, because I'm going to tell you."

"I don't want to know."

"She lives at 15 Great Road in Wichita."

Damn it.

"Addy...I didn't want to know."

"Yes, you do. You should also know that she's married."

My heart sank.

"What?"

Goddammit. If I hated her so much, why did that news devastate me?

"Something is not right with her, Sevin."

"What do you mean?"

"I don't know. I got a really bad feeling. She seemed reluctant to say her address, made me promise not to go there if she gave it to me. We need to check things out."

My chair skidded as I got up and walked toward the window. "I'm checking out, alright. Checking out altogether from this. I can't go down this road with Evangeline again."

"I don't get why you're acting like this toward her," Luke said. "She seemed really sweet, and she's definitely sorry for what she did. You should at least talk to her."

I walked over to my brother and flicked one of the cards at him. "If you weren't gay, I'd think she put you under the same spell she put on me when I was your age."

"Ain't that the truth," Addy said. "Listen to your little brother, though. Vangie's a good person and deserves forgiveness. I'm not saying that has to happen overnight or even soon. But you know our girl has always allowed herself to be led by fear and her conscience. She left because she felt she had no choice, probably couldn't handle the guilt given Elle's predicament. Whatever the reason, it was the wrong decision; we know that. But we can't change the past. She's married anyway now. It's not like we're suggesting you take up where things left off. Probably too late for that. You just need to find it in yourself to forgive her."

I took a sip of my beer and swallowed. "I'll never forgive her."

"I'm not saying you should forget, but you need to ask God to help you forgive."

***

Two months had passed since she showed up at my door. Despite my vow to try to forget her, there wasn't a day that went by that I didn't think about Evangeline or try to piece together what happened to her in the years we were apart.

I was never the church going type. Growing up, church was simply an opportunity to get out of Lillian's stagnant house or maybe meet some good girls to corrupt.

The period after Elle's death was the first time in my life that I'd used church as a place to meditate, to meet with God and channel his guidance on my inner struggles.

Not wanting to deal with people from Sutton Provisions, I chose not to attend service at the main church in Dodge City. Instead, I went to the one in the next town over. That was where I met Nancy. She was a widow whose husband died in combat overseas, but she had no children. Nancy moved back home to Kansas to be closer to her parents and had been a shoulder to lean on for me lately given our similar situations. She'd meet me at service, sitting next to me and would sometimes drop meals off at my house during the week. Some evenings, she'd stay for a while, and we'd just talk. Nancy was there the day that Evangeline showed up at my door. Thankfully, she never pried about my strange reaction to my "sister in law." While I was in no way ready for a relationship with someone, I had a feeling that Nancy wanted more with me and was just waiting in the wings for enough time to pass where it would be appropriate for me to start dating. I honestly didn't know whether things with her would evolve into something. If she were truly looking for another husband, I needed to be careful not to get myself in over my head. For now, we were friends, and her presence was comforting.

On that particular Sunday, Nancy and I were holding hands during a prayer when I noticed a family a few pews up from us. I couldn't put my finger on where I knew the father from. When he turned around to hand the donation basket to the people in front of us, his face just seemed familiar to me. The family had four daughters, three of them with lighter hair and a little darker-haired girl at the end of the pew who was missing the bottom half of her left arm. It dawned on me that they probably had her sit on the leftmost corner so that she could use her right hand to hold her sister's during the prayer. It made me think about the fact that everyone has their own unique challenges. This little girl's struggle was a lot different than my internal ones, but nevertheless, we all came together on Sunday to seek guidance from the same power. Something about that realization gave me renewed strength, like I wasn't alone in this crazy life.

That afternoon, Nancy followed me home. It was just like any other lazy Sunday at first. We watched a movie together in the living room, but when it was finished, she disappeared into the bathroom off of my bedroom for almost fifteen minutes.

I knocked on the door. "Everything okay in there?"

"Yes. Everything is fine."

"Alright. Let me know if you need anything."

A few seconds later, the door creaked open. Nancy was standing there in a white lace bra and matching underwear.

"What are you doing?" I snapped.

"I thought maybe this would help."

I swallowed. She looked beautiful, but it didn't feel right. "Help with what?"

Dumbest question ever.

"I know you feel guilty, like maybe I'm not ready or you're not ready for this because of our situations, but I think it's something we both need. I want to make you feel good, Sevin. It doesn't have to mean anything more than that. I haven't been touched in so long."

"Nancy, I ca—"

Before I could get the words out, she leaned in and planted a long kiss on my lips. My body tensed. My cock stiffened, even though I was trying to fight the physical reaction. Having not been inside of a woman since

Evangeline, of course my body was going to react. I just couldn't handle anything else that might come along with taking that step with someone.

Still, with each push of her tongue inside of my mouth, I felt weaker. A part of me wanted to drown my sorrows in Nancy, let her help me forget Evangeline even if for just a matter of minutes. When she started to undress me and took a condom out of her bra, I surrendered and closed my eyes. The sound of the wrapper crinkling prompted me to open them. After she sheathed me, everything happened so fast.

While being inside her had felt good, it lacked intimacy and passion. It was just sex. We both came, and it was just enough to make me temporarily feel something other than numbness or anger. It reminded me of the kind of sex I'd had before Evangeline, the kind that was used as an escape. It felt good, but it wasn't mindblowing.

Nancy slept over for the first time that night. I couldn't exactly tell her to go home after we'd had sex.

In the morning over coffee, she startled me with a question. "Evangeline is your sister-in-law's name, right?"

My hand, which had been reaching for the coffee pot, froze in mid-air. "Why do you ask?"

"You were saying her name in your sleep."

"I was?"

"Yes. You were saying, 'Evangeline, I'm so sorry. It's only ever been you.' And you kept apologizing."

In silence, I poured the coffee, trying to absorb what she'd just admitted. Taking a big gulp of the piping hot liquid I nearly burned my mouth before I said, "Well, that's bizarre."

"I thought so, too."

Thankfully, Nancy dropped the subject soon after and eventually left the house shortly before I had to go into work.

That entire day at the plant was spent obsessing over the fact that I'd been dreaming about Evangeline. So much effort was expended each day trying to forget her, but apparently I had no control over my weak subconscious mind. That really pissed me off.

***

Knowing where she lived was a curse. I truly wished Addy never blurted it out. Even though I knew I couldn't trust myself to be around Evangeline, curiosity was killing me. I wanted to see her but didn't want her to see me.

Evangeline was married. *Married.* Addy had left me with a bad feeling when she said she sensed Evangeline might be in some kind of trouble. It made me feel guilty for not checking in on things at least once. That was my official excuse as I headed down Route 54 toward Wichita. Borrowing my co-worker's car, I needed to make sure my truck didn't give me away.

What the fuck are you doing, Sevin?

Sweat was pouring off my forehead. Blasting the music, the vibration of the bass competed with my pounding heart. The Kansas night sky had transformed into a deep midnight blue. It was the kind of night made for parking in an open field and staring up at the stars—not stalking the married ex who devastated you.

When I pulled up to the address on Great Road, I couldn't believe my eyes. It was a small white one-story house surrounded by junk. On the dried-up lawn out front were a couple of abandoned cars, a broken-down Winnebago, old lawnmowers and half-burned pieces of furniture. It looked like the epitome of trash.

I sat parked across the street, unsure of what my next move would be. After about an hour, the front door opened, causing me to duck down into my seat.

The lights of the departing truck lit up the street. I wasn't certain whether Evangeline was inside but decided to follow it anyway.

After a three-mile ride, it stopped in front of a black building. The passenger door opened, and her long raven hair was the first thing that caught my eye as she exited the truck.

Evangeline.

My heart was now hammering against my chest.

She slammed the door, and the truck sped off. The jackass didn't even wait for her to safely enter the building.

If I thought my heart was pounding fast before, it nearly combusted when I got a look at the flashing neon sign out front: *The Pink Lady Gentleman's Club.*

No.

God no, Evangeline.

I tried my best to convince myself not to jump to conclusions. She could have simply worked the desk, waitressed or bartended. Just because she was walking into this dive didn't mean she was one of the strippers for God's sake.

Techno music was pumping through the room as multi-colored lights illuminated the dark and gritty space. Smoke filled the air, and the smell of booze was pungent. Evangeline was nowhere in sight as I looked around with my black hood over my head.

Taking a seat in the corner, I let out a deep breath as a blonde waitress approached my table. "What can I do you for, handsome?"

"Give me the strongest drink you have. Please."

She returned with an unidentifiable amber-colored liquid that smelled medicinal.

"Thanks."

"It's my pleasure. Guys like you don't walk in here every day. You should take that hood off. Show your gorgeous face and eyes. Let me know if you want a lap dance. The girls will be fighting over who gets to do it."

I breathed out a sigh of relief when she walked away. The last thing I needed was someone drawing any attention to me.

A quick scan of the room revealed that Evangeline was still nowhere to be found. On the stage, two redheads with fake breasts were dancing together and rubbing up on each other. Their bodies were well-oiled as they grinded together. They exited the stage and were quickly replaced by a blonde with pigtails and a short skirt doing a schoolgirl routine to a Britney Spears song. Her tits were hanging completely bare out of her open collared shirt while she sucked on a rainbow-colored lollipop. I watched for a while before turning my attention away and getting lost in my own thoughts.

The more time that passed, the more on edge my mood became. When the music suddenly stopped and the lighting changed, my full attention returned to the stage. My breath caught as a slow and sultry Amy Winehouse song began to play. It was a rendition of *Will You Still Love Me Tomorrow*.

A spotlight landed on the mane of black hair cascading down her back. *Fuck.*

My breathing became labored, and I sucked down my second shot.

How the hell in God's name had it come to this? How did she end up in this place?

Her back was facing me. The entire routine was performed from the chair she was straddling. She'd cross her legs or flip them around slow and sensually with graceful precision. She was basically making love to that chair. I stood up in amazement, still far enough away that she wouldn't have been able to see me.

So many mixed emotions were running through me. Sadness, because I couldn't understand why someone as bright as she was needed to exploit her body for money. Fear, because I worried about what else may have happened to have gotten her to this place. Anger at myself, because I cared so fucking much.

Most troubling was the intense desire awakening in me. I was supposed to hate this person for ruining my life. Instead, I stood there captivated, enraptured, wishing desperately to be that chair under her. It was a stark reminder of the sexual power she'd always had over me. But this situation—being a mere spectator, unable to touch her—took it to a completely different level. I was hard as a rock.

Equal parts disturbed and aroused, I continued to watch every movement of her body. Evangeline was wearing an open white dress shirt with a black bra underneath. When she took the shirt off, I swallowed hard because I knew what was coming. With her eyes closed, she gyrated her hips slowly as she unsnapped the back of her bra. It fell lazily to the floor. Those big, beautiful pear-shaped breasts that once belonged to me now hung freely for all the world to see. I looked around me for the first time. Almost all eyes in the room were planted on her, and then I felt sick to my stomach. Just sick. Sick that they were all watching her and even sicker for my body's reaction to it.

Exactly how far did Evangeline take things? I was still standing at my table when the waitress came back with another drink.

I pointed to the stage. "How much for a lap dance with her later?"

"Sienna? She doesn't do lap dances, honey. Sorry. She's one of the conservative ones. Probably why every guy that walks in this place wants her. But there are plenty of other girls that will do that...and more for you. I can bring you to the back room if you want?"

Sienna.

Fuck.

She was using the name Sienna.

"No. Thank you." A sense of relief coursed through me, knowing that at least she'd set some boundaries. But why did she have to do this at all? And how the fuck could her so-called husband drop his own wife off to strip for other men?

Downing the last shot in one gulp, I anticipated the song was about to finish. Before I knew it, she'd exited the stage. I didn't understand why, but all of a sudden my emotional state felt so out of control. Confusion. Jealousy. Curiosity. Desire. Possession.

Sadness.

Pure sadness.

The last five years might as well have been five minutes.

I needed to see her.

Walking over to the waitress, I made a rash decision. "I would like a private dance with Sienna."

"I told you, honey, she doesn't do that."

"Tell her I'd be willing to pay ten-thousand dollars."

"You're not serious."

"Would the money be going to her?"

"All but 10 percent."

"Taking my credit card out of my wallet, I said, "Run it."

I knew the amount had to be an offer that she couldn't refuse. Seeing the squalor she lived amongst, I suspected she might be willing to consider my proposition.

"I'll be right back. I need to talk to her."

"Please don't tell her my name."

"Don't worry. We use upmost discretion here."

So much time passed that it became doubtful she was going to go for it. The waitress reappeared, and I stood up.

"She's agreed to it provided it's just a lap dance you want, nothing more. There wouldn't be any sex involved. I do have other girls who would be willing to do that for that kind of money."

"No. I told you. I just want a lap dance. It has to be Sienna."

"Let me verify your card."

My palms were sweaty as I waited for her to come back.

She waved her hand. "Alright. Come right this way." The woman led me down a dark hallway and into a dimly-lit room tinted with red light.

The long wait was excruciating. Finally, the door slowly opened.

Evangeline entered with her head down, black strands of hair covering her half-naked body. When she finally looked up at me, I took down my hood.

Our eyes locked.

Gasping, she covered her breasts and froze.

CHAPTER 21

EVANGELINE

When Wilma walked into the dressing room and told me that there was a man who offered ten-thousand dollars for a lap dance, I couldn't believe it. Who would pay that kind of money for something that didn't involve sex? I asked her if he was a businessman-type, and she said he wasn't. Just a younger guy in a black hoodie. She said he was gorgeous. That made it seem even more bizarre.

At first, I had adamantly refused. I'd never given a lap dance before and swore I never would. I wouldn't even take my panties off during my performances. The club allowed me to get away with my hard limits because the regular patrons seemed to love me. Just my dancing topless brought in a lot of repeat business.

As the offer started to sink in, I thought about what that money could mean for me. Dean didn't know about my secret bank account. I'd only bring home half of the tips I made. The rest was put away. When there was enough cash in it to stand on my own, my plan was to eventually leave Dean and go back to school, start a new life. I'd have to figure out how to leave him carefully, though. Somehow, it had to seem like it was his idea. I couldn't just leave him on my own accord, because he would come after me. That ten-thousand dollars would give me a huge head start toward my dream.

So, I reluctantly agreed.

I took my phone with me in case I needed to call for help. Wearing nothing but my black lace bra, underwear and stilettos, I was covered in goosebumps as I walked down the hall to the back room.

I felt like a whore.

After opening the door, I couldn't bear to look at his face. The man had great stature from what I could see through the hair covering my eyes. His intoxicating cologne seemed oddly familiar. I finally looked up. When he took down his hood, my heart nearly stopped.

Covering my chest, I lost my breath.

Sevin's voice gave me the chills. "Don't hide. I want to see you."

I backed up against the door. "What are you doing?"

"What are *you* doing?" he seethed.

"Why did you come here? I thought you didn't want to see me. Hated me."

"That's how I *should* feel, isn't it? That's why this is so fucked up."

A wave of nausea hit me. Holding my stomach, I said, "I'm gonna be sick. This is a shock."

"Maybe I wanted to shock you the way you shocked me when you came back."

"Well, it worked. We're even. Were you watching me out there, too?"

"Yes. You put on quite a show."

"I can't believe this."

He walked slowly toward me. "Come here."

Shaking my head, I said, "No."

"No? You already agreed to it."

"I don't normally do this, Sevin."

"But apparently, you *can* be bought."

That was a low blow, but he was right. I felt like a cheap slut.

"Tell me why you paid ten-thousand dollars to talk to me now after you turned me away at your house. Why?"

"Because I didn't pay to talk to you. I paid for you to sit on me."

His words, and the tone in which he said them jarred me.

"You're not serious…"

"Do you see me laughing?"

"This is insane."

"Sienna, huh? Just like the first day we met."

"Yeah…"

'"Come here, Sienna." He'd emphasized the 'S' sound tauntingly.

What kind of a game was he playing? And what was wrong with me? Because as mean as he was being, I was aching to touch him. Sevin walked over to the plush seat, sat down and leaned his back into it.

He was gonna make me go through with this.

I slowly inched toward him until my knees were touching his.

"Give me my money's worth," he said huskily. For the first time, the alcohol on his breath registered. Maybe it was impairing his judgement, contributing to his aggressive behavior toward me, which was out of character. Or maybe Sevin had just changed. A twinge of fear had developed at the pit of my stomach.

It was quiet in the room aside from the muffled beat of the club music in the distance. My thighs were trembling as I wrapped them around him one by one and sat on his lap. His chest was heaving as he looked up at me, his eyes reflecting a wild intensity.

I wouldn't move at first. His pupils seemed to darken with each second that passed as he continued to stare at me.

Waiting.

With his more muscular build, grown out hair and chin scruff, age had definitely become him. Despite my fear, sexual awareness overtook my body, which had been longing for him. I never thought I would have the opportunity to be this close to Sevin again in my lifetime.

At the same time, I didn't deserve to be deriving pleasure from the contact. Aside from the differences in his physical appearance, I knew that the changes inside of him were far more profound. I had wrecked him, and then Elle's death had wrecked him all over again. I thought about what my mother said, about him being in "a bad way." I closed my eyes to fend off thoughts of Elle, thoughts of everything that might have happened—that did happen—after I left.

His calloused fingertips landed on my chin. "Open your eyes and look at me."

I kept them closed.

"Evangeline."

When he said my name, I opened them.

"I know you hate me," I whispered.

"I don't want to talk."

"What do you want?"

"I want what I came in here for, what I paid for."

It occurred to me that this was a form of payback. He wanted to humiliate me. It also occurred to me that I owed him. If this was what made him feel better—to shame and punish me—then I was going to give him whatever he needed.

It was better than him grilling me for information. I couldn't tell him everything that happened while I was away. So, I would give him anything else he asked for in return. I would play along.

"You want a lap dance? I'll give you a lap dance."

Sliding slowly toward him, I could feel the heat of his rock hard cock under me. Pushing his shoulders back onto the small loveseat, I gyrated my hips slow and hard over him. He let out a stifled moan. My nipples hardened, and wetness developed between my legs as the material of my underwear rubbed against his jeans.

This was a mistake.

He looked deeply into my eyes as I continued straddling his lap. We never took our eyes off each other the entire time.

He slipped his middle finger under my bra strap and nudged it. "Take this off."

Every word that came out of his mouth added to my aroused state.

I obliged, unhooking it at the back and throwing it to the ground. His eyes never left mine despite my undressing. His stare was a mix of anger, bewilderment and unadulterated lust.

Placing his palms on my breasts, he began to slowly massage them. He rubbed the tips of his thumbs roughly along my nipples.

Sevin's mouth curved into a slight smile. "You're getting turned on, aren't you?"

I wouldn't answer, but I didn't have to.

He continued, "I can feel how wet you are through your panties. Fuck." Grabbing the back of my ass, he pushed me down onto him harder. "What kind of a man lets his wife work here?"

I stopped moving. "I told you. I've never done this before."

He placed his hands on my hips to show me who was in charge and began moving my body over him again. "How much more money would it take to fuck you?"

I jumped off of him. "Stop. I get it. You hate me! You want me to pay for what I did to you. Just call me a whore and get it over with. Then leave." I walked over to the opposite side of the room, covering my breasts. "This is a losing game, Sevin. You can't possibly make me feel worse about myself than I already do. I wish it were me instead that died. I wish I were dead every single day. If I had the balls, I would just—"

"You would what?"

I gave him the honest answer.

"End it all…"

He looked like my admission had inflicted physical pain on him.

Sevin got up from his seat and rushed toward me. "Don't say that. Don't ever fucking say that!" Pulling me into his arms, he held me tightly. When he looked at me again, it was as if he'd just woken up out of a trance. "Oh God, I'm so sorry. So sorry. Forgive me. Forgive me for this. Forgive me."

He kept repeating himself, asking for forgiveness.

I ran my fingers through his hair as he buried his forehead into my chest.

"I understand," I said. "I deserve every bit of this."

He spoke into my chest, "I'm just so angry at you. I don't know how to handle it."

The heat of his breath warmed my skin in the otherwise freezing room. Then, I felt wetness fall onto the bare skin of my breasts. He was crying. I'd never seen Sevin cry, not even at Elle's funeral.

I held his face into me for several minutes.

"Why?" he whispered over my skin.

I wasn't able to give him that answer.

"You left me." He repeated louder, "Why? Why did you just give up?" He wiped his eyes and looked up at me. "You really think I hate you? I wish I fucking hated you, Evangeline. I'd give anything. I wish I could rid you from my heart, but you *are* my fucking heart."

Walking over to the other side of the room, he picked up my bra off the floor and handed it to me. He no longer looked angry. Just sad and a little ashamed of his actions.

"I have to leave."

"Are you okay to drive?"

"I'll be fine."

After I put the bra back on, he took off his hoodie and wrapped it around my shoulders.

Holding out his hand, he said, "Give me your phone." He took it and programmed his number into the contacts. "You have my number now. In case you need it."

After he left, I sat in the empty room, huddled in his sweatshirt, breathing in his scent, not knowing where things stood with Sevin.

I later hid the hoodie in my dressing room locker so that Dean wouldn't see it when he picked me up.

***

Several weeks went by before an opportunity to head to Dodge City arose again. Not having a car was a huge disadvantage but one that Dean carefully manipulated, refusing to let me buy my own vehicle.

I had stared down at Sevin's number almost every day, wanting to call but not knowing what to say. We'd left things on a very strange note, but in a sense, he'd left it up to me to make further contact. I wasn't sure if it was a good idea. I wondered if he told Addy where I was working and if she was disappointed in me.

Emily had made me promise to come see her, so a visit to my parent's house was long overdue. When Dean announced that he was taking off for a guys' trip over the weekend, the wheels in my head began to turn.

"So, where exactly are you guys going?"

"Not sure if they decided yet."

"You said Nelson is going to pick you up?"

"Yeah…why?"

"That means you're leaving the truck. Can I use it?"

"You can use it to go to work, but that's it."

"Why not? I was gonna take a couple of nights off and go to Dodge City for the weekend to see my parents."

"No. The truck needs new struts. You can't drive it far until I fix it."

"I can fix it myself for crying out loud."

"You think I'm gonna let you touch my truck, Evie? There's enough shit for you to do around the house anyway. You've been slacking this week. I don't need to be worrying about you while I'm away."

"I want to go home."

"This is your home."

No. It's not.

"Yes, bu—"

"Are you forgetting that you'd run away from that place when I found you? If it weren't for me, you'd be out on the street. Where was your fucking family then, huh? They wouldn't even want anything to do with you if they knew about your whorish ways. I'm the only reason you're straightened out. Now, you want to visit them on weekends all of a sudden? What a crock of shit, Evie…"

Evie. He was the only person to ever call me that. I hated it. It reminded me of *evil.*

"I have a right to see my parents and my sister."

"Well, it's not gonna be this weekend."

It was rare that Dean went away. I couldn't waste the opportunity and had to figure out a way to get back home.

***

Since there were no easy bus routes to Dodge City from Wichita, one of my co-workers, Liz, came through, letting me borrow her SUV for the weekend.

Dean's friend picked him up at 8AM. Nelson had brought over glazed donuts and boxed coffee from Wally's. I joined them in the kitchen, trying my best to act nonchalant. Dean thought I'd be spending the day catching up on laundry.

Fifteen minutes after they left, I walked the mile to Liz's and took off in her car down Route 54.

After three hours of driving, I finally arrived at my parents' property.

My relationship with Daddy was still strained, although at least he was talking to me.

Emily, our parents and I sat at the dining room table for lunch. Emily tried to lighten the mood by taking over the conversation, talking about her pursuit to convince my father to let her apply to a couple of out of state colleges. It didn't take long before Daddy began to interrogate me.

"I thought you said the next time you set foot in this house, you would bring that husband of yours."

I would have never promised that.

He will NEVER be coming here.

"I don't plan to bring him here, Daddy."

"You mind telling me why not?"

"Because you wouldn't approve of him, and I don't want to disrespect you."

"Since when do you care about respecting our opinion?"

My mother put her hand on my father's arm. "Lance, please. We're trying to have a nice lunch."

The rest of the meal was spent eating in silence with nothing but the sound of silverware clinking. I'd come to expect this as the new normal, feeling like an outcast among my own family. I suppose I was lucky that Daddy even let me back into the house after my disappearing act. It would have been unreasonable to expect a warm reception on top of that.

I couldn't help but ask, "How is Sevin doing?"

When my parents didn't answer, Emily chimed in, "Probably hanging out with that girlfriend of his. She's been coming around a lot. I see her car parked outside the guesthouse all the time."

My food felt like it was coming up on me. "Girlfriend?"

"Well, he says she's not, but I think he's just trying to be respectful of our feelings…because of Elle."

"Who is she?"

Emily finished her sip of water before she said, "Name's Nancy. That's all I know."

Forget Evie; *Nancy* was my new least favorite name in the world.

Even though I had no right to this jealousy, my heart was clamoring in protest.

"Does she drive a Toyota?"

"Yeah. Beige. That's the one."

A lump formed in my throat at the realization that it was the same woman I met the day I showed up at his door. That was a while ago, which meant they'd been seeing each other for some time.

My mother had turned mine and Elle's old bedrooms into guest suites. The plan was for me to spend the night in my old room.

On the way down the hall, I stopped into Elle's.

Collapsing on her bed, I broke down and spoke into her pillow, "I'm so sorry. I promise you, I would trade places with you if I could."

Breathing in, trying in vain to find some recognition of her scent, I sobbed for what must have been close to an hour. I suppose wherever she was, she knew everything now.

When I finally emerged from the room, I decided to take a quick ride to the nearest grocery store. Emily had made me promise to make her these cookies I used to bake for her when she was younger. It was the least I could do after having abandoned her for much of her formative years.

His truck was parked in front of the guesthouse, so I assumed he was inside. A few seconds later, just as I was getting into my car, headlights from an oncoming vehicle hit me in the face.

I froze as I realized it was Nancy's Toyota. They both got out, slamming the doors shut. Sevin didn't notice me at first. I wasn't going to say anything, but then he turned around and spotted me standing in front of the SUV.

From across the grass, our eyes met. He was silent as I walked from my parents' driveway over to his.

"Hi," I said.

"What are you doing here?"

"I'm spending the weekend with Mama and Daddy."

"You didn't tell me you were coming."

"I didn't think you'd want to see me."

He looked at his girlfriend. "This is Nancy. Nancy, this is…"

She interrupted, "I know. Evangeline. Your sister-in-law. We met briefly."

I nodded. "Well, I better let you two get on with your night. I'm just going to do some food shopping."

Hurrying away, I escaped into the car before anyone could say another word. Glancing over briefly again at Sevin, I noticed he hadn't moved from the same spot as he continued to look at me.

When I returned from the store, her car was still parked outside. It stayed there the rest of the evening. Even though I tried not to focus on it, it was constantly on my mind as I spent time with my sister, baking cookies and catching up on all of the things I'd missed during her teenage years.

Before going to bed, I looked out the window one last time and noticed that the car was still there. Nancy was definitely spending the night. The lights at the guesthouse were on. I wondered whether Sevin was thinking about me or worse, whether Nancy was helping him forget.

***

The next morning, I laced up my sneakers and pounded the pavement outside of my family's property for the first time in years. The sun hadn't yet fully risen, and the morning fog greeted me in all of its glory.

I couldn't even remember the last time I'd gone out for a jog. Gasping for air, it was clear that my body was no longer used to running.

Everything looked and smelled the same as I remembered. The sound of imaginary footsteps played in my head, footsteps I knew would no longer be appearing behind me. My chest tightened as I thought about our secret runs back when things were so different. As scandalous as everything was, the memories seemed inexplicably innocent. I would have given anything to go back and change so many things. Could I have changed falling in love with him? Probably not.

I would have definitely stopped Elle from riding Magdalene that day. That was the thing I was sure I would change.

Tears started to fall. What was it about jogging that made me so emotional? The endorphins always brought out my feelings in full force, yet also provided me with clarity. How had I stayed away from home for so long?

I made it about two miles before deciding to turn back around. My body wasn't used to this level of exercise anymore. It was important to pace myself, or I wouldn't survive the two miles back.

Halfway through, it felt like making it all the way home was an impossibility. My heart was beating out of control. Maybe it was overexertion. Or maybe it was more of a premonition. Because soon after, I heard them. Footsteps. Not coming from behind me but coming toward me.

Then, I saw him.

Hooded gray sweatshirt.

Tall stature.

Big sneakers digging into the dirt.

My heartbeat accelerated with every step Sevin took toward me, and then I completely lost my ability to breathe.

Resting my hands on my thighs for balance, I tried to catch my breath.

His footsteps slowed to a halt in the gravel. The next thing I knew, I felt him lift me up. Weightless, I rested my head into his chest as he walked, carrying me several feet until he put me down on the grass.

Taking out a bottle, he said, "What did I tell you about running without water?"

He handed it to me. I downed half the bottle as he watched every movement of my mouth.

"Thank you."

Sevin twisted the cap closed and dug the bottle into the dirt.

He wrapped his arms around his shins. His sleeves were rolled up, and for the first time, I noticed the letter E tattooed on his right forearm. My heart skipped a beat. He must have gotten that sometime after Elle died.

Clearing my throat, I asked, "Where's Nancy?"

"She's sleeping back at the house."

I nodded silently.

"Is your husband with you?"

"No." Wanting to skirt the subject of Dean, I said, "Thank you for not telling my parents about… you know…"

"Nothing good could possibly come from them knowing."

"You're right."

A long moment of silence passed as we both looked around, at our feet, up at the sky, anywhere but at each other.

I felt it coming.

The moment where I finally explained myself to him. I couldn't tell him everything, but he deserved as much of an explanation as I could give.

"You're probably wondering how I ended up in this place in my life."

"Not really…unless you count every single moment of every day since I got back from Wichita."

"Where do I even start?"

"How about start with why the fuck you left me in the first place. That would be good."

My mouth was dry. *How could I possibly explain?*

"Can I have some more water?"

He handed me the bottle.

I drank until it was so empty that the plastic bent. I finally spoke, "I don't know how to explain my actions to you, except to say that I couldn't be around Elle anymore. The guilt was too much to bear."

"Clearly not having to feel guilt meant more to you than anything. Did running away help you find your inner peace?"

"No."

"You found your inner slut instead?"

"Sevin…"

He rubbed his eyes. "Fuck. I'm sorry. That was uncalled for. I'm finding that I just don't know how to curb my anger around you."

Taking a deep breath in, I said, "I was in a very bad place that first year that I ran away. I was living with an old woman who took me in and let me stay in one of her spare bedrooms. But things changed, and I had to leave."

"What happened?"

"She died, and I had to find a new place to live. Her family let me live there until they sold the house."

"When did you meet him?"

"I was actually staying in a few different places, with some friends I met while waitressing, but I was virtually homeless. What I made wasn't enough to pay for an apartment. Anyway, Dean was a regular at the restaurant. That's how I met him. He was really nice in the beginning. We got to talking, and over time, he eventually helped me get on my feet."

"So you *married* the guy?"

I realized that my story seemed off. I was omitting the biggest part, and without it, nothing made sense.

"He took me in. I was screwed up mentally. I didn't really want anything but to just survive day to day. Back then, Dean was a different person. But over time, one of the conditions of his continuing to support me financially was to marry him. I didn't really feel like I had anything to lose. It had already felt like my life was over. At the time, I had no plans to ever come back here."

Sevin squinted his eyes, trying to make sense of everything. "How did Olga know where you were? She was obviously in contact with you if she told you about Elle."

"I called her at one point. I needed someone to know I was alive. I wouldn't tell her where I was, but she had a cell phone number."

"Why didn't she tell any of us?"

"I begged her not to."

"Did you know about me and Elle? That we'd gotten married?"

"Yes. That was really hard to take, but I understood."

"You said back when you first met this guy, you felt safe with him. What about now?"

"A lot's changed. I need to leave him, but I'm scared."

"Why?" The vein in his neck looked like it was going to pop out. "Does he hurt you?"

Yes.

He verbally abuses me and hits me sometimes.

I used to think I deserved it.

I can't tell you why. I'm afraid you'll go after him, and then he'll tell you everything.

You'll never want anything to do with me again.

You can't ever meet him.

"He doesn't hurt me...exactly," I lied. "He's just not right for me anymore. It's hard to make changes in your life when you've become accustomed to a certain way of living."

"What are you talking about? You're living in squalor!"

"Dean put a roof over my head, and he got me the job at *The Pink Lady*. His friend owns it. Stripping is the last thing you probably expected me to be doing, but it turned out to be the best way for me to make a living without a degree. I'm not sure how I would survive without being able to put some of that money away. If I left him now, I'd lose the job. So, I'm trying to save enough to stand on my own. That's the only reason I do it, Sevin."

"The ten-thousand dollars isn't enough for a start?"

"I asked them to credit back your card, told them to keep their fee and credit the rest."

"What? Why would you do that?"

"Because I can't take money from you, Sevin."

"I would rather you have taken the money and gotten away from that guy."

"It's not that simple."

"I don't want you to be miserable, Evangeline. You think I hate you, but I don't. I'm angry that you left, angry at life. I'm not sure that's ever going to change. I would never wish the kind of life you're living on you. If you're staying in a bad situation because you think you deserve it, you're wrong. Come home. Your parents will take you in."

Dean will come after me, and he'll tell everyone.

I need to make him leave me first somehow.

I haven't figured it out yet.

"That's not an option right now."

Desperate to change the subject off of me, I asked the question that had been nagging me. "How did you meet Nancy?"

He paused, seeming hesitant to talk about her. "At church. She's a widow. So, we have that in common."

"Are things serious?"

"I can't get serious with anyone at this point in my life. I'm too fucked up in the head."

"So, you're not…"

His eyes widened. "Are you asking if I'm fucking her?"

"I don't really want to know that."

"Because you run from things that hurt…"

"Yes. Knowing that would hurt."

"In that case, you should know that I *am* fucking Nancy. She gives good head, too."

The abrupt admission had shocked me into silence. Then, it was like something erupted inside of him as he continued, "Did it hurt to hear that? You want to talk about hurt? Hurt is finding out that all of this time, you've given yourself to someone you don't even love. Hurt is knowing that you've been fucking him with my heart still inside of you. Hurt was trying to convince Elle that you didn't leave because of her, when I couldn't tell her that you left because of me. Hurt was trying to be a good husband to your sister, making her feel like a woman, kissing her, sucking her tits, going down on her when she couldn't even feel my fucking mouth. All just to make her feel beautiful so she wouldn't wish she were dead—something she often admitted feeling. Hurt was making her believe that I loved her when I only ever loved you. Hurt was feeling so much guilt that I was betraying *you*, even though you abandoned me. How fucked up is that? The *truth* hurts. But you know what hurts the most? After everything, I still fucking love you more than life itself."

Sevin stood up and walked a few feet away to grab his composure. Each sentence that had come out of his mouth suffocated me more than the last.

After a few minutes, he returned to the spot next to me.

"I'm sorry. I just needed to get it all out."

Yearning to comfort him, I grabbed his hand. I was expecting him to push me away, but he opened his fingers and intertwined them with mine.

"Did Elle really say she wished she were dead?"

"Your sister had her days, but in the end, she died feeling loved. When it came to me, she never knew that she wasn't the one. I couldn't have played the husband role if you were around, couldn't have pretended. So, in that sense, you did her a favor in leaving. That's the one consolation you can take from all this. Your sister died as happy as she could have been under the circumstances."

Hearing that was truly a gift. It meant the hell I'd been living wasn't totally in vain. "Thank you for your honesty."

We sat in silence for a while until he turned to me. "I've been struggling with my feelings, doing a lot of thinking, especially since seeing you at the club. Even though I was so angry at you—still am—ultimately, a part of me does understand why you did what you did. Luke and I have become really close in the past few years. In retrospect, if I were in your shoes—if it were my brother—I might have done the same thing. That's a perspective I have now that I didn't have then."

"What are you saying?"

"I'm saying…I'm trying. I want to forgive you, but I'm not there yet."

His words cut deep. He wanted to forgive me. He could only forgive what he knew about, though. There was so much more about me that he didn't.

I asked Sevin to tell me more about his life with Elle. We sat for over an hour. Even though it was all hard to hear, it was something I needed to endure if I was ever going to move on.

We eventually jogged in silence back to the property.

Soon after, I left to return to Wichita to ensure I got there well before Dean returned from his trip.

Guilt consumed me in the days that followed.

Sevin was trying to forgive me.

For the first time, I seriously doubted whether I was capable of hiding the truth from him about what really happened anymore.

CHAPTER 22

SEVIN

A couple of weeks after Evangeline and I had our talk, Nancy was washing the dishes while I wiped them after dinner. She'd been acting strange all day.

Out of nowhere, she said, "Please don't be mad at me."

"Why?"

"I found something in your room. I was looking for my shoe under your bed, and there was a book of drawings. I opened it. They were of naked women. They all looked like your sister-in-law, Evangeline."

Fuck.

That was the first time I'd ever been careless and left the sketchpad out. I normally hid it in the closet but had slipped it under the bed when Nancy rang the doorbell earlier that day. I must have forgotten to put it back.

"Did something happen between you and her?"

Caught off guard, I stopped drying the plate in my hand but said nothing.

Nancy went on, "The couple of times she was here, there was this weird vibe between the two of you. Not to mention that dream you had. Now, the drawings…"

I was sick of living a lie. If Nancy and I were going to continue to be together, she needed to know everything. From her perspective, it would probably explain a lot about how I acted in general.

Leading her over to the couch, I said, "Forget the dishes and come sit down for a minute."

Over the next hour, I proceeded to tell her the full story about Evangeline and Elle from start to finish, leaving nothing out. Even though a part of her was mortified, she seemed relieved to not have to wonder about my strange behavior toward Evangeline anymore.

"Do you still love her?"

I looked straight into her eyes and told the absolute truth. "Yes. I don't think that will ever change."

Nancy seemed truly affected by my revelation. "Wow. This is all so much to take in. I don't know what to say."

"To be honest, I'm not sure what to say, either. I don't know where things stand right now. My life has been turned upside down in the past year. This is a big part of why I put up so many walls with you. You've been so good to me, and you deserved the truth."

"When I met you, I thought what we had in common was that we had each lost the love of our life. Yours is very much still alive. This changes things for me. My feelings for you are strong, but I can unequivocally say that Mason *was* the love of my life. No one will ever replace him. If he were still walking this earth, and I were in your situation, I would need closure."

"What are you getting at?"

"You obviously have unfinished business. I really like you, Sevin. *Really* like you. I would even venture to say I might be falling in love with you. My feelings have been growing, but I need to protect myself. Things can't get to a level where I could end up with a broken heart. I can't handle that after losing Mason. I think it's best for me to step away for a while until you figure things out. I mean, can you honestly look me in the eyes and tell me there's no chance that something could ever develop between you and her again?"

I couldn't.

Shit.

"I'm sorry, Nance."

The chaste kiss she gave me on the lips felt a lot like goodbye. "It sounds like the story isn't finished. If you're able to close the door on this chapter in your life, and I'm still around, please come find me."

***

The story wasn't finished.

Deep in my heart, I'd always known that. Nancy being out of the picture allowed me more time than ever alone with my thoughts. And all thoughts pointed to Evangeline. One evening, the urge to contact her became too strong to fight. Reaching over to my nightstand, I picked up my phone and texted her.

When can you talk?

A full thirty minutes went by before she responded.

Evangeline: Will you still be up at midnight?

Sevin: Yes

Evangeline: I have some time right after my shift before he picks me up. I can call you then?

Sevin: I'll be here.

The moon was bright as I gazed out into the starry night while anxiously awaiting her call. My window was wide open, letting in a cool breeze and the sound of crickets. At twelve on the nose, my cell phone vibrated over my comforter, and my heart came alive.

"Evangeline."

"Hi. Is everything okay?"

"Everything is fine," I said.

"It's so good to hear your voice."

"So, you're done for the night?"

"Yes. I finish at midnight. Then, I hang around and decompress until 12:30."

I relaxed into my pillow. "What do you think about when you're on stage?"

"Anything but what I'm actually doing. That way, it goes by pretty fast."

"No part of you enjoys it?"

"Not really." After a long pause, she asked, "Are you disappointed in me? For choosing to do this for money?"

"It makes me jealous, but that's my own issue. It's nothing to be ashamed of. You have an amazing body. As long as no one is touching you or hurting you, I'm okay with it."

"There was this one guy once…in a hood…he touched me. He terrified me a little."

I got an adrenaline rush for a split second, thinking she was referring to someone else before it sunk in that she was talking about me.

"That guy terrified me, too. I don't ever want to go back to that place with you ever again…that place of anger."

Evangeline changed the subject. "How are things with Nancy?"

"Things are on hold."

"What happened?" When I didn't answer, she must have sensed my apprehension. "Sevin?"

Exhaling, I wasn't sure whether to admit to everything. "You remember my drawings?"

"Of course. I still have the one you drew of me locked away in a place no one can find it."

"Well, Nancy found some of them."

"She got mad at you and left because of that?"

"You're gonna think I'm weird."

"Too late."

This was starting to feel a little nostalgic, like one of our old conversations.

"It had been so long, Evangeline, since I'd drawn a woman. Everything

206

that happened with Elle, I didn't have any alone time. I hadn't picked up my pencil in years until I saw you at *The Pink Lady*. I returned from that trip kind of fucked up. I was so angry at myself, shocked, frustrated, sad, longing for you—aroused. So fucking aroused. I started drawing you that next night and the next one and the next. I kept on with it any spare chance I got. It was sort of like spending time with you in a strange way. Anyway, Nancy was looking under my bed one day and found the sketchbook.

"Oh my God. She knew they were of me?"

"Yes. So, I used that opportunity to tell her about everything."

"About the fact that you have more naked women stashed away than Hugh Hefner?"

"No, not about that. Wiseass." I smiled. "About you and me."

"I'm sorry for joking about it."

"Are you kidding? I'm relieved you're joking around with me after the shit I pulled on you at the club."

"I know you weren't in your right frame of mind that night."

"That night? Try five years."

"She broke up with you because of me?"

"It wasn't that she was mad at the drawings. She sensed that my feelings for you were unresolved. She's afraid of getting hurt."

"I'm sorry."

"Don't be. She was right."

"So, what now?"

"Nothing."

"Nothing?"

"No. Just this." He paused for a few seconds. "Hear that? You and me. Just breathing. Not thinking about the past. Just together. Talking. I just want to talk to you every day and know that you're alright."

"I would like that."

"So, is midnight my time?"

"What do you mean?"

"Is that the time he's not with you, when it's safe for you to talk to me?"

"Yes. My shift ends at midnight. But I tell him to pick me up at 12:30

because I need that half-hour to myself. If midnight isn't too late for you, then that can be our time to talk."

"I'll take it."

We spoke every night at midnight for weeks on end. Evangeline would go to one of the empty backrooms at the club. We'd talk about our days—nothing too deep or upsetting. We'd talk about work, Addy, Luke or what music we were listening to. She was learning what my day to day life was like now, and I was doing a pretty damn good job pretending I didn't want nothing more than to kidnap her from that hellhole in Wichita.

Just like I used to live for our runs, I lived for that thirty minutes every night where our history didn't define us. I was just Sevin, and she was Evangeline. It helped that the distance meant the strong physical temptation that existed whenever we were together was removed from the equation. That made it easier for us to just get to know each other again.

***

It was rare that I slept in late. It was almost noon one Saturday when the sound of a rock hitting my window woke me up. At first, I thought it was my imagination. But by the second hit, my heart jumped, and my body followed.

I opened the door to find her standing in the morning sunlight. It seemed like maybe I was still in the middle of a dream. "Evangeline?" Rubbing my eyes to make sure I wasn't imagining her, I stepped to the side as she entered.

"I knocked on your door first, but you didn't answer."

"I had the air conditioning on; I must have not heard it."

"I hope it's okay that I'm here."

"It's more than okay."

Her eyes dropped down to my bare abs and then back up to my face. The instant euphoria I felt was a little disturbing to me, how hard and easily I fell right back in. My brain kept reminding me that this was the same girl who'd abandoned me. My heart spoke louder, though, reminding me that she was also the same girl who fell victim to a set of horrible circumstances beyond our control, the same girl I loved with every inch of my soul. The heart always won when it came to Evangeline, and it was beating in celebration to see her there in the flesh. My abandonment issues would have to take a back seat for now.

Her question snapped me out of my thoughts. "Are you okay?"

I'd been daydreaming while taking her in. My unwavering physical attraction to her never ceased to amaze me. Just the smell of her was making my dick hard. My body never reacted to anyone the way it did to Evangeline. I shouldn't have been thinking about how long it would take before I could bury myself inside of her again. It was all I could think about; that I needed her more than I needed or wanted anything—that I needed to get her away from that so-called man she referred to as a husband.

I needed to bring her home.

"Does he know you're here?"

"No."

"You ran away?" The irony of that question didn't escape me.

"No. Dean was called away for a family emergency. His mother is not doing well. It's rare that he goes anywhere, so I took advantage and borrowed my friend's SUV again."

"Will he give you trouble?"

"He won't know. He's coming back on Monday. I'll just make sure I'm home by Sunday night. It's a risk, but I needed to see you. It was time."

"I'm glad you decided to come, but I worry about you. I can't wrap my head around why the fuck you're still with him. I lose sleep at night over it."

"I already explained that leaving him needs to happen a certain way."

"I'll protect you. Don't you know that?"

My gut told me there was something she wasn't saying; it was eating away at me.

Why the fuck does this dude have so much power over you?

"Can we please not talk about him? I just need a break from it all."

"Alright."

For now.

She walked over to my couch and curled into it, letting out a huge breath. "It feels so good to be back here."

Then you never should have left.

I had to bite my tongue so often around her. It was really easy to lose control of my emotions, but I didn't want this short amount of time with her to be filled with drama. If the goal was to rebuild our relationship, I had to curb my own selfish need to push guilt.

Recently, I'd accepted the fact that Evangeline could pretty much rip out my heart, stomp on it, then feed it to me, and I'd still hand it back to her. She owned it.

"Are you hungry?" I asked. "I can make you something."

"Starving. But let me cook for you. I make a mean breakfast. Do you have eggs and stuff like that?"

"Yeah. I just went shopping."

Evangeline wasted no time getting to work in the kitchen, whisking eggs, popping bread in the toaster, frying bacon. A tightness in my chest developed as I watched her looking so domestic in my house. It was a side of her I never got to experience. It felt so good having her here.

At one point, she'd just placed the scrambled eggs onto our plates when she opened the cupboard.

I walked over to help her. "What do you need?"

"Do you have salt?"

"It should be in there."

She was shuffling through things then suddenly stopped. She was holding the box of Pop Tarts. "These are dated from over five years ago. Are these the same ones you had the last time I was here?"

I looked into her eyes and whispered, "Yeah."

"I don't understand."

"What's there not to understand?"

"You never threw them away..."

I shrugged. "I couldn't. Stupid, right? Like somehow having them was going to make you magically come back?"

The sadness in her eyes cut through me. I didn't mean for her to find them.

She shocked the shit out of me when she suddenly opened one of the individual packages and began stuffing her mouth with the stale pastry.

"What are you doing? Are you fucking crazy? Those are just artifacts. They're not meant to be eaten."

"You're right. I should have been here…to eat these with you," she said with her mouth full. Her eyes were filling with tears as she chewed.

"I didn't keep them so you could sicken yourself with them five years later!"

"If that happens, I deserve it. I'm a bad person. You have no idea. I—"

"Evangeline, stop." I took the box, threw it in the trash and pulled her into me. "You don't deserve botulism." I laughed.

When she cracked a slight smile at my comment, I added, "Well, maybe you deserve to get the shits."

She smacked me lightly in the chest, and we both had a good laugh. The toast had burned. The eggs were cold. None of it mattered, because she was safe in my arms.

"I ruin everything," she said. "I can't even make you breakfast without ruining it."

I held her closer. "I'm glad it burned."

She pulled back. "Why?"

I grimaced. "Because now I get to take you out. In fact, I think we should stay out for the entire day."

"What do you want to do?"

An idea suddenly came to me. "Stay here."

I went to my room and returned with a piece of paper.

"That time in the barn shortly after I moved in…you listed your dreams to me. Do you remember that?"

"Yes."

"I came back here that night and wrote them down as best as I could remember them. At the time, I didn't really understand why remembering them was so important to me. I later realized it was because I wanted to help you make them come true and because many of them were my own dreams." I showed her my handwritten list.

To be independent
To experience love without settling
To be loved back
To make a difference in the world
To be comfortable in her own skin
To make love in the rain
Skydive
To have no regrets
To be true to herself

"If my calculations are correct, you've achieved most of these except for the last three."

"How so?"

"Well, you're independent from your family. At least, you work and make your own money. You've experienced love. You've definitely been loved back. You've made a difference in *my* life. You take off your clothes in public. If that's not being comfortable in your own skin, I don't know what is!"

We both chuckled. It felt so good to laugh with her.

My voice lowered. "You've made love in the rain. I was there."

"Yes, you were."

"But the last three: skydiving, living with no regrets and being true to yourself…those I still need to help you with. We can start with the easiest."

***

Evangeline made it down before me. At least, I hoped to heaven she did.

There was a loud popping noise when the instructor pulled the handle to activate the parachute. Skydiving seemed like a piece of cake compared to the past year of my life. It was strange, but I wasn't as scared as I thought I might be to jump out of that plane; my life experiences as of late had toughened me up that way.

The relief that came over me when the parachute opened was euphoric.

Everything slowed down dramatically. Slowly descending and floating in the air, I let myself relax. The ground was rapidly approaching.

I ended up landing on my ass.

Evangeline was running toward me with a huge smile on her face. "That was freaking amazing! Oh my God!"

"Was it everything you hoped for?"

"The greatest adrenaline rush I've ever experienced. I can't wait to do it again."

I kissed her forehead. "We both needed this."

Later, after we calmed down and returned to my truck, her face was still red with excitement when she turned to me. "What are we doing now?"

"You want more? We could go bungee jumping."

"You're not serious?"

I laughed. "Actually, I thought we could have dinner at Addy's. I know she wants to see you."

"I would really love that," she said, looking more relaxed than I'd probably ever seen her. Life shouldn't have been as complicated as ours was up until now. All I ever wanted was to make her happy. For today, at least, I'd succeeded.

After I called Addy to let her know we'd be bringing dinner over, Evangeline and I returned to my house to clean up. I closed my eyes and listened to the sound of the shower running, thinking about how incredibly good it felt having her here, knowing she was away from him.

She emerged from the bathroom with her hair wet, running my hairbrush through the long strands. She'd changed into a red dress that hugged her curves. A pair of matching flip flop wedges made her shapely legs look even longer.

I couldn't take my eyes off her, and truly didn't know how I was going to possibly let her go back to Wichita.

I couldn't let her go back to him.

Evangeline must have been able to read my inner thoughts by the look on my face as I gazed at her. She stopped brushing and walked over to me. "I don't want to go back."

Sitting on the bed, I leaned my head gently into her stomach as she pulled me into her and wrapped her arms around my neck.

"Stay." When I spoke into the material of her dress, her body quivered.

"How can I?"

"You don't need to ever go back there. We'll serve him with a letter, send someone for your things, or I can go with you when you break the news to him."

She shook her head as if to rule out that last option.

"There are things you don't understand, Sevin, things I haven't told you."

"Do you really think there is anything at this point that could fucking shock me? I didn't know if you were even alive. Anything is still a step up from thinking you might have been dead."

"I'm sorry." Evangeline backed away and started to pace.

I got up and put my hands on her shoulders to stop her. "What exactly will he do? Because I'll fucking fight him to the bone for you. You only ended up with him anyway because you were running from me. You don't belong there."

"I was very lost when he came into my life. He feels that I owe him for a lot. All I want is to stay with you, but he won't let me go that easily."

Her fear was palpable. I didn't want to ruin our day by pushing her to tell me everything. She was clearly upset. I decided to back off for now despite my mind racing to think of ways to get her to consider never going back to Wichita.

"Let's just have a nice dinner at Addy's, okay?"

She wiped her eyes and smiled. "Okay."

***

After stopping at the market, we prepared a spaghetti dinner at Addy's, insisting our hostess not lift a finger. The small kitchen was filled with the smell of fresh basil and garlic bread baking in the oven. The tense mood from earlier had transformed into a comfortable camaraderie again as Evangeline and I cooked side-by-side, sipping wine and stealing glances at one another.

It was the first time everyone I cared about sat down for a meal together.

Luke passed Evangeline the salad. "So, Addy's told me lots of stories about the days when you used to sneak over here and work at the garage."

"Yeah…it was my favorite place in the world. She taught me a lot about fixing cars, but more about life in general."

He looked over at Addy affectionately. "I hear that. I've learned a lot from this woman, too."

"Well, thank you, baby." She turned to Evangeline. "Vangie was probably better and faster than most of the men who'd been mechanics half their lives."

"I used to dream about taking the business over. You know that."

I put my hand on Evangeline's arm. "Maybe you can still do it."

"There's no business to take over anymore," Addy said.

"Sure, there is. All of the foundational stuff is still locked up in the shop. We'd just need to be creative, come up with a business plan. We'd rename it and do a grand reopening."

Addy slapped the table. "We'll call it the GAY-rage, paint it in rainbows. People around here would love that," she said sarcastically.

"I'm all for that, Mama," Luke said as he high-fived her.

I slammed my drink down. "Will you two be serious for five seconds? Why not try to get it back up and running?"

Addy shook her head. "Because there was a reason I shut it down in the first place."

"Didn't you say that for a while you had to temporarily turn people away when Marty and Jermaine took other jobs? It was only after they left that business really slowed because those customers you turned away found other mechanics and never came back."

"That's true. Yes."

"I bet if you had the right staff, you could start it up again."

My life had been too hectic over the past several years to really come up with a plan to help Addy get back on her feet. Now that I had a little more time on my hands, I was getting pumped to be able to help her. The fact that this endeavor might lure Evangeline back to Dodge City was an added benefit. Addy had no clue that Evangeline was working as an exotic dancer. Evangeline preferred she not know, and I didn't betray her trust.

Evangeline was being awfully quiet, just looking back and forth between everyone. The conversation turned serious once Addy actually conceded that I was making some sense. She agreed to let me at least develop a business plan for her and said she'd consider reopening the shop.

At one point, Evangeline got up from the table, looking upset.

When she took a long time returning from the bathroom, I got up and knocked on the door. "Are you okay?"

"No."

"Open the door."

When she slowly opened it, her eyes were red.

"I didn't want you to see me like this."

"What's wrong? I thought we were having a good night."

"We were. Nothing is wrong. That's the problem. Everything is too perfect. This dinner. The talk about reopening the shop. The way you've been looking at me tonight like I never caused you all that pain…God, Sevin."

I grabbed a tissue and wiped her eyes. "I haven't forgotten the pain of you leaving or the broken heart you left me with. But you're also the only one who can heal it. There might have been times when I thought I hated you. But the fact is, I could never hate you more than I love you. You're the love of my life."

"I love you so much. That's why I can't forgive myself."

"You're punishing yourself by staying with that trailer trash. This is your home. We can go to Wichita tonight and get your stuff before he comes back."

She was shaking. "There's something you don't know. You will *hate* me, Sevin."

Placing my hands on her shoulders to still her body, I said, "Please stop being cryptic. Tell me what the fuck happened!" Immediately regretting my tone, I took a deep breath.

Addy interrupted us. "Everything alright in here?" She took one look at Evangeline's face and knew the answer. "Vangie, what's going on?"

Evangeline was coming apart. Whatever it was she was keeping from me had slowly been eating away at her and was now totally consuming her. We needed to be alone, and I needed to get her to open up to me on her own without forcing it.

"I think I'm having a nervous breakdown, Addy."

"I think it's better if I take her home."

Addy looked surprised. "To Wichita?"

"No. I said *home*. To my house."

Evangeline nodded in agreement. She and Addy hugged, and we promised to call in the morning.

The ride back to my place was quiet. Evangeline rested her head against the seat. I wasn't going to try to drag anything out of her tonight because she could have very easily just gotten in her SUV and left if I upset her enough. I didn't want her driving in this condition and was still set on her never going back at all. I needed to make her feel safe tonight and make her believe that nothing she could tell me would change how I felt about her.

She'd run away and had been on her own for a long time before she met that weasel Dean; anything could have happened to her. My imagination was running wild. The theories running through my mind were making me sick to my stomach. I needed to let go of my own insecurities, make her my priority tonight.

Her black hair was splattered across my throw pillow as she lay down on the couch and closed her eyes.

"We don't need to talk about it tonight. It's been a long day. But I need to know everything that happened while you were away…when you're ready to tell me."

Her eyes reflected a deep sadness as she simply looked at me without saying anything before closing her eyes once again.

Rubbing her arm gently, I said, "I want you to take my bed. I'll sleep on the couch tonight."

"You don't have to do that."

"I insist."

Beads of sweat were forming on her forehead.

"Are you hot? Let me get you some water." I walked over to the kitchen to pour her a glass.

"It's weird. I have the chills, but sweat is pouring off of me."

"Are you getting sick?"

"No. It's nerves."

"I'm gonna draw you a bath. It will relax you, get your mind off things for a while."

She swallowed nervously and nodded her head. "I would love that. Thank you."

"Be right back."

My heart was pounding as I made my way to the bathroom off of my bedroom. I couldn't explain my own nerves except to say it felt like something earth shattering was about to happen, even though I had no clue what it was. I just sensed it.

I ran my hand through the water coming out of the spout until it was the perfect warm temperature. Remembering that Nancy had left some bubble bath soap under my sink, I took out the container and poured the remainder of it into the water. The tub was now filled with spongy bubbles.

Returning to the living room, I offered her my hand and gently lifted her off the couch, leading her into the bathroom.

"Let me know if you need anything. I'll be right behind that door."

"Okay. Thanks."

I neatened up my bed for her before sitting on the edge and closing my eyes. Listening to the sounds of the water bubbling as she moved her body around in it, I wished more than anything that I could be inside with her.

Be inside of her.

"Sevin?"

Her voice was so low that it was barely audible.

I got up and leaned my cheek against the door. "Yeah?"

"Can you come in?"

I slowly turned the doorknob. Only her head was visible as she lay beneath the suds. She didn't look relaxed at all. The expression on her face seemed even more tormented than before.

"What do you need, baby?"

Evangeline lifted her hand, reaching it out to me as a tear fell down her cheek. "You."

"You want me to come in with you?"

She nodded.

My nerves from earlier were tenfold as I lifted off my shirt. Her eyes followed the movement of my hands as I slid my pants off. Leaving my boxer briefs on, I got in the tub behind her and wrapped my legs around her body. Evangeline's head of wet hair leaned against my pounding heart. Her chest was rising and falling. I kissed the back of her head softly to try to calm her down.

This was the opposite of a fun jaunt in the tub. It felt more like we were washing away our sins in a quiet moment of repentance. That nagging feeling that something significant was about to happen wouldn't cease.

Whispering against her head, I said, "It's okay, Evangeline. Everything is going to be okay. I'm here. I'm never going to let anything bad happen to you again." I held her closer to me. "I love you. I don't even know who I am without you. Don't you know that? Even experiencing pain with you is better than nothing at all. Please tell me you'll stay. We'll work it out...as long as it takes. Whatever it takes, baby, we'll do it."

Evangeline reached her foot out to lower the stopper. The water slowly emptied out into the drain as she continued to rest her back on top of my chest. With each second that passed, her breathing became heavier.

With the water gone, there was nothing left except Evangeline's slick naked body against me. I lowered my mouth to her neck and began to kiss it. She flipped around to stop me.

"I'm not gonna try to have sex with you tonight," I said, defensively. "I just wanted to kiss your neck. That's all."

"That's not why I turned around."

"Why did you turn around then?"

Her lips were trembling. "I need to show you something."

"What?"

She straddled me, her warm pussy sitting atop my thighs. I was still wearing my boxer briefs which were wet and stuck to my full erection. Her hands were shaking as she took mine in hers and placed them below her stomach. She let go and watched as I traced my finger along her taut skin.

That was when I saw the thick reddish line.

My finger froze.

It looked like someone had sliced into her.

"What is this? Did someone stab you?" My blood was boiling. "Was it him?"

She slowly shook her head no, and a few seconds later, everything started to register.

No.

Instinctively, I straightened up, and my body went rigid.

Then, a flash of panic.

I covered my mouth as I looked down at her scar.

No.

No.

No.

"I need to hear you say it, Evangeline."

She cried harder.

I rubbed my thumb along her bikini line. "What is this? Say it."

She wouldn't answer.

I yelled, "Say it!"

"I had a baby!" she screamed.

I lowered my voice and repeated, "You had a baby."

"Yes," she whispered.

My heart felt like it was going to explode out of my chest.

Was it mine?

His?

It would be impossible to stomach either scenario.

"Whose baby?"

"Our baby."

Our baby.

No two words had ever had a greater impact on my life, yet I was so confused.

"You gave birth…to *our* baby?"

"Yes."

"Where is it?"

"I don't know."

"What do you mean…you don't know? You don't know. You DON'T KNOW? How the fuck can you NOT know?"

"I gave her away."

Gave her away.

Her.

A daughter.

Gave her away?

"Her? You gave our daughter away?" Dripping wet, I pushed past her out of the tub and stormed into the bedroom, pacing with my palm on my forehead. "Oh my God."

Trying to piece it all together, my thoughts were jumbled. It now made sense why Evangeline ran away when she did. We'd been careful most of the times that we had sex with the exception of one or two. I couldn't believe that I never once considered that she could have been pregnant when she left. I understood why she had to hide it from Elle, but how could she keep something like that from me?

She was wrapped in a towel when she came out of the bathroom. "I know it's incomprehensible. I have to explain what was going on in my head at the time."

Throwing on my pants and a pullover, I snapped, "There's no explanation that will justify your giving my child away without my knowing." I grabbed my keys. "I can't talk to you…can't be around you right now. I'll do or say something I'll regret. I need to process this."

"Wait…"

When she followed me and put her hand on my shoulder, I whipped it away from her. "Don't fucking touch me," I spewed before slamming the door shut and running off into the night.

CHAPTER 23

EVANGELINE

I shouldn't have expected anything different. I knew he would never begin to understand. How could he understand if I couldn't even fully understand my own actions? I left Sevin a note, letting him know that I was driving back to Wichita. I doubted he wanted to see the sight of me anyway.

As I drove down the freeway, I cursed at myself for ever believing that Sevin could look past something so deplorable. But earlier tonight, I started to feel hopeful that maybe he would find it in himself to forgive me. Even if he didn't, I knew I couldn't keep it from him any longer. This secret had ruled my life for years, and the weight of it was too heavy to bear anymore. It was the only reason I forced myself to stay with Dean, because he constantly threatened to find my family and tell them about the "pregnant whore" he rescued. Back then, I couldn't risk Sevin and Elle finding out about the baby. Dean always thought I never knew who the father was.

Now that Sevin knew the truth, I had no reason to stay in Wichita, imprisoned by Dean's threats. Plotting my exit from the marriage and home we shared would have to be done cautiously. He wasn't going to grant me a divorce easily. But I needed to leave either way. I just prayed he didn't kill me first.

It was the middle of the night when I got to our house. A light flashed on from the porch as soon as I pulled the SUV in front. Dread filled me as

I also noticed Dean's truck parked outside.

Fuck.

He'd come home early.

I had to make a decision whether to jet away or face the music. I decided that after the night I'd had, I had nothing to lose. I was no longer going to hide from my demons. Nothing could affect me like hurting Sevin had.

Dean stormed out from the house before I even had a chance to exit the car. "Where the fuck have you been? I just called the club, and they said you didn't work tonight."

"I went to Dodge City."

"I thought I told you not to leave while I was away."

"I wanted to go home."

"Get in the fucking house. We're not going to get into it in the middle of the street."

"Why? Are you afraid someone might hear the way you talk to me or see you shove me around?"

"Get the fuck inside!"

"No."

"Excuse me?"

"No! You're not going to hurt me. I'm not going inside."

"The fuck you're not."

Dean grabbed my arm and began to drag me across the lawn. When I resisted, he slapped me hard across the face.

"Let go of me!" I screamed.

Lights from an oncoming car distracted him momentarily. I tried to run, but he tackled me to the ground, pinning me down.

A car door slammed, and then I heard him.

"Get off her!"

Dean jumped off of me. "Who the fuck are you?"

Sevin charged toward him and shoved Dean in the chest with both hands. "Who am I? The last person you'll ever speak to alive if you don't leave her alone. I have a shotgun in my car, and I'll use it if I have to." He turned to me, helping me off the grass. "Evangeline, are you okay?"

"Yes."

"How the fuck do you know my wife? You some obsessed stalker from the club?"

"Your *wife* is my family."

"What?"

"She was running away from me when she met you."

"She was a pregnant whore when I met her, said she didn't know who the father was."

Sevin looked like he was about to blow. He closed his eyes briefly then looked over at me. "Evangeline, get inside my truck."

I grabbed my overnight bag from Liz's SUV and walked over to Sevin's Ford F150.

"Evie, you take off with this guy, you better never set foot in this house again."

"You can count on the fact that she won't. And if you think about coming after her, I'll call the cops to let them know about your pot growing operation in the basement. I've spoken to several people who've bought from you over the years, too. They're waiting on standby for hefty payoffs if I need them. You stay away from her, and no one gets called."

"Evie, you're gonna let this old boyfriend of yours bribe me after all I've done for you? I fucking saved your life!"

"You'll be hearing from her attorney," Sevin said before walking over to me.

I almost apologized to Dean for leaving him in that way but stopped myself. He didn't deserve my respect.

"Goodbye, Dean." I pressed the button to close the window.

Sevin started the truck and peeled out down the road.

***

The silence was deafening during the ride back to Dodge City. Sevin still looked like he was about to erupt. He wasn't ready to talk to me, and I couldn't blame him.

When he finally spoke, his voice rattled me. "You shouldn't have left my house. I was coming back to talk to you. I just needed the time to let it sink in."

"I wasn't sure if you ever wanted to see me again. How did you get here so fast?"

"I must have left immediately after you when I got your note."

"How did you know about Dean's marijuana plants?"

"I've had my eye on him for weeks," he simply said without looking at me. "We've both been through a lot tonight. It's too late to drive all the way home. We're gonna find a hotel, get a few hours sleep. When we wake up, you're gonna tell me everything. And I mean *everything*, Evangeline. Every last fucking detail."

I nodded and glanced over to make sure he saw it.

We stopped at a small hotel off the interstate in Hutchinson.

"How many beds?" the front desk clerk asked.

Sevin answered right away, "One."

I looked at him. He looked at me. His eyes were telling me not to question it, and I had no intention of protesting. I was confused, unable to understand how he could possibly want to share a bed with me after everything that happened tonight.

The room was small with one full-sized bed. It was dark, but neither of us turned on the lamp. We kept the bathroom light on, which allowed just enough illumination for us to see each other.

Sevin lifted his shirt and threw it on the chair. I honestly didn't know where his head was at. His specifically asking for one bed made me wary about the reason he wanted to sleep next to me. The truth was, if he planned to try to angrily fuck me to let out his frustrations, I would give him whatever he wanted. I'd do just about anything to comfort him tonight.

"Lie down," he said, his tone demanding as he undid the bedding and got underneath.

My back was facing him as I climbed into the bed with everything but my shoes on.

Sevin wrapped his arms around my waist and held me close. He was being so quiet that I wasn't sure whether he'd fallen asleep until he asked, "Has he always manhandled you like that?"

"Not in the very beginning, but in the past few years, yes. He's never beaten me really badly, but he slaps me sometimes or shoves me. And he's very verbally abusive."

Sevin started to breathe heavier, tightening his grip on me and pulling me even more firmly against him. Closing my eyes, I relaxed into him. After several minutes of quiet, he lowered his hand and placed it under my shirt over my stomach, gently caressing my skin with his thumb.

I knew he was thinking about our baby, searching desperately and in vain for something that was long gone. It was breaking my heart. How was I going to explain everything to him tomorrow in a way that could possibly justify my actions?

Sometime in those early morning hours, Sevin and I fell asleep, his hand never leaving my belly.

***

The morning sun streamed through the window. When I woke up and patted the bed around me, he was gone. Before I could freak out, the door creaked open and clicked shut behind him. Sevin was holding two bags of fast food breakfast and two coffees in a cardboard tray.

I sat up as he handed me a coffee and placed one of the bags on the night table next to me.

"Eat," he simply said. His mood was definitely darker than last night when he held me. He was probably gearing up for the conversation we were about to have.

As for me, there was no way to mentally prepare for it. As I sat up eating, the sun caught his dark blue eyes in such a way that it made my heart clench. His hair was unruly from sleep. It had been at least a few days since he last shaved. Sevin was such a beautiful man. I didn't know how I would be able to handle it if I had to live in Dodge City and not be with him, not be allowed to love him openly if he could never forgive me.

After breakfast, he told me to take a shower. Afterward, he stood in the doorway with his arms crossed and watched as I brushed my hair slowly. I was trying to delay the inevitable.

"Sit down," he said.

I knew it was time.

Sitting on the bed, I looked down at the floor and rubbed my sweaty palms along my thighs. Sevin stood leaning against the wall at the opposite side of the room as if to avoid being near me in the event that his anger became uncontrollable; at least, that was how I interpreted his standing so far away.

When I finally looked up at him, he offered me a simple nod.

I just started talking.

"I found out I was pregnant about a month before I left. You might remember I started to really distance myself. I wanted to tell you, but I knew if I did, that you would insist that we keep it. I just didn't see how that could ever be possible unless we both ran away. I just couldn't do that to Elle. At the same time, abortion wasn't an option. This was still our child. I needed help, so I made a decision that was risky. I told Mama about us…everything."

Sevin's gaze lifted from the floor, and his eyes were piercing. A look that was a mix of shock and rage washed over his face. "Your mother? Olga has known all this time?"

"Yes."

"What about Lance?"

"Daddy still doesn't know to this day. Neither does Emily. No one else knows."

"Fuck. I can't believe this."

"I confided in my mother instead of Adelaide, because I was afraid Addy might tell you. Mama set me up in a house in Wichita. The old woman who lived there was a second or third cousin of my grandmother's. My mother paid her to let me stay there while I was pregnant. I don't know if you remember her going away some weekends back then? She was visiting me."

"Yeah. I always thought it was strange that she would leave Elle…to supposedly visit some cousins."

"I also got a job waitressing at the time. That was when I first met Dean, although we never got together until after the pregnancy. He was a regular at the restaurant."

"Fucking asshole."

"I was really scared, Sevin. I missed you so much, yearned for you. I was carrying a part of you inside of me and couldn't tell you. I thought I would never see you again. I know it seems like I made a rash and irresponsible decision, but it felt like I had no choice. I just didn't see another solution at the time. I couldn't risk my sister finding out, especially in her condition."

"I had a fucking right to know!"

"Can you honestly say that you would have let me give the baby up for adoption?"

"I absolutely would *not* have."

"And I knew that. It wasn't fair to you. I know. But I made a decision based on what was best for my sister."

"What about what was best for our daughter…to have her mother and father in her life?"

"I didn't feel like I was fit to be a mother."

"I would've taken her and raised her myself. Elle would never have had to find out. I could have figured out *something*. Fuck…it was my daughter! *My daughter.* I would have figured it out! God, Evangeline! Where is she?"

My heart was breaking because I didn't have the answers he deserved.

"It was a closed adoption. I don't know, Sevin. I don't know. I know you hate me for this. It's why I've spent every day since she was born punishing myself. I won't ever forgive myself for what I took away from you, and you shouldn't forgive me, either."

I covered my face and burst into tears. I hadn't even gotten to the hard part of the story.

After a few minutes, his temperament calmed. He leaned his head against the wall, closed his eyes and whispered, "Tell me about the day she was born. Tell me everything."

"It was a rainy day. I started to feel some contractions while at work and called Mama right away. She'd set up a special cell phone just for my calls."

Sevin shook his head in disbelief.

"I was really scared. I'd never been in so much pain in my life. Mama got there a few hours later, and by that time, the contractions were less than five minutes apart, so we went to the hospital. She called the adoption agent she was working with to let her know that things were happening."

"They let you put her up for adoption without my permission?"

"We told them we didn't know who the father was. That's the only circumstance where the father doesn't need to sign off on it."

His face and ears were turning red as he muttered something to himself.

I continued, "The contractions were really bad, but I wasn't dilating at all. They figured out it was because the baby had flipped back around in the wrong direction. She was breach. That was why everything wasn't progressing enough for me to give birth naturally. I was so scared because they told me they were going to have to do an emergency C-section. I don't remember much right after that." I stood up and walked around the room a bit before continuing, stopping at the desk and leaning against it for support. "Everything happened so fast. They rushed me into the operating room, pumped me with drugs. Mama was right by my head. I couldn't feel anything, and there was a blue divider in front of my face, so I couldn't see what the doctor was doing. I thought about you in that moment, how you would have been there by my side, holding my hand. I wanted you there. It was so scary, but the fear was nothing compared to the massive amount of guilt I remember feeling."

"You're damn right I should have been there. Wherever I was, I was thinking it was just another fucking day, maybe at work or at home with Elle. All the while, you were giving birth to my child. I can't even comprehend that. That is so fucked up."

When he walked over to me suddenly, I instinctively backed away against the wall.

"Why did you just back away from me like that?"

"I don't know."

I guess after years of living with Dean, it was second nature for me to feel as though someone approaching me in anger would mean ending up getting physically punished.

"Did you think I was going to lay a hand on you?"

"I'm not sure why I did it. Maybe that was my instinct."

"I would never hurt you like he did. Do you understand me?"

"Yes."

In fact, Sevin didn't touch me at all. I felt like I needed him to hold me but wouldn't dare ask. He made his way back to the opposite side of the room away from me.

He was silent for a while then asked, "Did you even hold her, or did you just have them take her away?" His tone was bitter.

"I didn't feel her come out. I heard her cry, and that was how I knew she'd been born. They brought her around to me and put her close to my face. I tried not to look at her. I was afraid if I did, I'd never be able to let her go. Her skin was so soft when it brushed against my cheek. She had the sweetest smell. I went to turn my face to kiss her with my eyes closed, but they took her away too fast."

"That was it?"

I shook my head no. "There was a 48-hour waiting period required before I was allowed to sign the papers…in case I changed my mind. I'd made it clear that they shouldn't bring her to me, though. Sometime in the middle of the night that first night, I was trying to take a walk. The C-section left me in a lot of pain, but they told me I needed to try to move around. I ended up accidentally passing by the nursery. My mother was in there holding her. I felt like she was being such a traitor in that moment because she'd been the one pushing me the hardest to give her up. Mama had tears in her eyes. The baby was crying uncontrollably. I guess they were having trouble getting her to take the formula."

I had to stop to sit down. This was the first time I'd ever spoken aloud about the birth, and the memories were hard to handle. While unable to make eye contact, I could feel Sevin's pain emanating from him without even looking at his face.

"I was angry at my mother for sneaking time in the nursery when she'd been adamant about my not seeing the baby. I walked over to her and took the baby from her." Tears started to fall freely down my cheeks just thinking about what happened next. "She stopped crying a few seconds after I took her into my arms. She somehow knew it was me."

Sevin sat down on the bed and covered his face. I couldn't tell if he was crying. A part of me wanted to stop the story, but he needed to know everything. It wasn't going to be any easier telling it another time.

I wiped my eyes. "She was searching with her little mouth for my breast. My milk had just started to come in. I knew feeding her was a huge no-no given the situation, but in that moment, all that mattered was comforting my baby. I ordered my mother to get out of the room. Then, I sat down, opened up my hospital gown, and she latched right on. The nurse came in and told me to stop feeding her, that it was a bad idea to get her used to breast milk when she needed to become accustomed to formula. But I just couldn't stop. It was all I could give her...all I would ever give her. I never imagined how much I was going to fall in love with her so quickly. I loved her so much, not just because she was mine, but because she was yours."

The next part of the story was the hardest for me to grapple with.

"She spit up a little, so I undid her blanket to clean her..." I closed my eyes. "That was when I noticed that..." I hesitated.

"What?"

"She had a birth defect. No one had told me."

"What are you talking about?"

"The bottom half of her left arm was missing."

"What?"

"None of the ultrasounds caught it. They said it was just a genetic blip, nothing specific that I did to cause it."

His ears were turning red as he kept his head in his hands. Maybe I needed to stop.

He turned to me, his eyes swollen and red. "How could you give her away after that?"

The pain in my chest worsened as I forced myself to go on with the story.

"The adoptive family was told about her arm. They also found out that

I was having doubts, and threatened to back out if I didn't sign the papers soon. They said they weren't going to wait forever only to have me change my mind. I was scared she wouldn't have a good home. Mama kept pressuring me, reminding me of all the reasons I ran away in the first place and saying that it would be harder to find another family because of the baby's imperfection."

"So you did it...just...signed the papers," he said incredulously.

"I didn't even say goodbye to her because I couldn't. How ironic is that? I gave up our baby in the same way I left you. So, see? All of this...it's why I'm such a terrible person, why I deserved every bit of the type of life I've had since."

"There's no way to find out where she is?"

"Like I said, it was a closed adoption. I don't even know the family's last name."

A long moment of silence ensued before he turned to me. "What did she look like?"

Telling him would be like pouring major salt in his wound, but there was no holding back anymore.

"She looked like you. Just like you."

Sevin shot up from the bed. "I need some air."

He walked out the door, slamming it behind him.

Feeling empty, I curled into the bed, wishing I had drugs to numb the pain.

After everything sunk in, a strange, almost calming fogginess came over me. It was similar to how you feel after a long run or after coming down from a panic attack. It was a feeling of relief at the same time, like the worst was over. It couldn't get any worse than admitting to Sevin that I gave his child away.

An hour later when the door burst open, Sevin's eyes were wide and frantic upon returning from his walk.

Alarmed, I straightened my back against the headboard. "What happened?"

He clutched his chest, trying to catch his breath. "I know where she is."

CHAPTER 24

SEVIN

"I've seen her...our daughter."

"What?"

"Your mother lied."

"That's not possible."

"She lied! She knows where our daughter is."

"How do you know that?"

"It all hit me just now on my walk." The words were spilling out of me so fast. "I've been going to this church for a while in Spearville. I go there to clear my head a couple of Sundays a month. I always sit in the back row. There was this family that caught my attention a couple of times because one of their daughters was missing the bottom half of her arm. Her hair was darker than her sisters'. I remember thinking how much they reminded me of my half-brothers and me, three blondes and a dark-haired child that stuck out like a sore thumb."

"But it could be a coincidence. That doesn't mean it's her, Sevin."

"Let me finish. What also made me pay attention to this family was that the father always looked so damn familiar. The one or two times he'd turned around to hand the donation basket to the people behind him or offer a sign of peace, I swore I knew him from somewhere but could never figure it out. Well, one day I did. I remembered that he was the same guy who showed up at Sutton once. This guy was in the lobby. The receptionist handed him an envelope, and then he left."

"I don't get it."

"It seemed a little suspicious to me at the time, so I asked Jeannie if she knew what was in the envelope. She said that it was cash and that Olga had come into the office and instructed her to give it to the guy. She must have not wanted her business done at home. I assumed it was some kind of charity donation, that maybe they were poor or something. I never gave it another thought again…until now."

She covered her mouth. "Oh my God."

"I've seen her, Evangeline. Only from the back. She has long, black hair—just like you—except she's a little pudgy and precious. It's her. I just know it is. Your mother must have been giving them money for her all this time."

"I can't believe this."

I started to pack up our things. "I have to think about what I'm gonna do."

"What do you mean? There is nothing you can do. She's legally theirs."

"She's still my daughter."

***

I told Evangeline it was best if she moved in with Addy and Luke for a while until we could figure things out. It was too soon after her dropping that bombshell to think about repairing our relationship. I was still in shock and trying to figure out how to proceed. I wanted to be armed with as much legal information as possible before confronting anyone.

Unfortunately, everything I read basically stated that it wasn't cut and dry. I could legally challenge the adoption, claiming parental rights, but it wouldn't be an easy process, and nothing was guaranteed. Was it even fair to put my little girl through that?

My little girl.

It still hadn't sunk in completely.

So much was uncertain, except for the fact that I knew I needed to see her. The one time since finding out the news that I returned to church, she wasn't there.

Only one person knew where to find her. It was time to confront Olga.

It was the middle of the afternoon. I checked to make sure Lance was at Sutton Provisions and that Emily was gone before heading over to the main house.

Olga was holding a laundry basket when she opened the door. Looking surprised to see me at that time of day, she tilted her head. "Sevin."

Maybe it was the look on my face. Or maybe it was the fact that I said nothing at all in response. The smile on her face quickly faded.

I gritted my teeth. "Where is she?"

"Who?"

"My daughter. Where does she live?"

Olga dropped the laundry basket, and her face turned white. With her head down, she moved aside to let me enter.

"When did she tell you?"

"Several days ago."

"You can't do anything, Sevin."

I repeated, "Where does she live?"

"Promise me you will not try to make trouble for that little girl."

"Answer me!"

"Spearville."

"Who are these people?"

"Robert and Genia Simonsen. They're good people."

"You chose them?"

"The adoption agent found them. I helped select the family based on the one I felt had the best values and the fact that they were local."

"You give them money?"

"They're hard working, but they're not well off. I just give them a little extra to make ends meet."

"Why didn't you tell Evangeline that you were in on all of this?"

"It was best that she not be involved. She was too vulnerable back then. We both know that it had to happen this way, Sevin. Imagine if Elle—God rest her soul—were to have found out what you two did…"

"Don't say that like we committed a crime. We didn't do anything but fall in love. I'm pretty sure I made up for my sins when it came to Elle, and you know it. I didn't see you helping her wipe her ass as much I did." Immediately regretting that comment, I said, "I'm sorry, Olga. But you need to understand why this is wrong."

"Lance can't find out I kept this from him. This family has been through enough."

"So, I'm just supposed to forget she exists…shut up about it…so Lance doesn't get upset? This is about me and my child. This has nothing to do with you or Lance or even Evangeline at this point. What's their address?"

"What are you going to do?"

"I don't know. But I need to know where to find her. You gave me their names. If you don't tell me, I'll find them anyway."

"Ten Lowell Lane in Spearville."

"What's her name?"

"Rose."

Rose?

How could that be?

"Rose?"

"Yes."

"That's my mother's name."

"I know, Sevin."

"Who gave her that name?"

"Evangeline."

"I don't understand. Why did she want to name the baby Rose if she was just going to give her away?"

"She wouldn't sign the papers unless they agreed to keep the name. It was a verbal agreement. She has no way of really knowing whether they followed through. They weren't obligated to. The Simonsens didn't know the significance of the name. Evangeline felt incredibly guilty, and I think she wanted to believe that if the baby were named Rose, that maybe a part of you would somehow always be with her."

***

With my baseball cap on, I sat at the far end of the bleachers on the highest row. You could say I blended in. No one ever questioned me. I could have been anyone's father, brother or uncle. A fixture at these T-ball games every Tuesday and Thursday at Greenbush Field, I never missed one.

After Olga had given me the Simonsens' address, I'd held onto it for several days before doing anything with it. My initial plan was to knock on their door and explain who I was, demanding they let me see my child.

When I got to their modest two-story house that first night, I used my binoculars to peek into their window from my car. For the first time, I saw the face of my beautiful raven-haired little girl. Even though she had Evangeline's long, thick hair, her facial features were all me. It was like looking into a mirror. I couldn't believe it. She was slightly chubby, had long bangs that nearly covered her eyes and was wearing pig tails. She reminded me a little of the character Boo from *Monsters, Inc.* This was my daughter. Holy shit.

Slowly dropping my binoculars, I wiped the tears from my eyes and tried to regain my composure. She was watching something on television with her sisters and belly laughing. Suddenly, my plan to barge through their door and stake claim on her didn't seem like such a bright idea. It seemed asinine, in fact. I didn't want to scare her. So, I put everything off and just enjoyed this beautiful child from afar for a while. Every trip, I'd go with the intention of making my presence known, and each time, I'd decide against it.

The more I acted as a spectator, the clearer it became that Rose had a good life. She was a happy little girl, well-cared for and genuinely loved. The realization of that made it even harder to reveal myself.

So, I became The Invisible Dad.

For weeks.

Evangeline had no idea what I was up to on Tuesdays and Thursdays. Our relationship was temporarily at a standstill. We were giving each other space. She spent her days with Addy, helping to reorganize the shop for the reopening. Evangeline probably thought I was avoiding her for other reasons, but it was mainly my needing to focus on the situation with Rose for a while that kept me away.

While Lance and Olga knew that Evangeline was getting divorced and living with Addy, no one had yet told Lance that he had a granddaughter. Certainly, no one told him who the father of said granddaughter was. For the time being, it was better that way.

Evangeline knew I had gone to see Rose that first time, but she had no clue that I returned to Spearville twice a week after work. She made it clear that she was opposed to the idea of my disrupting Rose's life in any way. But I just needed to see my daughter. Rose's games were my own private time with her. So private, the poor little girl didn't even know about it. No one got hurt this way.

Until the one day I slipped and unintentionally revealed myself.

It started out just like any other Thursday. It was late in the afternoon, and the sun was starting to go down over the grassy field that was filled with five and six-year-old T-ball players and their parents. Some people set up folding chairs while others hung out on the bleachers.

I assumed my spot on the top row with my travel mug of coffee. There was so much waiting involved with that sport. I'd spend every second of it watching her, whether she was just staring into space, giggling with the other kids or actually playing. Whenever she'd step up to the plate, my heart would do flips. Filled with pride, I'd always stand up so that I could see her better. It was amazing what she could do with one arm. She'd whack the ball with her one right arm and run to first base. She'd hit it on the first try almost every time. The cheers for her were always the loudest. I had to give the Simonsens credit for putting her in a sport that would defy her disability. They could have stuck to soccer or something where she didn't have to use her arm, but clearly they wanted to show her that she could do anything if she put her mind to it.

A stray ball made its way to the corner of the field near where I was sitting. For some reason, Rose separated from everyone to go after it. A rush of adrenaline hit me. My heart was pounding faster with every step she took toward me. She'd never travelled in my direction before. The ball ended up rolling toward the bleachers. She went in search of it.

Unsure of whether it was the right thing to do, I walked down the bleachers and made my way behind them to where she was looking for the ball. She was tiny. She shouldn't have been back there by herself. What if I were a bad person? And why hadn't anyone noticed her leave the game?

"Do you need help?"

"I'm looking for a ball."

I closed my eyes briefly, cherishing the moment of hearing the sound of her sweet little voice clearly for the first time. It travelled through me and squeezed at my heart.

"I'll help you find it."

She followed me around behind the bleachers. There was no sign of any ball.

"I'm sorry. I don't think it's back here."

"Okay."

She started to walk away.

I wasn't ready to let her go. "Wait."

She stopped and turned around.

I took a long look at her confused little doe eyes. I smiled upon realizing that even though she was the spitting image of me, her eyes were actually brown like Evangeline's.

"Do me a favor, okay? Don't wander away like that anymore. And don't talk to strangers. I'm a good guy, but not everybody is. You should never follow anyone anywhere, especially when there are no other adults around."

"I'm sorry."

"It's alright. Just don't do that again, okay?"

"Okay."

She started to walk away again. I was struggling with my emotions because I didn't want to let her go. My eyes wandered to the left and suddenly landed on a bright white softball sitting on the grass.

"Rose!" I called out.

She turned around.

"I found the ball! It's over here." I ran over to pick it up then walked over to where she was waiting, knelt down and handed it to her.

"How did you know my name?"

Shit.

"Wild guess. You look like a rose maybe?"

"Thank you for the ball."

Thank you for existing.

I stayed kneeling, waiting for her to leave. For some reason, she didn't. She just stayed there looking into my eyes. It was like some weird cosmic connection that could only exist between a parent and a child. Something came over me, and against my better judgement, I lifted my hands to her face and pulled her toward me, kissing her forehead. My palms remained wrapped around her cheeks. In that moment, an epiphany came to me. It was the answer to the one question I'd spent my entire life asking. I finally knew my purpose, what I was put on this Earth for, why I was allowed to live when my mother died. I was born to give life to this precious human being.

I must have gotten carried away in my thoughts because I'd forgotten my hands were still on her face. The next thing I knew I heard footsteps, followed by a man's voice.

"Hey! Get off of my daughter!"

I jumped back.

He knelt down and placed his hands on her shoulders. "What did this man do to you?"

"Nothing, Daddy. He just helped me find my ball. Then, he kissed me."

His eyeballs nearly popped out of his head as he slowly turned to me.

Holding my hands up, I pleaded, "It's not what you think."

"My daughter disappeared from the field, she turns up with a strange man who kissed her, and it's not what I think! It's not what I think? You'll be telling that to the police!"

"Mr. Simonsen...Robert..." I said.

He squinted. "How do you know my name?"

I couldn't say it in front of Rose, but I needed to explain myself if I didn't want to be carted off to jail. "My name is Sevin Montgomery. You know Olga Sutton…"

He released his grip on her. "Rose, go back to your coaches." She hesitated to leave, looking between him and me. "Go on!" he yelled. She glanced at me one more time before running toward the other players. When Rose was out of earshot, he looked at me. His voice lowered. "What about Olga Sutton?"

"Five years ago, Olga Sutton arranged the adoption of my child without my knowledge."

"That's insane. Olga's daughter didn't even know who the father was."

"It was a lie. I'm the father."

"You can't prove that."

"Look at my face, then look at Rose, and tell me I can't prove it."

CHAPTER 25

EVANGELINE

Addy was pressing her uniform in preparation for the grand reopening next week. A loud whooshing sound escaped from the iron as she let some steam out onto the thick navy material. "Have you heard from him?"

I was sitting on a stool watching as she took each wrinkle out. "No. Not since last Thursday night. The more days that go by, the more I'm seriously starting to worry that we'll never be able to repair our relationship."

It had been nearly a week since Sevin's last visit to Addy's. While he'd been helping her with the business side of the reopening through emails mostly, he was keeping his physical distance from me.

Last week, though, he'd come over to confess what happened with Rose's adoptive father at the baseball field. I had no clue he'd been going to Spearville every week. It helped explain his temporary absence from my life. Sevin's resilience was not a surprise. Even though I'd made it known that I felt it was a bad idea for him to confront the Simonsens, I knew that it was inevitable.

Apparently, when Sevin made his identity known that day, Robert Simonsen softened, begging and pleading with him to stay out of Rose's life, pointing out that it would devastate the little girl to discover that everything she knew to be true was a lie; Rose obviously had no clue that she was adopted. Robert told Sevin that if he really cared about Rose, he wouldn't try to disrupt her life. Sevin left Spearville feeling defeated and confused, especially since having the close contact with her had only reinforced his feelings of unconditional love and attachment. At the same time, he felt a responsibility to protect her from getting hurt. The situation was left unresolved for the time being.

Not a day went by when I didn't think of Rose. The fact that they'd kept the name I'd chosen for her both broke and warmed my heart at the same time. Sevin was a lot stronger than I was, because I couldn't even bear to see her face, knowing what I did.

Addy now knew the whole truth about my time away and the reasons behind it. She spent almost every day trying to encourage me not to give up on a future with Sevin.

Fluffing out her newly pressed uniform, she hung it up and took a seat. "Five years of damage is not going to undo itself easily. This is going to be a battle you may have to fight for a very long time. You betrayed him. But guilt and self-punishment are a waste of energy. Let me ask you this. Why did you stay married to that donkey for so long?"

God bless Addy for always finding a way to make me laugh under the worst circumstances. I chuckled at her use of that term to describe Dean, who luckily had left me alone and was cooperating with the divorce. The threat against his marijuana operation apparently worked.

"Primarily, it was out of fear that Dean would find my family and tell them about the pregnancy, but it was also because I felt like I didn't deserve any better after both betraying my sister and giving Sevin's and my baby away. At my worst, I wasn't even sure I wanted to live anymore. My depression made me indifferent about things, especially the marriage. The stripping, too, was just another display of my own self-loathing and lack of respect for myself."

"Okay...so you spent all of these years focusing on self-punishment, which really got you nowhere. I'd say you put enough time and energy into that, wouldn't you? It's time to find your inner-strength—we all have it. Sometimes, it gets buried by fear, depression...all the negative stuff. It's time to focus your energy instead on getting your life back—getting Sevin back—if that's what you want."

"Of course, it's what I want. How do I do it, though, if I've shattered his trust?"

"You don't do it by sitting around focusing on guilt and shaming yourself, baby girl. He needs to know that you're strong, here for the long haul, that even when he's trying so hard to punish you with distance, that you'll be waiting for him when he's ready."

"But what if he can never forgive me for giving Rose away?"

"It took two people to create that precious baby. Don't undermine his own sense of responsibility in all this. Yes, he's mad that you made a decision without including him, but he's also angry at himself. He's admitted that he feels guilty for not being more careful with you, for getting you into that predicament in the first place. I can't guarantee you that he can get over it completely. Sometimes, we don't get over painful things, we just learn to live with them."

Addy was so wise. She always made me see things in a different light.

"Okay, so if I want to earn back his trust…where do I start?"

"You start with you. I think you need to talk to someone other than me—a professional—to come to terms with the guilt first. Only then will you regain the strength you need to fight for Sevin."

***

I ended up taking her advice and booking an appointment with a local therapist, Dr. Zinger. It took a while to get in to see him, since there weren't many practices taking new patients locally.

After several sessions, he'd helped talk me through the subjects that I'd been avoiding the most. Nestled into his tweed loveseat while overlooking the oak tree outside his office window, I'd opened up about the most upsetting things, like Sevin's intimacy with Elle, the circumstances of her death and giving up Rose. Lots of tears were shed on that couch. Facing those tough topics wasn't easy, but it was necessary to my eventual recovery. Dr. Zinger's goals for me were a lot like the serenity prayer: gaining the strength to change the things I could and to accept the things I couldn't.

Sevin was making it extremely clear that the ball was in my court. He hadn't come around except on the shop's reopening day. I'd catch him sneaking looks at me while I was working, but he avoided conversation and never stayed for the celebratory supper that night.

One of the realizations I'd come to through my sessions with Dr. Zinger was that Sevin had always been the fighter when it came to us. Even in the early days, he was always the one so sure and confident in what we had. He always maintained that nothing could break us, as long as we stuck together. I was always the one who ran. Not anymore. It was my time to step up to the plate, prove my love to him—run *to* him, not away from him.

***

I'd rehashed what I planned to say over and over during the drive to Sevin's that night. He'd recently moved out of the guesthouse and purchased a small two bedroom home on the outskirts of Dodge City. It was further away from everyone and in my mind, the move represented his alienating himself from us.

I double checked the address written down on a slip of paper to make sure I was pulling up to the right place. When I confirmed Sevin's house number, all of the practiced words in my head seemed to evaporate when I spotted a familiar beige Toyota parked out front.

Nancy.

What was she doing here?

The old Evangeline might have turned right back around and returned to Addy's. Instead, with my heart palpitating, I got out and slammed the door to the used Chevy that I'd recently purchased, unintentionally closing it on the skirt of my dress.

Overcome by a feeling of wild possession, I marched to his door and knocked hard. My breath was visible in the cold night air as I exhaled.

I was not going to lose him now.

When he appeared at the door, relief washed over me upon the realization that he was fully clothed. She was sitting at the kitchen counter.

Sevin looked shocked to see me. "Evangeline…"

"What is she doing here?" I asked.

"Nancy was just visiting."

Stepping down from the stool, she said, "I'd better leave…"

"Yes. You should," I retorted.

Sevin lifted his brow at me, his mouth curving into an unexpectedly amused smile in reaction to my blatant jealousy.

"I'm sorry, Nance. Thank you for coming by."

"Of course." She forced a smile at him. Without looking at me further, she grabbed her brown leather satchel.

He walked her to the door, and she whispered something to him before lightly kissing him on the cheek. I knew I had no right to feel this way, but I was burning with jealousy. I'd been working so hard to get myself to a place where I could muster up the courage to see him, and her presence was a really unwelcome surprise.

After she left, his stare was penetrating, even though his expression still reflected a slight amusement. "Well, that was rude."

"I don't want you with her."

"I'm not with her. She came by to check on me. I told her about Rose. You're seriously jealous after everything you've put me through?"

"Yes. I'm jealous. And angry at so many things. But I'm done running from them all. I want to be here with you. I want you to open up about Rose to *me*, not her."

"I don't know if I'm ready for that."

His admission caused a lump in my throat.

"I know. Even if you're not ready to open up to me…I want you to know that I am here, that I'm not going anywhere. We shouldn't have to face things alone anymore. I want to be here when you're thinking about Rose or Elle or the poor decisions I've made. I want to share in your pain. If you're mad at me, I want to be here so that you can unload your feelings onto me even if it hurts me. I don't care what Daddy or anyone thinks anymore or who finds out the truth. You're my truth. The only thing that has ever felt natural to me is loving you. No one is going to tell me I can't love you openly anymore. I'm done running, Sevin."

"You're done running from reality?"

"Yes."

He gestured with his fingers. "Come here."

I wasn't sure what he was going to do. Instead of touching me, he reached into his pocket and grabbed his phone. After swiping through a few times, he faced it toward me.

On the screen was a picture of a beautiful little girl with dark hair. Unprepared for the image—one I was never supposed to see—my chest suddenly felt heavy. At the same time, it was an unexpected gift. The photo was taken from the side. With a beaming smile, Rose was in a royal blue baseball uniform and clearly didn't know her picture was being taken.

"Look at what we lost," he said.

Taking the phone from him and choking back tears, I whispered, "I'm so sorry."

"I'm not gonna fight the adoption. My mind is made up. I don't want to rip apart her world. I love her too much."

I looked over at him. "I think that's the right decision."

His indignant stare permeated me. "One I should never have had to make."

"You're right."

"But I take some responsibility too, you know. I should have been more careful with you back then. I was so crazy in love with you that I didn't always make the most responsible decisions."

"Both of us."

"I still have very little control of my feelings around you. That's why I needed to stay away, why you haven't heard from me while I tried to come to a decision on Rose. I'm still working on coming to terms with it. That's partly why Nancy was here. She's actually adopted. I wanted to pick her brain about her feelings toward her birth parents, stuff like that."

"No explanation needed. And I totally understand why you've stayed away."

"It hasn't been easy keeping my distance from you." He took the phone from me. "Addy told me you've been seeing a therapist."

"Yes. He's really helped me see what I need to do moving forward."

We spent the next couple of hours opening up to each other about our feelings when it came to Rose. Sevin confessed that he, too, had been seeing a therapist to come to grips with his anger issues.

Finally, I built up the nerve to suggest something I'd been holding in. "I need to be here with you, Sevin. Everyday. I need to prove to you that I'm in this with you for the long haul—not just with my words but with my actions. My car is filled with all of my things. I—"

"Wait." He wrinkled his forehead incredulously. "You want to move in with me?"

"Yes."

"I'm not sure I'm ready for that."

"I wouldn't be sharing a room with you. I just want to take care of you for a while. Will you let me?"

"I don't know if that's a good idea."

Not beyond begging, I pleaded, "Please."

The look in my eyes must have shown him how serious I was, because he simply nodded.

That night, Sevin helped me move my things in, setting me up in the spare bedroom. I prayed to God that it would be my last move for a while.

***

The next few weeks were all about adjusting to the new routine. Sevin and I were living in his home, but there was no intimacy. He was still acting closed off toward me for the most part. We'd sit and have dinner together or talk about our days, but he didn't make any physical contact.

It was painful, but I vowed to push through, reminding myself that only through the passage of time could my intentions be proven. Even though he was being cold, I still wanted nothing more than to just be with him every day and try to give him the kind of life he always deserved.

On the way home from work at Addy's shop, I would stop daily to purchase more items to make his house a home. Sevin's house had a cute farmer's porch, so I picked up some potted plants to hang up across it. I painted the white living room a terracotta color and hung several canvas paintings. I put out candles and hung up inspirational wooden words, like "home" and "hope" as well as organizing all of his music. Everything was perfect on the outside but broken on the inside.

The hardest of my efforts was the cooking. I was determined that we would sit down together to a nice meal every night but couldn't cook for the life of me unless it was breakfast or dessert. Everything else sort of went to hell. I would intentionally race home from Addy's to arrive before him and sift through recipes online. It was hard to tell if Sevin was enjoying what I'd make half of the time. I was pretty sure my meals were at least edible. Enjoyable might have been too much to ask from me. Dean always preferred crap food that was easy to make, like hotdogs, frozen chicken nuggets or macaroni and cheese. He never liked vegetables. So, cooking healthful and tasty food was fairly new for me.

As the weeks went by, Sevin was softening toward me a little bit, but it seemed to be at a snail's pace. And he never touched me. Ever. That was painful. Sitting across from him at night while we watched TV, I could smell him and practically feel the heat of his body. I'd catch him looking at me when he thought I was fully immersed in a show. I knew he was holding back intentionally, that even though he wanted me, he wasn't ready to let himself cross that line. Understanding his reasoning, though, did nothing to ease the cumulative ache building inside of me. My physical attraction to him was at an all-time high, not only because I hadn't been touched in so long but because at nearly twenty-seven, he was truly all man and more handsome and built than he'd ever been in his life.

So, frustration was really starting to get the best of me. It all came to a head one night when the house phone rang during our TV time. Sevin got up to answer it before taking the handset into his bedroom. Bogged down by a mixture of fatigue and jealousy, I knocked on the door.

"Who are you talking to that you have to take the phone into the other room?" Before he could answer, I snatched it from him.

"Who is this?"

"It's Nancy," she said.

"Nancy."

"Yes."

About to explode, I had so many words at the tip of my tongue. But I knew that none of it was fair. She was there for him when I wasn't. To expect him to just drop her from his life and take me in was unfair. Instead of going off on her, I gave him the phone and marched out.

Sevin was visibly upset when he emerged from the room. "She's just a friend, Evangeline."

"Then why did you have to walk away to talk to her?"

"Because I didn't want to upset you."

Having reached my wits end, I cried out, "I've been trying so hard. I don't know what else to do to get you to forgive me. I just want to make you happy. I'm so tired. Just tell me what you need, and I'll do it!"

"I wish it were that simple."

"Do you want me to leave?"

Rubbing his eyes, he breathed out slowly. "No. I like having you here."

"You just seem so complacent about my being here."

"I'm trying to protect myself. There is no halfway when it comes to you, Evangeline. There never was. It's all or nothing. Finding out about Rose rocked my entire world. I just need time to forgive you organically. It's not something I can force. I can't be with you until my head is in the right place again."

"What do I do in the meantime?"

"Just keep doing what you're doing."

"Trying to kill you with my cooking?"

We both broke out into much needed laughter.

He surprised me when he leaned in and cupped my cheeks gently. "Don't leave."

Hearing him say that he wanted me to stay was all the motivation I needed.

I smiled. "Okay."

***

Nothing that's worth it comes easy. But when the payoff comes, it can be spectacular.

In the weeks after my outburst, Sevin seemed more cognizant of my need for reassurance. One of the changes was that he started to cook alongside me at night. His fingers would sometimes brush along my back as he passed me in the kitchen. Even the slightest touch sent shooting tremors of sexual awareness through me. I savored every last bit of subtle contact he offered me.

Another thing was that he started to leave me little sticky notes around the house. Some were just standard thank you notes: *My clothes have never smelled cleaner. I don't know what the fuck you're doing to them, but I can't stop sniffing myself. It's a problem.* Others were polite suggestions about my less than gourmet meals: *Maybe let's not do Chicken Piccata again.* Some were downright funny, like one I found on the bathroom mirror: *Your hair sheds more than an Old English Sheepdog. I'm collecting it to make sweaters for the poor.*

For several days, the notes were pretty vanilla. Then one day, I was putting some laundry away in Sevin's room. A note on top of his chest of drawers was staring me in the face. I had to clutch my chest because this one made my heart feel like it was going to leap out.

You looked so fucking beautiful at breakfast this morning. You make it really hard to want to go to work.

We never talked about the notes. I took each one and kept them in a box in my room. He'd leave me new ones every day. While his actions toward me at night hadn't changed much, the notes were his safe way of expressing the evolution of his feelings.

Another afternoon, I had just returned home to change my clothes when a yellow sticky taunted me from my nightstand.

That shirt you were wearing last night with no bra…wear it again.

That night at dinner, his eyes travelled down to my breasts, and he simply said, "I see you got my note."

Flushed in the best possible way, I smiled and answered, "I did."

That kind of innocent flirting went on for a while. It was a slow burn until one afternoon when the note on the kitchen counter was anything but innocent.

Don't bother with dinner. The only thing I'll be eating tonight is you.

I stood there in shock for the longest time, my heart pounding and my body buzzing with excitement. Looking over at my alarm clock, it hit me that he'd be home in a little over an hour. Stripping off my clothes, I ran to the bathroom to get myself ready for him.

Unprepared, I hadn't shaved my legs in days. After I finished making sure I was clean and smooth, every orifice of my body was tingling from the anticipation as I closed my eyes and let the water pummel down on me.

The door suddenly burst open, causing me to jump.

He was early.

Panic quickly transformed into excitement once everything registered. Through the foggy glass, I could see him, the defined muscles of his chest and arms. He was wearing black pants. Metal clanked as he whipped his leather belt out and threw it on the floor before stepping out of his clothes.

The door slid open. The hunger in his eyes was like nothing I'd ever seen from him. His manly scent saturated the steam-filled tub.

"You ready for me?"

I nodded eagerly. "You know I am."

He stepped in and flipped me around. "You'd better hold onto the wall."

Those words caused a shiver to roll down my spine. As he pressed his chest to my back, his hot erection slid against my ass. I held both of my palms against the tile wall and closed my eyes. The past several weeks had been one long bout of foreplay, so I was already wet. He opened the door briefly again to get something. I turned around to see him savagely ripping the packaging of a condom with his teeth. He spread the rubber over his cock before sinking all the way into me in one slow thrust.

"Oh God," he muttered. As he began to move inside of me, he groaned, "Holy hell...I've missed fucking you. I've dreamt about it so damn much.

I've been dying for this."

"Me, too," I breathed out.

He began to fuck me harder. At one point, I winced.

"Too rough?"

"No."

"Good. I don't think I can do it any other way right now. You feel incredible."

Our wet bodies slapped together as he slammed into me, my finger nails digging into the grout. His thrusts were rough and sometimes painful, but even when it hurt a little, it felt so right, so perfect. I couldn't get enough of him.

His breathing became suddenly uneven. "I can't…too much…I'm gonna…"

"It's okay. Let go, Sevin."

"Fuck…" A second later, his moans echoed through the bathroom while he pulled me even tighter into him. My muscles contracted around his cock as he came, my own climax spasming through me. I'd nearly forgotten how intense sex with him was. Nothing compared to it.

He stayed inside of me, breathing against the back of my neck. He turned me around and kissed me tenderly then surprised me when he dropped to his knees on the shower floor. The water ran down over his silky black hair as he gently kissed my stomach and whispered, "Don't ever leave me again."

Kneeling down to meet his eyes, I clutched the back of his neck. "I would rather die than ever hurt you again."

Offering his hand, he lifted me to a standing position before shutting off the faucet and squeezing the moisture out of my hair. He grabbed a towel and wiped my body and his own then led me next door into his bed.

He got on all fours over me, locking me in with his arms. "You're not gonna sleep in there anymore, okay? I want you right here with me every night."

My eyes began to well up upon hearing him say that. Even though I understood it, my having to sleep in the guestroom always hurt like hell.

"Nancy's not gonna call or come around anymore, either," he said.

"You don't have to do that. She's been a friend to you."

"Yeah, but she's also an ex-girlfriend, and I don't want to upset you. I would expect the same from you. We're done hurting each other, okay?"

When I nodded, he just continued to hover over me in silence. So much loss, so much pain and he was still able to look at me with the same love shining through his eyes.

"Lie back."

"What are you doing?"

"I intend to make good on my promise about dinner."

My eyes trailed down his neck to the carved V beneath his abs and down to his cock that was once again gloriously hard.

"You like what you see?"

"Your body is even more incredible than I remembered."

He spread my legs open and rubbed his palm slowly down the length of my torso then cupped my pussy possessively in his hand as he said, "This body is mine. Promise me you won't show it to anyone else ever again."

"I promise."

He then lowered his face between my legs. My eyes rolled back the second I felt the wetness and warmth of his lips on my tender skin. Applying pressure on my clit with his tongue, he licked and sucked until he brought me to orgasm. He was the only person to have ever gone down on me.

We made love slowly two more times that night in his bed—our bed. It felt monumental, because for the first time since running into each other on that dirt road years ago, we were truly free to do what came naturally.

All I ever wanted was to love him. Still, things would be far from perfect so long as the biggest representation of our love continued to be missing from our lives. There would always be a hole in his heart. I needed to figure out a way to fix it.

CHAPTER 26

SEVIN

Evangeline and I were officially done hiding. We finally came out to Lance as a couple, making it seem like we'd only gotten close in the months after her divorce. Of course, Olga knew the truth about our secret past but continued to play dumb. No one said a word about Rose. That was the best decision for now. Surprisingly, Lance and Emily seemed to accept the fact that we were together.

My role at Sutton Provisions had only gotten bigger over the years. I was now the Operations Manager, overseeing beef processing and fabrication. Someday, I would replace Lance as the company president. With Elle gone, I guess my being with Evangeline helped solidify me as a permanent member of the family in Lance's eyes. While his acceptance almost seemed too good to be true, I would gladly take it.

Evangeline was still working at Addy's shop, which was renamed SEAL Autobody. SEAL was a play on our names: Sevin, Evangeline, Addy and Luke. Sometimes, I'd sneak home early to arrive before she got home from work. Catching her all greased-up and dirty was a huge turn on.

One such afternoon, I was waiting impatiently for her to walk through the door when the house phone rang.

"Hello?"

"Is this Sevin Montgomery?"

"Yes."

"My name is Genia Simonsen. I'm—"

"I know who you are." My stomach dropped. "Has something happened to Rose?"

"No. I'm sorry to have alarmed you."

Letting out a massive sigh of relief, I asked, "What's going on?"

"I'm not supposed to be in contact with you. If Robert knew, he would be irate."

"How did you get this number?"

"Evangeline has been in touch with me several times in recent weeks. She gave it to me."

"She has?"

"She found me online, and we've been going back and forth a bit."

Evangeline never said anything about contacting the Simonsens. It touched me that she'd been pushing for contact, especially since I knew she was personally against disrupting our little girl's life. She was making the effort for me.

"What have you been discussing?"

"Evangeline has tried to connect with me, woman-to-woman, hoping to convince me to allow you both to spend some time with Rose."

"Your husband made it very clear to me that seeing her wouldn't ever be an option."

"Evangeline asked if I could arrange something, maybe where Rose didn't know who you were, but where you two could still see her on a semi-regular basis. I spoke to Robert about it, and I'm afraid he's dead set against it."

"So, you're just calling to let us know that?"

"Well, actually, something's come up."

The tone in her voice prompted me to sit down. "What happened?"

"Robert was let go from his job a couple of months ago. He was just offered a position that's out of state."

"Out of state? Where?"

"Oregon."

As soon as she uttered the word, my chest felt like it had been crushed.

"You're moving? Leaving with her?"

"I'm afraid we are. We have no choice."

"What does Robert do? I could give him a job at Sutton. I—"

"You know he wouldn't accept that. Arrangements for the move are already being made. I just somehow felt that you had a right to know."

"I appreciate that, but honestly, I'm in absolute shock. Even though I can't see her on a daily basis, there was solace in the fact that she was just a town over."

"I was thinking that maybe you would want to see her before we leave. I can bring her to a public place. We could make it seem like a coincidental meeting. You just wouldn't be able to tell her your real names in case she mentions something to her father."

Her father.

This moving bombshell she dropped had stunned me into silence.

Genia continued, "I know Evangeline was hoping for more, but that's not going to be possible, especially now that we're moving." She paused. "Robert is out of town tomorrow. He's chaperoning a field trip with my older girls. Would you be available? I could pack her lunch, meet you with Rose at a playground somewhere in between both of us."

"Of course, we'll be available. There is nothing I could possibly have to do that would be more important. Just let us know the time and place. We'll be there."

***

Evangeline and I arrived early. We didn't want to risk missing any of the time that we were allotted with her. The sun was blazing onto the blue rubber playground surfacing. I could see our shadows as we sat on one of the benches aligning the edge of the park.

We'd gotten coffee on the way, and Evangeline was now ripping apart the Styrofoam cup.

"Don't be nervous."

"I can't help it," she said, continuing to destroy the cup.

Wearing a skirt and fancy blouse, Evangeline was overdressed for the occasion. I didn't say anything because I knew it made her feel more confident; she wanted to make a good impression.

My own nerves were also acting up. Closing my eyes, I listened to the sounds of bouncing basketballs from the nearby court along with children playing tag in the crowded playground area.

Suddenly, the smell of hot dogs hit me, prompting me to open my eyes. A food truck had parked just outside the fence behind us.

I turned to her. "You want one?"

She shook her head. "I have no appetite. You do?"

"No." I smiled.

A few minutes later, I heard her name before I spotted her.

"Wait, Rose!"

Her black pigtails were swinging back and forth as she ignored her mother and ran straight to the climb-up tower above the red tube slide.

Evangeline and I both stood up from the bench in unison as Genia Simonsen walked toward us.

She was holding a small cooler and said, "Sorry. She has a mind of her own. She'll come back when she's hungry or thirsty. How long have you been waiting?"

"Not long," Evangeline lied. We'd actually arrived so early that we were the first people here.

"We've been so busy packing for the move. She's just a little overly excited to be out of the house."

"I can imagine," Evangeline said as she licked her lips and flashed a fake smile.

We made awkward small talk until Rose ran toward us. "Mommy, I'm thirsty."

Genia reached into the cooler. "I have your water here."

Rose chugged it down before closing the cap. She hadn't looked at us and started to take off again.

"Wait a minute, missy!" Genia shouted after her. "Say hello to my friends before you run off again."

"Hello." She made eye contact with me in particular then seemed to examine my arm. "I remember you."

"You do?"

"Uh-huh. You helped me find my ball."

Wow.

"That's right. That was many months ago. I can't believe you remembered me."

"I remember the E on your arm."

I chuckled as I looked down at the tattoo on my forearm.

"You're very sharp."

"What does the E stand for?"

Curious as to what she would say, I responded with a question. "What do you think it stands for?"

"Elmo?"

While the three adults laughed at her response, Rose looked so cute as she stood there confused. Little did she know that just beneath my shirt was a tattoo of her own name. I'd recently had *Rose* inked over my heart.

"The E stands for Evangeline."

Genia glanced over at me with a slight look of warning. I'd forgotten that we weren't supposed to say our names. I wasn't thinking. Evangeline looked at me, too, seeming surprised at my answer. She'd once wrongly assumed that the E stood for Elle; it always stood for Evangeline.

"Who's Evangeline?" Rose asked.

"Someone special."

"Like your dog?"

"Something like that. Do you have a dog?"

"No. My mom won't let us get one."

I would SO get you a dog.

Anything you wanted.

She turned to Evangeline for the first time. "I like your hair."

"Thank you. I like yours, too."

They had the same exact hair.

Out of nowhere, Rose suddenly bolted in the direction of the slide. Evangeline stayed quiet but wouldn't stop staring at Rose. I suspected she was going through the same emotions I was the first time I got to see our daughter in person. It was one thing to think about her, but another altogether to see your flesh and blood right in front of you, especially when it was as precious as Rose.

Continuing to keep her eyes on Rose, Evangeline finally spoke up. "How does she handle her disability in general?"

"It's all she's ever known, which in some ways makes it easier than losing functionality later in life." My thoughts immediately turned to Elle as Genia continued, "We've always encouraged her not to give up on the things she thinks she can't do. Like baseball. That took a while, but eventually she was able to play almost exactly as well as the other kids."

I nodded in agreement. "I admire what you've done, encouraging her to be the best that she can be. Thank you."

"Thank *you* for not fighting the adoption. I can't tell you how much that means to me."

"Are you going to tell her someday?" I asked.

"We're not sure."

"She has a right to know."

"We're considering it, just not anytime soon."

"She's never asked why she looks so different from her sisters?"

Before Genia could answer me, Rose ran toward us. She had dirt all over her bottom.

"Can I have my Capri Sun?"

"That's for lunch. You want to sit down and eat now?"

"Yes."

Genia handed Rose a peanut butter and jelly sandwich along with the pouch of juice. Taking a spot on the bench, she began to devour her lunch then turned to me with her mouth full. "Why are you named after a number?"

"What do you mean?"

"Your name…Seven."

Genia's eyes widened.

"I never told you my name."

"You told my Daddy once."

I'd forgotten I'd told Robert my name before he shooed Rose away that day at the baseball field.

"How did you remember that?"

"It's easy to remember a number."

She turned to Evangeline. "What's your name?"

Hesitating, she finally said, "Sienna."

"That's pretty."

"Thank you. So is Rose."

Rose did this thing where she hummed when she chewed. At one point, Evangeline and I, who were fixated on her, looked at one another and smiled with a look that said, *We did that?*

Rose handed me the rest of her sandwich. "You want this?"

Genia laughed. "Rose, I don't think he wants to eat your scraps."

"Are you kidding?" I joked, "I love peanut butter and jelly!" I took it from her and stuffed my face, making noises that sounded sort of like Cookie Monster. Rose started to laugh.

When her cackling died down, she casually swung her legs back and forth and randomly said, "We're moving to Origami."

"Oregon?"

"Yeah. Oregon."

"I heard. How do you feel about that?"

"I don't want to go."

"I know how you feel."

"You're moving there, too?"

I wish.

She didn't realize I was referring to my own feelings about her leaving.

"No, but I've moved away before. It can be scary, but when I moved here to Kansas from Oklahoma, I met some really great people who changed my life. Some amazing things happened. I don't regret any of it. For one, if I hadn't moved, I wouldn't be here with you right now."

Of course, she didn't really get it. She wasn't supposed to.

"You wouldn't be eating peanut butter and jelly."

"Right…yeah." I grinned. "Just remember that sometimes, good can come out of things that seem bad or scary at first."

"Like my arm? How I'm missing half? Someday, I'll be happy about it?"

I had to think about how to respond to that.

Unable to really answer her question, I simply answered, "I saw the way you play baseball. You should be very proud of yourself."

In typical fashion, Rose suddenly jumped off the seat and turned to Genia. "Can I play a little longer?"

"Sure, honey."

She ran off toward the jungle gym.

We watched her quietly for several minutes while Genia packed up the cooler. At one point, Rose was standing at the bottom of the monkey bars, looking up. She was watching another girl climb. It broke my heart because she looked like she wanted to do it so badly.

I got up and ran over to her. "You want some help?"

"Yeah."

I lifted her up as she grasped the first bar with her right hand. She let herself hang, and when she started to lose strength, I'd balance her up for a bit before moving her along to the next bar. She'd hang for as long as her one little arm could sustain on each one. We did the monkey bars like this a few times until she tired of it.

"What did you think?"

She shrugged her shoulders. "It wasn't all that."

I bent my head back in laughter at her response. "It was more fun when you thought you couldn't do it, huh?"

"Yeah."

When she giggled, it caused a dull ache inside of my chest.

Genia waved her hand at us. "We'd better get going, honey."

The sun shined into Rose's big brown eyes as she looked up at me. "I don't want to go."

It pained me to say, "I know, but you have to listen to your mom."

Feeling defeated, I walked ever so slowly with Rose back to the bench where Genia and Evangeline were waiting.

Rose was drinking some water when I pulled Genia aside.

"There's something I'd like to give you for her before you leave. How can I get it to you?"

"What is it?"

"It's a letter and a family heirloom. If you ever decide to tell her, I'd like her to have it."

"I can drop by alone to pick it up sometime this week before we leave town."

"Thank you. I really appreciate it."

Rose ran to a recycling bin to throw out her water. When she returned, she waved her little hand and said, "Well...bye." As if her leaving right then wasn't about to devastate our world.

Genia lingered, knowing that we would need more than just a casual goodbye.

"Can I have a hug?" I asked. Without waiting for her response, I knelt down as she walked toward me and into my arms without hesitation.

So trusting.

Please be careful, Rose.

Before finding out about Rose, I never truly vocalized my prayers. Now, I prayed every single night, asking God to watch over her. Maybe I never truly believed in God until Rose. She was my first living proof of his miracles—the personification of love. Maybe for me, God *was* love.

She smelled liked peanut butter and fresh air. Burying my nose in her pigtail, I tried to burn her scent into memory while praying for the tears stinging my eyes to just go away. I didn't want to scare her. As much as I was holding back, there was another part of me that had the urge to just blurt out, *"I'm your Daddy."* I'd always thought the love I had for Evangeline was the strongest kind; it didn't compare to my love for Rose, which seemed infinite.

She was the true love of my life.

Pursing my lips together to grab my composure, I cherished the last seconds of our hug before pulling away.

Evangeline hadn't said a word in a while. She surprised me when she asked, "Can I have one, too?"

"Okay."

Rose's back was facing me, so all I could see was Evangeline as she shut her eyes so tightly to fend off the tears. When she released Rose, she turned around ever so quickly to wipe her eyes before anyone could see.

"Take care," Genia said as she took Rose by the hand, leading her to the parking lot.

Evangeline and I stood frozen, watching every last movement they made until Rose disappeared from sight into the car.

Knowing that they would be driving by our spot again in order to exit the lot, I stayed in place. When the green Subaru passed, Rose waved at us one final time from the backseat. I smiled at her, but then a second later when she was gone, the tears finally came. Evangeline buried her face in my chest, and we both let out everything we'd been holding in.

When I released her, I wiped the tears from her eyes and said, "She'll come back to us someday. I know it. They'll tell her."

Sniffling, she cried out, "What if she hates us?"

"Then, we'll explain everything the best we can."

It was too easy to let my sadness fester into anger. I couldn't live like that anymore. In a sense, losing Rose was the ultimate test of my love for Evangeline. Unconditional love isn't possible without forgiveness. If we were ever going to truly move on, there was something I needed to say to her even if I wasn't one-hundred percent sure I truly meant it yet. It had to be said.

I pulled her back into me and whispered into her ear, "I forgive you."

She sighed into my shoulder. "How could you?"

"Because that's how much I love you."

"Today really made me realize everything we lost."

"We did lose something. But she also gained a family that loves her...three sisters. She's happy. That counts."

She released herself from my arms. "She's happy, but what about us?"

"We'll get there." Seeing the look of doubt on her face as she looked down at the ground, I placed my hand on her chin, prompting her to make eye contact. "Hey. You're enough for me."

That assurance became more important than I could have ever known.

***

In the years that followed, we'd tried everything, but Evangeline was never able to get pregnant again. It was a sad irony, considering her one pregnancy with Rose had such a profound impact on the course of our lives.

A year after Rose moved away, Evangeline and I got married in the same way that our relationship started: alone on a grassy knoll, the only witness being a cool Kansas breeze. Evangeline carried two roses, one for our daughter and one for my mother, along with blue hydrangeas, which were Elle's favorite flowers. A reception followed in the form of a Texas-style barbecue in Addy's backyard. The few guests included Emily and a guy named Zachary, who was courting her. Also in attendance were Luke and his new boyfriend, Alexander.

We stayed childless, living a life that I would imagine some people with kids occasionally fantasized about: eating out a lot, going on vacations, having total freedom to do whatever we wanted, whenever we wanted. It was Evangeline and me against the world. We would have given anything to share our lives with a child; it just wasn't in the cards. That was the thorn in our side to an otherwise beautiful life. In many ways, life was like a rose—beautiful but not without the sometimes painful thorny path leading up to the gorgeous red flower. If the red flower represented the best of life, then our flower bloomed on an ordinary Monday afternoon ten years after our playground date with Rose.

Evangeline had gone out to check the mail and came inside the house with an envelope that was shaking in her hands. When I took one look at the name on the return address label, it all made sense.

Rose Simonsen.

CHAPTER 27

ROSE

Dear Rose,

If you're reading this, your parents have obviously told you the truth.

I'm finding it hard to sum up in one letter all that I want to say to you. I guess I should start by saying hello. My name is Sevin Montgomery, and I'm your father. Jesus, I sort of feel like Darth Vader right now. (I just realized, you probably don't know who that is!)

We've actually met a couple of times. I don't know if you can remember. You were about five, going on six. The first time, you had lost a ball at your T-ball game, and I helped you find it. The second time we met, your mother, Genia, brought you to the playground right before you moved from Kansas to Oregon. Your birth mother, Evangeline, was also with me that day. Genia brought you to the park so that we could see you before you moved. You didn't know who we really were. Do you recall the monkey bars? Think back. Try to remember. That was me.

Anyway, you're probably wondering how your mother and I could have given you up. It's a very long story, one I'm not sure you're ready for. I have no way of knowing how old you are as you read this. What I can tell you is that at the time, your mother, Evangeline, felt she had no choice. She believed that your parents would give you a better life than she ever could. I promise to explain everything to you honestly someday and answer every question you have about the circumstances that led to that decision.

Unfortunately, I didn't find out about you until several years later – shortly before we first met at the baseball field. By that time, you were already happy and settled with your adoptive family. Your parents weren't ready to tell you the truth, and I couldn't in good conscience rip your world apart. That was the only reason I didn't fight them for you, Rose. Please believe that. It had nothing to do with not wanting you. I fought long and hard with my decision.

I need you to know that from the first moment I discovered your existence, I fell hopelessly in love with you. Not a day has gone by or will go by when I'm not thinking about you and wishing we could be together. I will pray every day that you come back to me when you're old enough to decide whether that's what you want. Please don't be mad at Evangeline for deciding to give you up. She loves you very much, too.

I gave your mother, Genia, a ring to go along with this letter. It was my mother's wedding ring. You were named after her—your grandmother Rose. Actually, you look exactly like her because, well, you look just like me. Every time I was supposed to give the ring to someone, something happened to prevent it. That's probably because it was never meant for anyone but you. I hope you get to wear it and that it reminds you of how much you are loved.

I'm so proud of you, Rose. If I never accomplished another thing in this life, that would be good enough for me. Because you are my greatest accomplishment. Your existence is enough to make me glad that I was born. I spent a lot of my early life wondering about my purpose for being alive. That's a story for another day, too. I hope we get that day, but the choice is yours, my precious girl.

This letter was not meant to upset you. And you certainly don't have to see me or Evangeline if you don't want to. (Your mother and I got back together around the time you moved away.) Just know that we love you and always will. Our address is: 11 Briar Road in

Dodge City, Kansas. I don't plan to ever move, because I want you to always be able to find me. Till that day comes...I love you.

—Dad (or Sevin...whatever you prefer.)

Wiping my eyes, I refolded the letter for the umpteenth time and placed it back inside the envelope. Reading it never got easier. The most telling part was the fact that the blue ballpoint ink over the last few sentences was smeared. It looked like it had been hit by water and made me wonder if a teardrop had fallen from his eye toward the end, landing on those words.

I'd had a lot of time to rehash everything in the letter over the past few months. He was probably right. If my parents had told me that I wasn't really their biological child back when I was five, it would have devastated me. My sisters, Janelle, Cassie and Trinity, were my entire world. Even though we were inseparable, I'd always felt different as it was, because of my darker features. So, to have found out back then that I truly wasn't related to them would have wrecked me. I might not have been emotionally mature enough to really understand or accept it.

That's not to say that finding out at sixteen was all that much easier. It wasn't entirely clear to me why sixteen was the magic number for them. My parents sat me down alone one night after my softball game and told me everything. I hadn't even changed out of my uniform.

My sisters had later entered the room together as if on cue and joined in on the conversation after the shock wore off a bit. It had all seemed so surreal. At the same time, the inexplicable feeling of incompleteness that I'd carried around my entire life now made total sense.

There was no doubt about the fact that my childhood was blessed. After my father took the job in Oregon, things got easier for our family. We moved into a bigger house, into a great neighborhood. It was the perfect all-American upbringing. Yet, something unidentifiable always seemed to be missing. Maybe, I couldn't identify it because it was coming from deep within my soul.

The night of my parents' revelation, my mother walked into my bedroom holding an envelope and a small blue box. She explained that the items were from my birth father and asked if I wanted her to stay in the room while I read the letter. I preferred to process it alone, so she left.

I hadn't expected the immediate connection I felt to him through his words. What I really never expected was to find out that we'd actually met...and that I remembered.

I remembered him.

Not clearly. But I remembered meeting a handsome stranger with black hair when I was young. I remembered him helping me on the monkey bars. I remembered feeling a connection with him but not understanding why. I didn't remember much of what was said. I also couldn't remember Evangeline or what she looked like at all.

Obviously, the letter didn't provide me with all of the information since much was left unexplained. I still really knew nothing about what happened to Evangeline that was so bad or what he was referring to when he said he always questioned why he was born. I was grateful, though, for what answers the letter did give me and for what uncertainties it ruled out. Without it, I might have wrongly assumed that my birth parents gave me away because of my birth defect.

When I opened the box that night, inside was a small but sparkly marquise-shaped diamond set in between two sapphires. Using my prosthetic left hand, I'd placed it over my right ring finger. My grandmother must have had dainty fingers, because it fit perfectly.

Since finding out the truth, I'd reread the letter several times, dissecting every last sentence. My parents were clear that the choice of how to proceed was all mine. Unsure of whether I was ready to face all of the details of how I came to be, it was many weeks before I conjured up the courage to reach out to him.

***

The car stopped in front of the gray house. From what little I could remember about Kansas, it seemed like nothing had changed.

In the side yard, I spotted a woman with dark hair kissing a blond man as they sipped drinks. It alarmed me. Was that Evangeline? Had something happened to Sevin? I'd sent a letter back to him a few weeks ago, acknowledging receipt of his own letter. I asked him for more time to process things and promised to write him back again. Instead, I made the rash decision to fly out here during my school break. My parents were adamantly against my coming to Kansas without calling first, but I didn't have his number and really just had to see things for myself.

"This is 11 Briar Road?"

"Yes, this is it. We've arrived," the driver said. "You have my number when you'd like me to come back and take you to your aunt's house."

My parents had hired a car service to drive me from the airport all the way to Dodge City. I'd insisted on coming here alone. They agreed so long as I stayed with my mother's sister in Spearville.

"Do you mind hanging out for just a few minutes…in case the people I want to see aren't home?"

"Sure thing. You just text me, let me know what you want me to do."

Slowly approaching the canoodling couple, I cleared my throat. My heart was pounding.

Was that my mother?

"Hello?"

"Can I help you?" she asked.

"Does Sevin Montgomery live here?"

"What's your name?"

"Rose."

Her mouth was agape as she examined my face.

"Did you say Rose?"

"Yes. Who are you?"

"Emily…Evangeline's sister." She looked anxiously behind her shoulder. "They didn't know you were coming?"

My aunt.

"Do you know who I am?"

Her eyes started to water. "Yes. Yes, I do. I…I only recently found out…like very recently. Oh my God." She covered her mouth and repeated, "Oh, my God. I can't believe this." Then, she suddenly pulled me into a hug. The man standing next to her looked really confused. Still flustered, she turned to introduce him. "Um…sorry, this is my husband…um…"

"Zachary," he reminded her.

I waved at him before asking, "Where are they?"

Emily was still examining my face when she said, "They're inside getting ready to bring the food out. We were just about to eat dinner outside."

I pointed my thumb back to the waiting car. "I can come back."

"Are you kidding?" She held out her hands to stop me from leaving. "Don't you move! Stay right there." She kept muttering as she walked away, "Oh my God. Oh my God."

Zachary and I smiled awkwardly at each other while we waited in silence. My throat felt dry. I really needed a glass of water. My thoughts were racing. *What was I going to say? Would I call him Sevin? Mr. Montgomery? Her…Evangeline? Were they even married? Mr. and Mrs. Montgomery? No…I'd call them Sevin and Evangeline.*

I was nervously removing pieces of lint from my dress when I heard footsteps and looked up. My heart beat faster.

He was holding her hand as they both rushed out before stopping short to take me in.

The two people who'd given me life.

Evangeline was stunningly beautiful, her long black hair tied up into a messy knot. She was holding a wooden spoon that looked like it had Cool Whip on it, an indication that she was literally whisked out of the kitchen. She lifted her trembling hand to her mouth and froze, while Sevin approached me slowly.

Choking back tears, he placed his hands on my shoulders and just looked at me for the longest time before finally whispering, "Hello, Rose."

My own tears really caught me off guard as he pulled me into him. His heart was hammering against mine as he started to full on cry. I didn't know what the future held, certainly not when it came to a relationship with Evangeline. While there was so much I still didn't know, there were a few things I *was* sure of. One, that this man loved me. Two, that tears definitely smudged the ink on that letter. Three, that there was no doubt in my mind anymore about what I should call him.

When he pulled back, I looked into his glistening eyes and answered, not with my head—but with my heart.

"Hello, Dad."

FOR MORE TITLES,
VISIT PENELOPE WARD'S WEBSITE:

www.penelopewardauthor.com

SUBSCRIBE TO PENELOPE'S NEWSLETTER:
http://bit.ly/1X725rj

Other Standalones by Penelope Ward:

COCKY BASTARD
New York Times and USA Today Bestseller

STEPBROTHER DEAREST
New York Times, USA Today and Wall Street Journal Bestseller

JAKE UNDONE (Jake #1)
JAKE UNDERSTOOD (Jake #2)

MY SKYLAR
USA TODAY Bestseller

GEMINI

ACKNOWLEDGEMENTS

First and foremost, thank you to my parents for your love and support, even though my mother still insists I try writing a G-rated book (probably not likely).

To my husband: Thank you for your love, patience and humor, for inspiring the music in my books and for coming up with the name Sevin.

To Allison, who believed in me from the beginning: Thank you for pushing me to pursue my dream.

To my besties, Angela, Tarah and Sonia: Love you all so much!

To Vi: I don't remember a time without you. Thank you for always being there in the early AM hours and beyond. We should write a book together…oh, wait…

To Julie: Thank you for your friendship and for being an overall awesome indie rogue friend. Can't wait to see what's next from you!

To my editor, Kim: Thank you for your undivided attention to all of my books, chapter by chapter.

To my invaluable facebook fan group, Penelope's Peeps and to Queen Amy for steering the ship: I adore you all and don't know what I would do without you!

To Erika G: Thank you for your kind spirit, punky power and all things E.

To Luna: Thank you for your friendship, protective nature and your immeasurable creativity and devotion to my books and characters—especially your Jake.

To Mia A.: Thank you for bringing humor to my life on a daily basis via text and private message—sometimes simultaneously.

To Aussie Lisa: What a gift to have been able to finally meet you this year!

To Natasha G.: Thank you for our chats and your admirable patience. (Bas!)

To all the book bloggers/promoters who help and support me: You are THE reason for my success. I'm afraid to list everyone here because I will undoubtedly forget someone unintentionally. You know who you are and do not hesitate to contact me if I can return the favor.

To Lisa of TRSoR Promotions: Thank you for handling my blog tour and release blitzes. You rock!

To Ellie from Love N Books: Thanks for your help in obtaining the cover photo.

To Letitia of RBA Designs: Thank you for always working with me until the cover is exactly how I want it. Your covers are all phenomenal.

To my readers: Nothing makes me happier than knowing I've provided you with an escape from the daily stresses of life. That same escape was why I started writing. There is no greater joy in this business than to hear from you directly and to know that something I wrote touched you in some way.

Last but not least, to my daughter and son: Mommy loves you. You are my motivation and inspiration!

ABOUT THE AUTHOR

Penelope Ward is a *New York Times, USA Today* and *Wall Street Journal* bestselling author.

She grew up in Boston with five older brothers and spent most of her twenties as a television news anchor before switching to a more family-friendly career.

Penelope lives for reading books in the new adult/contemporary romance genre, coffee and hanging out with her friends and family on weekends.

She is the proud mother of a beautiful 11-year-old girl with autism (the inspiration for the character Callie in Gemini) and a 9-year-old boy, both of whom are the lights of her life.

Penelope, her husband and kids reside in Rhode Island.

She is the author of *Stepbrother Dearest,* which hit #3 on the *New York Times* bestseller List. Other works include the *New York Times* bestseller *Cocky Bastard* (co-written with Vi Keeland), *My Skylar, Jake Undone, Jake Understood and Gemini.*

Email Penelope at: penelopewardauthor@gmail.com

Newsletter Signup: http://bit.ly/1X725rj

Facebook Author Page: https://www.facebook.com/penelopewardauthor

Facebook Fan Group (Request to join!)
https://www.facebook.com/groups/715836741773160/

Instagram: https://instagram.com/PenelopeWardAuthor

Twitter: https://twitter.com/PenelopeAuthor

Website: www.penelopewardauthor.com

Made in the USA
Las Vegas, NV
08 February 2025

17763956R00163